• GEOFFREY CHAUCER •

Canterbury Marriage Tales:

The Wife of Bath, The Clerk,
The Merchant, The Franklin

CANTERBURY MARRIAGE TALES

GEOFFREY CHAUCER

THE WIFE OF BATH, THE CLERK, THE MERCHANT, THE FRANKLIN

The original words put into modern spelling and edited by

MICHAEL MURPHY

Conal & Gavin

Canterbury Marriage Tales:
The Wife of Bath, The Clerk, The Merchant, The Franklin

Copyright © 2000, Michael Murphy

Publisher's Cataloging-in-Publication
(Provided by Quality Books, Inc.)

Chaucer, Geoffrey, d. 1400.
    Canterbury marriage tales : The wife of Bath,
The clerk, The merchant, The franklin : the
original words put into modern spelling / by
Geoffrey Chaucer ; edited by Michael Murphy. --
1st ed., reader friendly ed.
    p. cm.
    ISBN: 0-9679557-1-8

    1. Christian pilgrims and pilgrimages--England
--Canterbury--Poetry. 2. Marriage in literature.
I. Murphy, Michael, 1932- II. Title.

PR1867.M87 2000   821'.1
                 QBI00-427

Published by
Conal & Gavin
641 East 24 St., Brooklyn, NY

A Note to the Reader

This edition is designed to make the text of a great medieval English classic more reader- friendly to students and general readers, especially to those who are not English majors and those not interested in becoming medievalists.

It is **NOT** a translation. The words are Chaucer's line for line. Only the spelling is modernized, as it is in Shakespeare texts.

It is more faithful than a translation but is a lot less demanding than the standard Middle English text. It is better than a translation because it keeps the verse and in Chaucer's own language, but in a friendlier form than the old-spelling version.

With this text, readers have the language that Chaucer wrote, but without the frustration of trying to master the vagaries of Middle English spelling. The change in spelling is meant to allow the reader to enjoy Chaucer not merely endure him. Even so, this edition is a good deal more conservative than the great poet and critic Coleridge was prepared to accept :

On Modernizing the Text

Let a few plain rules be given for sounding the final è of syllables and for expressing the termination of such words as ocèan, and nation, etc, as disyllables—or let the syllables to be sounded in such cases be marked by a competent metrist. This simple expedient would, with a very few trifling exceptions where the errors are inveterate, enable any reader to feel the perfect smoothness and harmony of Chaucer's verse. As to understanding his language, if you read twenty pages with a good glossary, you surely can find no further difficulty, even as it is; but I should have no objection to see this done: Strike out those words which are now obsolete, and I will venture to say that I will replace every one of them by words still in use out of Chaucer himself, or Gower his disciple. I don't want this myself: I rather like to see the significant terms which Chaucer unsuccessfully offered as candidates for admission into our language; but surely so very slight a change of the text may well be pardoned, even by black-letterati, for the purpose of restoring so great a poet to his ancient and most deserved popularity.

Coleridge, *Table Talk*, March 15, 1834

To my family
in gratitude and love

OTHER CHAUCER TITLES EDITED BY MICHAEL MURPHY:

Canterbury Quintet: The General Prologue and Four Tales
Miller, Wife, Pardoner, Nun's Priest
A Reader-Friendly Edition
published by LittleLeaf Press (2000). ISBN: 1-893385-02-7

**For more information or to order copies of
Quintet or *Marriage Tales*, contact:**

LittleLeaf Press
P.O. Box 187, Milaca, MN 56353
Toll Free: (877) 548-2431 Fax: (320) 556-3585
E-mail: littleleaf@maxminn.com
http://www.maxminn.com/littleleaf

Geoffrey Chaucer: *The Canterbury Tales*
The General Prologue and Twelve Major Tales
University Press of America 1991. ISBN 08191-8149-8

Audio tapes of this book in modern English pronunciation were recorded by professional actors and published by Recorded Books, 270
Skipjack Rd, Prince Frederick, MD 20678. ISBN 1-55690-652-8

The Canterbury Tales
An electronic edition in modern spelling on the World Wide Web (1999)
http://academic.brooklyn.cuny.edu/webcore/murphy/

Chaucer's *Troilus and Criseyde* and Henryson's *Testament of Cresseid*
An electronic edition in modern spelling on the World Wide Web (1999)
http://academic.brooklyn.cuny.edu/webcore/murphy/

TABLE OF CONTENTS

Introductory Note

 This is a selection of four stories from Geoffrey Chaucer's **Canterbury Tales,** as told by four of the pilgrims on that famous fictional pilgrimage to Canterbury somewhere around the year 1390, to the shrine of St. Thomas Becket, who had been martyred there in the year 1170. We have also included the beginning and end of the General Prologue, and the pen portraits of those four pilgrims from it. The General Prologue is an introductory section in which the poet tells us how he happened to meet these "nine and twenty" pilgrims on the way to Canterbury, how they agreed to tell the tales at the suggestion of the landlord of The Tabard (the inn where they stopped in Southwark in south London), and how they all appeared to the poet: their habits, their speech, their clothes, their attitudes, and so on. This account of the pilgrims, before any of them gets to tell a tale, is a verbal portrait gallery with word pictures of the individuals who will later tell the famous tales. We reproduce here those parts of the General Prologue most immediately relevant to the tellers of the tales we have chosen: the beginning and end, and the four individual portraits.

It has often been remarked, and it is worth remarking again, that this portrait gallery provides pictures of a considerable cross section of fourteenth-century English society. Not a complete and comprehensive survey, for Chaucer is a poet not a sociologist, but it is a sampling remarkable for its diversity: there are men and women, clerics and laymen; young, middle aged and old; people who differ widely in their spiritual lives, their economic status, their tastes in clothes, books, and food; those who need to travel constantly and those for whom this will be the one major journey of their life. There are rogues and innocents, introverts and show-offs, saints (few) and sinners (many).

The people in this varied group tell an equally varied selection of tales. The four tales that we have included here are often known as the Marriage Group for the simple reason that they all deal in a significant way with the subject of marriage and, in the case of the first three, they are connected with each other even by clear textual reference.[1] That is, the Clerk clearly refers to the Wife of Bath, and the Merchant refers back to both the Clerk and the Wife. Your appreciation of *The Clerk's Tale* is enhanced if you have read *The Wife of Bath's Tale* that precedes it, and *The Merchant's Tale* that follows it, for *The Clerk's Tale* is a sly response to the rollicking Wife on the subject of marriage; in turn, it provokes a sharp, dissenting reply from the Merchant. The tale of the Franklin seems to promote a humane compromise among the views of the preceding three:

> *friends ever each other must obey*
> *If they will longe holden company.*
> *Love will not be constrained by mastery.*
> *When mastery comes the God of love anon*
> *Beateth his wings, and farewell, he is gone.*

---

[1] The term *marriage group* was first used by Eleanor Hammond in *Chaucer: A Bibliographical Manual* (1908), p. 256 to characterize the Wife of Bath's Prologue and the tales of the Franklin and Merchant. Her single sentence was elaborated by George L. Kittredge in *Modern Philology* (1912) and in *Chaucer and His Poetry* (1915). Kittredge added the Clerk's Tale to the group, and since his time the term has been widely used, with some difference of opinion as to the extent or even the existence of such a grouping.

Here we have some of the best tales from the most famous of Chaucer's works and one of the most famous works in English literature.

THE LANGUAGE OF THIS EDITION[1]

 Geoffrey Chaucer, the author of the Tales, died in the year 1400, rather more than 200 years before the death of Shakespeare.

Since living languages are always changing, it follows that Chaucer's language will be more different from ours than Shakespeare's is. This is most noticeable in the medieval spelling that is preserved in most editions of the Tales. By contrast, the spelling in any current edition of Shakespeare is modern, even if some of the words are obsolete. This sensible editorial convention makes it unnecessary for Shakespeare readers to wrestle with the needless difficulties and uncertainties of the actual spelling of Shakespeare's own day. Shakespeare's verse is difficult enough as it is.

By contrast, the archaic spelling in every edition of Chaucer's verse except ours is a severe obstacle for many people who do not want to fight the difficulties of the fourteenth-century spelling of Chaucer any more than the oddities of the sixteenth-century

---

[1] For full development of the argument sketched here see my articles "On Not Reading Chaucer—Aloud," *Mediaevalia* 9 (1986 for 1983), 205 - 224, and "On Making an Edition of The Canterbury Tales in Modern Spelling," *Chaucer Review* 26 (1991), 48-64. As the present edition indicates, I have since modified my views enough to restore the "pronounced" – *e*'s in most words.

spelling of Shakespeare. That is why the spelling in our printed edition has been modernized **without changing anything else.**

Somewhere near the front of most editions of Chaucer's work there is nearly always a Guide to Chaucer's Pronunciation, and it is customary in college Chaucer classes to insist that the students *pronounce* the words as Chaucer was supposed to have pronounced them. The accuracy of this re-constructed pronunciation is quite dubious, as it is now 600 years since Chaucer was writing and speaking, and the evidence from that period of how English was pronounced ranges from slim to non-existent. There is some reason for scholars to try this reconstructed pronunciation, but not enough reason to impose it on general readers and on students most of whom do not intend to be professional medievalists.

Phonetic Version

Whan that Avril with his shoorez sote-eh
The druughth of March hath perséd toe the rote-eh,
And baathéd every vein in switch licoor
Of which vertúe engendréd is the flure,
Whan Zephirus ache with his swayt-eh braith,
Inspeeréd hath in every holt and haith
The tender croppez, and the yung-eh sun-eh
Hath in the Ram his hal-f coorse y-run-eh,
And smaaleh foolez maaken melody-eh
That slaipen al the nicked with awpen ee-eh
So pricketh hem Nat-yóor in hir cooráhjez—
Than longen fol-k to gawn on pilgrimáhjez
And pal-mers for to saiken straunj-eh strondez
To ferneh halwehs couth in sundry londez
And spesyaly from every sheerez end-eh
Of Engelond to Caunterbry they wend-eh
The hawly blissful martyr for to saik-eh
That hem hath holpen whan that they were saik-eh.

This passage and others are reproduced in the International Phonetic Alphabet in Helge Kokeritz's pamphlet *A Guide To Chaucer's Pronunciation* (Holt, Rinehart: N.Y., 1962). Even in Kokeritz, which is the standard version, the uncertainties of the phonetics are clear from the fact that he gives fifteen alternative pronunciations in sixteen lines. The Chaucer Studio has produced tape recordings of many of the tales by academics spoken in this reconstructed dialect. (Department of English, Brigham Young University, Provo, Utah 84602).

For readers and listeners interested in how Chaucer's verse **might** have sounded I have provided a *rough* "phonetic" version of a short passage opposite its manuscript version:

Hengwrt Manuscript

Whan that Auerylle with his shoures soote
The droghte of March / hath perced to the roote
And bathed euery veyne in swich lycour
Of which vertu engendred is the flour
Whan zephirus eek with his sweete breeth
Inspired hath in euery holt and heeth
The tendre croppes / and the yonge sonne
Hath in the Ram / his half cours yronne
And smale foweles / maken melodye
That slepen al the nyght with open Iye
So priketh hem nature / in hir corages
Thanne longen folk to goon on pilrymages
And Palmeres for to seeken straunge strondes
To fernè halwes / kouthe in sondry londes
And specially / from euery shyres ende
Of Engelond / to Caunterbury they wende
The holy blisful martir / for to seke
That hem hath holpen whan at they weere seke.

The conviction behind this present edition is that Chaucer can be read in standard modern spelling, and heard in any standard spoken English. And by Chaucer we mean the language of Chaucer himself, NOT a translation. The language of this edition is **Chaucer's** language line for line, word for word—Chaucer's vocabulary, Chaucer's word order, Chaucer's sentence structure. The only things that we have modernized, in accordance with the practice for all other authors, are spelling and punctuation. But this makes all the difference.

Some obsolete and archaic words and forms remain, but this is true of the work of any author from a former era, and even with an author as old as Chaucer these expressions are never so numerous as to hold up seriously the meaning of the narrative. Moreover, all unusual words are glossed in the right margin. But it is probably unwise and certainly unnecessary to stop your reading to look up every unfamiliar word or for other small difficulties. The narrative itself will often explain these.

There are tape recordings by professional actors of the tales as printed in this edition (for details see p.8 above). Listeners without any acquaintance with the theories of Middle English sounds can enjoy the tales spoken in modern English. A combination of the tape and the edition is an excellent way to get a good grasp of Chaucer's work with a minimum of wrestling with the oddities of spoken or written Middle English, as Chaucer's English is called. These tapes are especially useful for those who have to use an old-spelling edition. They can thus listen to the modern pronunciation while reading the old spelling. Much of the pain of fighting the archaic spelling and sounds is thus eliminated, so readers and hearers learn quickly to **enjoy** Chaucer not merely endure him. The poetry remains great after the elimination of the difficulty of old spelling and old pronunciation, a difficulty that did not exist, remember, for Chaucer's contemporaries.

Brief Life of Chaucer

 Geoffrey Chaucer was born in London in the early 1340's. His father, a prosperous wine merchant, had enough money to provide his son with an education that grounded him solidly in French and Latin, and enough influence to have the boy taken into an aristocratic household for another kind of education that would later fit him for diplomatic, court and public service. The early part of this training he got in the house of Lionel, one of the sons of King Edward III. At the end of that phase of his education, he went to France on one of the military campaigns of the Hundred Years War, but was captured. He was important enough to be ransomed by the king, but not as important as Sir John of Beverley's horse for which the king paid more ransom money than he did for Geoffrey. Some amused remarks have been made by modern students of Chaucer about the king's sense of priorities, but as Professor Lounsbury said while horses were still a functioning part of American life, there has never been a period in the history of our race when the average man could bring the price of a good horse. That still means that the king thought Geoffrey Chaucer was an average man. How unperceptive, we think.

After his rather inglorious military debut, Geoffrey may have been for a year or two a student at one of the Inns of Court, schools which prepared men for careers in law and administration. He married Philippa Roet (or Pan), a woman who had probably served in the household of Lionel and his wife Elizabeth. Philippa's sister was first the mistress and later the wife of John of Gaunt, another son of Edward III, and one of the most powerful men in the land. Already Geoffrey was well connected. In the 1360's Chaucer served on missions abroad for the king several times. In the early 1370's he visited Italy for the first time on a trade mission, and again in 1378. During these trips he made acquaintance with the work of Dante, Boccaccio and Petrarch, all of whom influenced him profoundly.

In the meantime, in 1374 he had been appointed Controller of the Customs in wool, skins and hides at the Port of London, probably both a demanding and remunerative post, and when he was appointed Controller of the Petty Customs on wines in 1382, he no doubt had more work and more money. These posts he kept until about 1386, when he seems to have lost them through a "change in administration." They were real jobs, and not sinecures. How he wrote as much as he did while travelling on diplomatic missions or working full time on the docks is something of a mystery. He himself lifts the veil just a tiny bit in a passage spoken by the Eagle to Geoffrey in his poem "The House of Fame":

> Thou hearest neither that nor this.
> For when thy labor done all is,
> And hast made all thy reckonings,
> Instead of rest and newė things
> Thou gost home to thy house anon,
> And all as dumb as any stone
> Thou sittest at another book
> Till fully dazėd is thy look.

For a man whose reading and writing were done in large part after his day's work, he produced a prodigious body of poetry of the very first rank.

For one year in 1386 he was even a Member of Parliament for Kent. From 1389-91 he was Clerk of the King's Works, in charge of maintaining some of the major royal buildings under the new king, Richard II. In the rest of the decade of the 1390's he does not seem to have had any official position, and there is some evidence that he was in serious debt. One such piece of evidence is a charming "begging poem" that he wrote "To His Purse," and directed to King Henry IV who had seized power from Richard II:

> *To you, my purse, and to no other wight*   *person*
> *Complain I, for you be my lady dear.*
> *I am so sorry now that you be light ...*
> *Me were as lief be laid upon my bier,*   *I'd rather*
> *For which unto your mercy thus I cry:*
> *Be heavy again or else must I die.*

And so on for three stanzas ending with a direct plea to the King:

> *O conqueror of Brutë's Albion ...*   *(Britain)*
> *Have mind upon my supplication*

He died in 1400, and was buried in Westminster Abbey, the first occupant of Poet's Corner.

Chaucer lived during trying and sometimes stirring years, and yet one hears very little of this in his poetry. He was a small boy when the Black Death struck for the first time in 1348, one of the most fearful calamities of the Middle Ages. In several visitations the bubonic plague wiped out at least one third of the population of England, striking quite democratically at all ranks of society. It must have left powerful memories, or at least yielded powerful narratives from his elders, yet there is hardly a reference to this traumatic event in his work. Partly as the result of the shortage of labor produced by the Black Death, the peasantry became rather more demanding. Repressive legislation produced only rebellion, notably the Peasants Revolt of 1381 which threatened the whole fabric of society. Again there is but one passing mention of it in Chaucer's work, though some marxist critics profess to hear its muffled reverberations throughout.

We do hear rather more about the major religious questions that beset people at the time. The profound dissatisfaction of many people with the institutional Church is reflected in Chaucer's satiric portraits of clerics in his General Prologue and in some of his tales. But his satire never shares the vehemence of a reformer like his contemporary John Wycliffe, a progenitor of the Reformation, who had to be protected from the wrath of senior churchmen by the power of John of Gaunt. Nor does it have the impassioned commitment of a different kind of reformer and different kind of poet, his other contemporary William Langland, author of *Piers Plowman*.

From his earliest years and over an extended period of time Chaucer had rather close contact with some of the most elevated and powerful people in the land, and yet in more than one place in his work he seems to deal in a very sympathetic way with the idea that true nobility, "gentilesse," is not a matter of "gentle" birth, but of moral quality. And his tales of "churls" (working people) show him at least as much at home with the world of the working class as with the aristocratic world portrayed in the Knight's tale. It is as well to remember that he did work for years in the customs at the port of London where he rubbed shoulders with everyone from common seamen through small-time pirates to merchant princes, who were often just bigger pirates.

It is hard now, after six hundred years and the writings of many great poets in English, to realize what a phenomenon Chaucer was. Every poet after him has had a great poet before him writing in English from whom to learn and borrow. Chaucer had no predecessor in English, for the literature of pre-conquest England which we call Old English was a closed book to him, and there seems to have been little English literature of any quality between the Norman Conquest and his time. His only serious models were the great Latin poets of ancient Rome and the vernacular poets of more modern France and Italy. It was probably from the French and Italians that he got the idea for the English iambic pentameter line which he invented, and which is the line of all his major poetry and of almost all other major poetry in English, rimed or unrimed, from his day until very recent times, when metrical verse has largely gone out of fashion. He was a diplomat, a senior civil servant who always worked for a living, and a scholar interested not only in poetry, but in science and philosophy. He translated the *Consolations of Philosophy* by Boethius, a book whose influence on him and on the rest of the literate medieval world it would be difficult to overestimate. And, because astronomy was one of his passions, he wrote for his "little son Lewis" a *Treatise on the Astrolabe*, an instrument for studying the heavens. He knew the standard theories on dreams, and the standard authorities on the theological-philosophical problem of Predestination. He was, in fact, the first of a long line of poets in English who were nearly as learned as they were poetically gifted.

A Short Note on How the Text May Be Read

 Readers are invited to pronounce or not, as they see fit, all instances of dotted ė, as in "Inspirėd," "easėd," "youngė," "sunnė".

This superscript dot indicates a letter that was probably pronounced in Chaucer's medieval poetic dialect, possibly with a light schwa sound, a kind of brief "-eh". Hence, this modspell text has kept some medieval spellings that differ somewhat from ours: "sweetė" for "sweet," "halfė" for "half," "couldė" for "could," "lippės" for "lips," and so on. This preserves the extra syllable to indicate the more regular meter that many scholars insist was Chaucer's, and that many readers will prefer. The reader is the final judge.

It is perfectly possible to read "With locks curled as they were laid in press" rather than "With lockės curled as they were laid in press." Some would prefer "She let no morsel from her lips fall" over "She let no morsel from her lippės fall". Similarly a sentence of strong monosyllables like "With scaled brows black and piled beard" should be at least as good as "With scalėd browės black and pilėd beard." As with these, an acceptable rhythm for the following lines without pronouncing the -ė-'s could be kept by crisp pronunciation of final consonants or by pauses at the breaks:

Madamè Pertelot, my worldè's bliss,
Hearken these blissful birdès—how they sing!
And see the freshè flowers—how they spring!

There is nothing to prevent any reader from ignoring the superscript -è- whenever you feel that is appropriate. Similarly you may wish (or not) to pronounce the ï of words like *devotïon*, to make three syllables for the word instead of two, etc. The text offers a choice. Blameth not me if that you choose amiss.

The medieval endings of some words, especially verbs, in -n or -en have been retained for reasons of smoother rhythm: **"lacken, sleepen, seeken, weren, woulden, liven, withouten."** Such words mean the same with or without the -n or -en. Also words beginning y- mean the same with or without the y- as in **y-tied, y-taught**.

An acute accent indicates that a word was probably stressed in a different way from its modern counterpart: **uságe, viságe, daggér, mannér, serviceáble** to rhyme with **table; sort / comfórt; dance / penánce; disáventure / measúre / creäture (3 syllables).** Some of these and other common words like **certain** are sometimes pronounced with emphasis on one syllable, sometimes on another: **cértain, certáin.**

The Beginning and End
of
THE GENERAL PROLOGUE

 The opening is a long, elaborate sentence about the effects of Spring on the vegetable and animal world, and on people. The style of the rest of the Prologue and Tales is much simpler than this opening. A close paraphrase of the opening sentence is offered at the bottom of this page[1]

	When that April with his showers soote	*its showers sweet*
	The drought of March hath piercèd to the root	
	And bathèd every vein in such liquor	*rootlet / liquid*
	Of which virtúe engendered is the flower;[2]	
5	When Zephyrus eke with his sweetè breath	*West Wind also*
	Inspirèd hath in every holt and heath	*grove & field*

---

[1] When April with its sweet showers has pierced the drought of March to the root and bathed every rootlet in the liquid by which the flower is engendered; when the west wind also, with its sweet breath, has brought forth young shoots in every grove and field; when the early sun of spring has run half his course in the sign of Aries, and when small birds make melody, birds that sleep all night with eyes open, (as Nature inspires them to)—THEN people have a strong desire to go on pilgrimages, and pilgrims long to go to foreign shores to distant shrines known in various countries. And especially they go from every county in England to seek out the shrine of the holy blessed martyr who has helped them when they were sick.

[2] 4: "By virtue (strength) of which the flower is engendered."

	The tender croppès, and the youngè sun	*young shoots / Spring sun*
	Hath in the Ram his halfè course y-run,[1]	*in Aries / has run*
	And smallè fowlès maken melody	*little birds*
10	That sleepen all the night with open eye	*Who sleep*
	(So pricketh them Natúre in their couráges),	*spurs / spirits*
	Then longen folk to go on pilgrimáges,	*people long*
	And palmers for to seeken strangè strands	*pilgrims / shores*
	To fernè hallows couth in sundry lands,[2]	*distant shrines known*
15	And specially from every shirè's end	*county's*
	Of Engèland to Canterbury they wend	*go*
	The holy blissful martyr for to seek,	*St. Thomas Becket*
	That them hath holpen when that they were sick.	*Who has helped them*

At the Tabard Inn, near London, the poet-pilgrim falls in with a group of twenty nine other pilgrims who have met each other along the way

	Befell that in that season on a day	*It happened*
20	In Southwark at The Tabard as I lay	*inn name / lodged*
	Ready to wenden on my pilgrimage	*to go*
	To Canterbury with full devout couráge,	*spirit, heart*
	At night was come into that hostelry	*inn*
	Well nine and twenty in a company	*fully 29*
25	Of sundry folk by áventure y-fall	*by chance fallen...*
	In fellowship, and pilgrims were they all	*...Into company*
	That toward Canterbury woulden ride.	*wished to*
	The chambers and the stables weren wide	*were roomy*
	And well we weren easèd at the best.	*entertained*
30	And shortly, when the sunnè was to rest,	*sun had set*
	So had I spoken with them every one	
	That I was of their fellowship anon,	
	And madè forward early for to rise	*agreement*
	To take our way there as I you devise.	*I shall tell you*

---

[1] 8: The early sun of Spring has moved part way through the sign of Aries (the Ram) in the Zodiac.

[2] 13-14: "Pilgrims seek foreign shores (to go) to distant shrines known in different lands." *Palmers:* pilgrims, from the palm-leaves they got in Jerusalem.

35	But natheless, while I have time and space,	*nevertheless*
	Ere that I further in this talė pace,	*Before I go*
	Methinketh it accordant to reason	*It seems to me*
	To tell you all the conditïon	*circumstances*
	Of each of them so as it seemėd me,	*to me*
40	And which they weren, and of what degree	*And who / social rank*
	And eke in what array that they were in;	*also / dress*
	And at a knight then will I first begin.	

The descriptions of the individual Pilgrims follow. We keep only the four relevant to our four tales; each will be found before its appropriate tale.

* * * *

The narrator continues

	Now have I told you soothly in a clause	*truly / briefly*
	Th'estate, th'array, the number, and eke the cause	*rank / condition*
	Why that assembled was this company	
	In Southwark at this gentle hostelry	*inn*
	That hight The Tabard, fastė by The Bell.	*was called / close*
720	But now is timė to you for to tell	
	How that we borėn us that ilkė night	*conducted ourselves / same*
	When we were in that hostelry alight;	*dismounted*
	And after will I tell of our viage	*journey*
	And all the remnant of our pilgrimage.	

Then the poet offers a comic apologia for the matter and language of some of the pilgrims

725	But first I pray you of your courtesy	
	That you n'arrette it not my villainy [1]	*blame / bad manners*

---

[1] 726: "That you do not blame it on my bad manners." *Villainy* means conduct associated with villeins, the lowest social class. This apologia by Chaucer (725-742) is both comic and serious: comic because it apologizes for the way fictional characters behave as if they were real people and not Chaucer's creations; serious in that it shows Chaucer sensitive to the possibility that part of his audience might take offence at some of his characters, their words and tales, especially perhaps the parts highly critical of Church and churchmen, as well as the tales of sexual misbehavior. Even the poet Dryden (in the Restoration!) and some twentieth-century critics have thought the apology was needed.

Though that I plainly speak in this matter

To tellė you their wordės and their cheer,   *behavior*

Not though I speak their wordės properly,   *exactly*

730   For this you knowen all as well as I:

Whoso shall tell a tale after a man

He must rehearse as nigh as ever he can   *repeat as nearly*

Ever each a word, if it be in his charge,   *Every / if he is able*

All speak he ne'er so rudėly and large,   *Even if / coarsely & freely*

735   Or elsė must he tell his tale untrue

Or feignė things or findėn wordės new.   *invent things*

He may not spare, although he were his brother.   *hold back*

He may as well say one word as another.

Christ spoke himself full broad in Holy Writ   *very bluntly / Scripture*

740   And well you wot no villainy is it.   *you know*

Eke Plato sayeth, whoso can him read: *Also / whoever*

"The wordės must be cousin to the deed."

Also I pray you to forgive it me

All have I not set folk in their degree   *Although / social ranks*

745   Here in this tale as that they shouldė stand.

My wit is short, you may well understand.   *My intelligence*

*After serving dinner, Harry Bailly, the fictional Host, owner of the
Tabard Inn originates the idea for the Tales:*

Great cheerė made our HOST us every one,[1]   *welcome / for us*

And to the supper set he us anon.   *quickly*

He servėd us with victuals at the best.   *the best food*

750   Strong was the wine and well to drink us lest.   *it pleased us*

A seemly man our Hostė was withall   *fit*

For to be a marshall in a hall.   *master of ceremonies*

A largė man he was with eyen steep   *prominent eyes*

A fairer burgess was there none in Cheap.   *citizen / Cheapside*

755   Bold of his speech and wise and well y-taught

And of manhood him lackėdė right naught.

---

[1] 747: "The Host had a warm welcome for every one of us."

Eke thereto he was right a merry man,	*And besides*
And after supper playèn he began	*joking*
And spoke of mirthè amongst other things,	
760 (When that we had made our reckonings),	*paid our bills*
And saidè thus: "Now, lordings, truly	*ladies and g'men*
You be to me right welcome heartily,	
For by my truth, if that I shall not lie,	
I saw not this year so merry a company	
765 At oncè in this harbor as is now.	*this inn*
Fain would I do you mirthè, wist I how,[1]	*Gladly / if I knew*
And of a mirth I am right now bethought	*amusement*
To do you ease, and it shall costè naught.	
You go to Canterbury, God you speed.	
770 The blissful martyr 'quitè you your meed.	*give you reward*
And well I wot, as you go by the way,	*I know / along the road*
You shapèn you to talèn and to play;	*intend to tell tales & jokes*
For truly, comfort nor mirth is none	
To ridèn by the way dumb as a stone;	
775 And therefore would I makèn you desport	*amusement for you*
As I said erst, and do you some comfort.	*before*
And if you liketh all by one assent	*if you please*
For to standen at my judgèment	*abide by*
And for to workèn as I shall you say,	
780 Tomorrow when you ridèn by the way,	
Now by my father's soulè that is dead,[2]	
But you be merry, I'll give you my head.	*If you're not*
Hold up your hands withoutèn morè speech."	
Our counsel was not longè for to seek.	*Our decision*

The pilgrims agree to hear his idea

785 Us thought it was not worth to make it wise,	*not worthwhile / difficult*
And granted him withoutèn more advice,	*discussion*
And bade him say his verdict as him lest.	*as pleased him*

---

[1] 766: "Gladly would I entertain you, if I knew how."

[2] 781: "Now, by the soul of my dead father ..."

To pass the time pleasantly, every one will tell a couple of tales on the way out and a couple on the way back

"Lordings," quod he, "now hearkèn for the best,   *Ladies & g'men*
But take it not, I pray you, in disdain.
790   This is the point—to speakèn short and plain:
That each of you to shorten with our way
In this viage, shall tellèn talès tway   *journey / two*
To Canterbury-ward, I mean it so,   *on the way to C.*
And homeward he shall tellèn other two
795   Of áventures that whilom have befall.   *events / in past*

The teller of the best tale will get a dinner paid for by all the others at Harry's inn, The Tabard, on the way back from Canterbury. He offers to go with them as a guide.

And which of you that bears him best of all,
That is to say, that telleth in this case
Talès of best senténce and most soláce,   *instruction / amusement*
Shall have a supper at our aller cost   *at expense of all of us*
800   Here in this place, sitting by this post
When that we come again from Canterbury.
And for to makèn you the morè merry
I will myselfèn goodly with you ride   *gladly*
Right at mine ownè cost, and be your guide.
805   And whoso will my judgèment withsay   *whoever / contradict*
Shall pay all that we spendèn by the way,[1]   *on the trip*
And if you vouchesafe that it be so,   *agree*
Tell me anon withouten wordès mo'   *now / more*
And I will early shapèn me therefore."   *prepare*

They all accept, agreeing that the Host be MC, and then they go to bed

810   This thing was granted and our oathès swore
With full glad heart, and prayèd him also
That he would vouchèsafe for to do so   *agree*

---

[1] The host will be the Master of Ceremonies and judge. Anyone who revolts against the Host's rulings will have to pay what the others spend along the way.

And that he woulde be our governor
And of our tales judge and reporter,
815   And set a supper at a certain price,
And we will ruled be at his device   *direction*
In high and low; and thus by one assent
We been accorded to his judgement.   *agreed*
And thereupon the wine was fetched anon.
820   We dranken, and to reste went each one
Withouten any longer tarrying.

The next morning they set out and draw lots to see who shall tell the first tale

A-morrow, when the day began to spring
Up rose our Host, and was our aller cock,[1]
And gathered us together in a flock,
825   And forth we rode a little more than pace   *no great speed*
Unto the watering of St Thomas.
And there our Host began his horse arrest,   *halt*
And saide: "Lordings, hearken if you lest.[2]   *if you please*
You wot your forward (and I it you record) *know y. promise / remind*
830   If evensong and morrowsong accord.
Let see now who shall tell the firste tale.
As ever may I drinken wine or ale,
Whoso be rebel to my judgement   *Whoever is*
Shall pay for all that by the way is spent.
835   Now draweth cut, ere that we further twinn; *draw lots before we go*
He which that has the shortest shall begin.
Sir Knight," quod he, "my master and my lord,   *said he*
Now draweth cut, for that is mine accord.   *draw lots / wish*

---

[1] 823: "He was the cock (rooster) for all of us." That is, he got us all up at cockcrow.

[2] 825-30: They set out at a gentle pace, and at the first watering place for the horses, (*the watering of St. Thomas*) the Host says: "Ladies and gentlemen, listen please. You know (*wot*) your agreement (*forward*), and I remind (*record*) you of it, if evening hymn and morning hymn agree," i.e. if what you said last night still holds this morning.

Come near," quod he, "my lady Prioress.

840 And you, Sir Clerk, let be your shamefastness,   *shyness*

Nor study not. Lay hand to, every man."

Anon to drawèn every wight began   *person*

And shortly for to tellèn as it was,

Were it by áventure or sort or cas,   *Whether by fate, luck or fortune*

845 The sooth is this, the cut fell to the knight,   *The truth / the lot*

Of which full blithe and glad was every wight.   *very happy / person*

And tell he must his tale as was reason

By forward and by composïtion   *By agreement & contract*

As you have heard. What needeth wordès mo'?   *more*

850 And when this good man saw that it was so,

As he that wise was and obedient

To keep his forward by his free assent,   *his agreement*

He saidè: "Since I shall begin the game,

What! welcome be the cut, in God's name.

855 Now let us ride, and hearkèn what I say."

And with that word we ridèn forth our way

And he began with right a merry cheer   *with great good humor*

His tale anon, and said as you may hear.   *at once*

The tale of the Knight is not included in this selection of Tales. We pass directly to the first of the Marriage Group, the Prologue and Tale of the Wife of Bath

THE CANTERBURY TALES

The Wife of Bath and Her Tale

The Wife of Bath's Tale

 Introduction

We remember the Wife of Bath, not so much for her tale as for Chaucer's account of her in the General Prologue and, above all, for her own Prologue. For one thing, the tale itself is a rather unremarkable folktale with a lecture on true nobility somewhat awkwardly incorporated. The tale is meant to illustrate the contention of her prologue: that a marriage in which the woman has the mastery is the best, and the conclusion of one closely coincides with the other. The tale also seems to express covertly her desire to be young and beautiful again. It is not a poor tale, but neither is it of unforgettable force like the Pardoner's or of unforgettable humor like the Miller's. Moreover, the Prologue is about three times as long as the tale to which it is supposed to be a short introduction. If that is appropriate for anyone, it is so for Alison of Bath, about whom everything is large to the point of exaggeration: her bulk, her clothes, her mouth, the number of her marriages, the extent of her travels, her zest for sex, her love of domination, her torrential delivery. The result is a portrait of someone for whom it is difficult to find an analogy in English literature except perhaps

Shakespeare's Falstaff or some of the characters of Dickens.

She is wonderful company provided one is not married to her and can contemplate from a distance the fate of the sixth husband whom she is seeking as voraciously as she did his predecessors: "Welcome the sixth, when that ever he shall." Shall what? Have the temerity to get too close to this medieval Venus Flytrap, and be devoured?

Oddly enough, this unforgettably ebullient figure is an amalgam of many features derived from Chaucer's reading. Many of the traits he attributes to her are essentially borrowed from that favorite of the Middle Ages, the long French poem *The Romance of the Rose*. She also embodies traits in women which misogynistic Church Fathers like Jerome and Tertullian denounced in their writings. All this illustrates what wonderfully creative work can be done with old material. The medievals liked to think that their tales were not original, that they were renewed versions of old authors who had become "authorities." Here Chaucer borrows very freely, and it is interesting to observe the result. While the elements are not original but largely borrowed from a variety of sources, the final product is the unforgettably original creation that is the Wife.

The Wife has attracted attention and comment over the centuries in abundance in contrast to, say, that pleasant and attractive lady, the Prioress. One reason is the intense personal quality that emanates from the character. Take her way of referring to herself or to women in general. Whether she is holding forth in her Prologue or telling her Tale, her pronouns slip with an engaging ease from "they" to "we" to "I" or from "women" to "we" to "I" or the other way round. Her talk is intensely *hers*, incapable of being confused with that of anyone else. As she is telling how she always made provision for another husband if her current victim died, she loses the thread of her discourse for a second, but only for a second:

> But now, sir, let me see what shall I sayn?
> Aha, I have my tale again.

As she is telling her folktale of the knight and the old hag, she refers to the classical story of Midas, and immediately wants to tell it:

> *Will you hear the tale?*

Her Prologue is, above all, about *her*—her experiences of love in and out of marriage, and her right to hold forth on that subject in spite of the "authority" of clerics who know nothing about the matter. A much-married woman, she has much more "authority" on love and marriage than any celibate clerk who knows only books, and she knows how to deal with books that do not please her too. Her outpouring is a confession of sorts but without a trace of the penitent's "mea culpa," for as she recalls with relish: "I have had my world as in my time." The only thing she regrets is that age "Hath me bereft my beauty and my pith."

Hers is the first contribution to the Marriage Group, and it is answered in one way or another by the Tales of the Clerk, the Merchant, and the Franklin. She asks her fellow pilgrims to take it "not agrief of what I say / For my intent is not but for to play " (191-192), but the force of her polemic and her personality has attracted far more attention from readers early and late than most other characters on that famous pilgrimage.

The Portrait, Prologue and Tale of the Wife of Bath

The Portrait of the Wife from the General Prologue

In the Wife of Bath we have one of only three women on the pilgrimage. Unlike the other two she is not a nun, but a much-married woman, a widow yet again. Everything about her is exaggerated: she has been married five times, has been to Jerusalem three times, and her hat and hips are as large as her sexual appetite and her love of talk.

A good WIFE was there of besidė Bath	*near*
But she was somedeal deaf, and that was scath.	*somewhat / a pity*
Her coverchiefs full finė were of ground;	*finely woven*
I durstė swear they weighėden ten pound	*dare*
That on a Sunday were upon her head.	
Her hosen weren of fine scarlet red	*stockings*
Full straight y-tied, and shoes full moist and new.	*supple*
Bold was her face and fair and red of hue.	*color*
She was a worthy woman all her life.	

460 Husbands at churchė door she had had five,[1]

Withouten other company in youth,	*Not counting*
But thereof needeth not to speak as nouth.	*now*
And thrice had she been at Jerusalem.	*3 times*
She had passėd many a strangė stream.	*foreign*
At Romė she had been and at Boulogne,	
In Galicia at St James and at Cologne.	*[famous shrines]*
She couldė much of wandering by the way.[2]	*knew much*

---

[1] 460: *at churchė door:* Weddings took place in the church porch, followed by Mass inside.

[2] 467: Chaucer does not explain, and the reader is probably not expected to ask, how the Wife managed to marry five husbands and take pilgrimage as almost another occupation. Going to Jerusalem from England *three* times was an extraordinary feat in the Middle Ages. This list is, like some others in the Prologue, a deliberate exaggeration, as is everything else about the Wife.

	Gat-toothed was she, soothly for to say.	*Gap-toothed/truly*
	Upon an ambler easily she sat	*slow horse*
470	Y-wimpled well,[1] and on her head a hat	
	As broad as is a buckler or a targe,	*kinds of shield*
	A foot mantle about her hippés large,	*outer skirt*
	And on her feet a pair of spurs sharp.	
	In fellowship well could she laugh and carp.	*joke*
	Of remedies of love she knew perchance	*by experience*
	For she could of that art the oldé dance.[2]	*knew*

The Prologue to the Wife of Bath's Tale

The Wife's narrative opens with a defense of her many marriages, all legal, as she points out, i.e. recognized by the Church even though some churchmen frowned on widows re-marrying. The Wife challenges anyone to show her where the Scripture sets a limit to the number of successive legal marriages a person can have in a lifetime. She claims that, because she has lots of experience of marriage, she is more of an authority on that subject than the celibate "authorities" who write about it. And she knows how to use "authorities" too, if it comes to it, as the many marginal references in our text show.

Experience, though no authority	*authors*
Were in this world, is right enough for me	
To speak of woe that is in marrïage;[3]	
For, lordings, since I twelve years was of age,[4]	

---

[1] 470: A wimple was a woman's cloth headgear covering the ears, the neck and the chin.

[2] 476: She knew all about that.

[3] 1-3: "Even if no 'authorities' had written on the subject, my own experience is quite enough for me to speak with authority on the woes of marriage." By *authorities* she means the Bible, theologians and classical authors.

[4] 4: *Lordings* means something like "Ladies and gentlemen." Twelve was the legal cononical age for girls to marry. Marriages took place at the door of the church followed by mass inside.

5	(Thankèd be God that is etern alive)	
	Husbands at churchè door I have had five,	
	(If I so often might have wedded be).	
	And all were worthy men in their degree.	
	But me was told certain not long agone is,	*(To) me*
10	That since that Christ ne went never but once	
	To wedding, in the Cane of Galilee,	*John II, 1-10*
	That by the same example taught he me,	
	That I ne shouldè wedded be but once.[1]	
	Lo, hark eke which a sharp word for the nonce[2]	
15	Beside a well Jesus, God and man,	
	Spoke in reproof of the Samaritan:	*John IV, 6-26*
	'Thou hast had fivè husbandès,' quod he;	*said he*
	'And that ilkè man which that now hath thee,	*that very man*
	Is not thy husband.' Thus he said certain;	
20	What that he meant thereby, I cannot sayn.	
	But that I ask why that the fifthè man	
	Was no husband to the Samaritan?	
	How many might she have in marrïage?	
	Yet heard I never tellen in mine age	*my life*
25	Upon this number definitïon;	
	Men may divine and glossen up and down.	*speculate & comment*
	But well I wot, express without a lie,	*I know / definitely*
	God bade us for to wax and multiply;	*told us to increase*
	That gentle text can I well understand.	
30	Eke well I wot he said that my husband	*Also I know well*
	Should let father and mother, and take to me;	*leave (Matt. xix, 5.)*

---

[1] 9-13: Jerome, one of the more ascetic of the Church Fathers, suggested that because Jesus is recorded as having attended only one wedding, people should not marry more than once. The Wife scoffs at this peculiar thinking.

[2] 14-16: "Now listen also to what sharp words Jesus, who is God and man, spoke on one occasion (*for the nonce*) when he reproved the Samaritan woman at the well." In the Gospel of John (4:4-26) Jesus tells a Samaritan woman whom he meets as she is drawing water from a well, but whom he has not seen before, that she has had five husbands, and that the man she is now living with is not her husband. He does not say why her present partner is not her husband.

But of no number mentïon made he,
Of bigamy or of octogamy;[1]   *2 or 8 marriages*
Why should men then speak of it villainy?   *speak badly*

Holy men in the Bible had more wives than one

35   Lo, here the wisė king Daun Solomon;
     I trowė he had wivės many a one.   *I believe*
     (As would to God it lawful were to me
     To be refreshėd half so oft as he).
     Which gift of God had he for all his wivės![2]
40   No man hath such, that in this world alive is.
     God wot, this noble king, as to my wit,   *God knows / I'll wager*
     The firstė night had many a merry fit   *bout*
     With each of them, so well was him alive.   *so virile was he (?)*
     Blessed be God that I have wedded five.[3]
45   Welcome the sixthė when that ever he shall,   *shall (come along)*
     For since I will not keep me chaste in all   *totally celibate*
     When my husband is from the worldė gone,
     Some Christian man shall weddė me anon.
     For then, the apostle says that I am free   *Paul (I Cor VII, 9)*
50   To wed, on Godė's half, where it liketh me. *w. God's consent / pleases me*
     He says that to be wedded is no sin;

---

[1] 33. "Bigamy" here means being married twice but not to two people at the same time. "Octogamy" = 8 marriages in a row. Later, however, the Wife seems to use the term "bigamy" in the sense of the sin or crime of bigamy (l.86).

[2] 39: This line means either that the gift was from God to him in granting him so many wives, or from Solomon to them, probably the former.

[3] 44a-44f: The following six lines do not appear in any Six Text MS, but they have been accepted by scholars as genuine Chaucer, and appear in many editions.

44a Of which I have pickėd out the best
     Both of their nether purse and of their chest.   *= lower purse = scrotum*
     Divérsė schoolės maken perfect clerks   *students*
     And díverse practices in sundry works
     Maken the workman perfect sikerly.
44f Of fivė husbands scholeying am I.   *I am the student*

	Better is to be wedded than to brinne.	*burn (I, Cor VII)*
	What recketh me though folk say villainy	*What care I*
	Of shrewèd Lamech and his bigamy? [1]	*(Gen.IV, 19)*
55	I wot well Abraham was a holy man,	*I know*
	And Jacob eke, as far as ever I can,	*also / I know*
	And each of them had wivès more than two,	
	And many another holy man also.	

Virginity is good, but is nowhere **demanded** by God

	Where can you see in any manner age	
60	That highè God defended marrïage	*forbade*
	By express word? I pray you telleth me.	*tell me*
	Or where commanded he virginity?	
	I wot as well as you (it is no dread)	*I know / no question*
	The apostle, when he speaks of maidenhead,	*St. Paul / virginity*
65	He said that precept thereof had he none.	*command*
	Men may *counsel* a woman to be one,	*advise / be single*
	But counselling is no commandèment;	*I Cor VII, 25*
	He put it in our ownè judgèment.	
	For haddè God commanded maidenhead,	
70	Then had he damnèd wedding with the deed.	*condemned*
	And certès, if there were no seed y-sow,	*certainly / sown*
	Virginity then whereof should it grow?	
	Paul durstè not commanden at the least	*dared not*
	A thing of which his Master gave no hest.	*no command*
75	The dart is set up for virginity,	*The first prize*
	Catch whoso may, who runneth best let's see.	
	But this word is not take of every wight,	*not meant / person*
	But there as God will give it of His might.	*only where / power*
	I wot well that the apostle was a maid,	*I know / virgin*
80	But natheless, though that he wrote or said	*I Cor. VII, 7*
	He would that every wight were such as he,	*wished t. e. person*

---

[1] 53-4: "What do I care if people speak ill of bad Lamech and his bigamy?" Though Lamech is the first man mentioned in the Bible as taking two wives, other more famous patriarchs did also, as she points out in the following lines.

	All n'is but *counsel* to virginity.	*is advice only*
	And for to be a wife he gave me leave	
	Of indulgence,[1] so n'is it no repreve	*it is no reproof*
85	To weddė me, if that my makė die,	*my mate*
	Without exceptïon of bigamy,	*accusation*
	All were it good no woman for to touch,	*Even if it is good...*
	(He meant as in his bed or in his couch)	
	For peril is both fire and tow to assemble;	*to join fire & flax*
90	You know what this example may resemble.	
	This all and some: he held virginity	*In short*
	More perfect than wedding in frailty:	*out of*
	(Frailty clepe I, but if that he and she	*I call it / unless*
	Would leaden all their life in chastity).	
95	I grant it well, I have of none envy,[2]	
	Though maidenhead preferė bigamy;	*is preferred over*
	It likes them to be clean in body and ghost.	*It pleases / b. & soul*
	Of mine estate ne will I make no boast.	*my state (as wife)*

Virginity is not for everyone

	For well you know, a lord in his household	
100	Ne has not every vessel all of gold;	
	Some be of tree and do their lord service.	*of wood*
	God clepeth folk to him in sundry wise,	*G. calls / different*
	And ever each has of God a proper gift,	*everyone / special*
	Some this, some that, as that him liketh shift.	*pleases him to choose*
105	Virginity is great perfectïon,	
	And continence eke with devotïon.	*And sexual restraint*
	But Christ, that of perfectïon is well,	*is the source*
	Bade not every wight he should go sell	*every person*
	All that he had and give it to the poor,	
110	And in such wisė follow him and his foor;	*fashion / steps*

---

[1] 83-4: "He gave me leave out of indulgence (for human weakness)" or "He gave me leave to indulge."

[2] 95: "I grant that readily. I am not envious if virginity is regarded as preferable to being married more than once."

He spoke to them that will live perfectly,   *wish to*
And, lordings, (by your leave) that am not I.
I will bestow the flower of all mine age
In the actės and the fruit of marrïage.

If virginity were for everyone, why do we all have sexual organs?

115   Tell me also, to what conclusïon   *for w. purpose*
Were members made of generatïon,   *sexual organs made*
And of so perfect wise a wright y-wrought?[1]
Trusteth me well, they were not made for nought.
Gloss whoso will, and say both up and down,   *Explain (away)*
120   That they were madė for purgatïon
Of urine, and our bothė thingės small[2]
Was eke to know a female from a male,
And for no other causė. Say you no?
The experience wot well it is not so.   *knows*
125   So that the clerkės be not with me wroth,   *clerics / angry*
I say this, that they makėd be for both,
This is to say, for office and for ease   *duty & pleasure*
Of engendrure, where we not God displease.   *procreation*
Why should men elsė in their bookės set
130   That man shall yield unto his wife her debt?
Now wherewith should he make his payėment,
If he ne used his silly instrument?[3]   *his blessed (?)*
Then were they made upon a creäture
To purgė urine, and eke for engendrure.   *also f. procreation*

Marriage is not for everyone either

135   But I say not that every wight is hold,   *person is required*

---

[1] 117: "And made (*y-wrought*) by so perfectly wise a creator (*wright*)."

[2] 121: "Both out small things". Whatever organs, male and female, the wife is thinking of, "small" is the surprising word.

[3] 132. Theologians wrote that in marriage each partner had an obligation to satisfy the other's sexual need—hence a debt that required payment when called for. This is one of the few theological teachings that appeals to the Wife, at least when she is the creditor.

That has such harness as I to you told,	*equipment*
To go and usen them in engendrure;	
Then should men take of chastity no cure.	*respect*
Christ was a maid, and shapen as a man,	*virgin, & formed*
140 And many a saint, since that this world began,	
Yet lived they ever in perfect chastity.	
I n'ill envy no virginity.[1]	*will not*
Let them be bread of purèd wheatè seed,	*refined*
And let us wivès hotèn barley bread.	*be called*

But marriage is for Alison

145 And yet with barley bread, Mark tellè can,	*St. M. says*
Our Lord Jesus refreshèd many a man.[2]	
In such estate as God has clepèd us	*career / has called*
I'll persevere; I am not precïous.	*not fastidious, snobbish*
In wifehood will I use mine instrument	
150 As freely as my Maker has it sent.	
If I be daungerous God give me sorrow.	*distant, frigid*
My husband shall it have both eve and morrow,	*night and morning*
When that him list come forth and pay his debt.	*it pleases him*
A husband will I have, I will not let,	*I won't be stopped*
155 Which shall be both my debtor and my thrall,	*Who / my slave*
And have his tribulatïon withall	*suffering*
Upon his flesh while that I am his wife.	
I have the power during all my life	
Upon his proper body, and not he;	*his own (Fr."propre")*
160 Right thus the apostle told it unto me,	*I Cor VII, 4*
And bade our husbands for to love us well.	*& Ephes V, 25*
All this senténce me liketh every deal."	*t. teaching pleases me*

An interruption from an unexpected quarter

Up starts the Pardoner, and that anon;	*suddenly*

---

[1] 142. As in many other places in Chaucer, the double negative is not bad grammar.

[2] 145-6: Probably a reference to the occasion where Christ miraculously multiplied a few loaves and fishes to feed a hungry multitude. See Mark 6: 38 ff

"Now, Dame," quod he, "by God and by Saint John,   *Now, ma'am*

165   You be a noble preacher in this case.

I was about to wed a wife, alas!

What! Should I buy it on my flesh so dear?

Yet had I lever wed no wife to-year."[1]

"Abide," quod she, "my tale is not begun.   *Wait*

170   Nay, thou shalt drinken of another tun   *barrel*

Ere that I go, shall savor worse than ale.   *(which) will taste*

And when that I have told thee forth my tale

Of tribulation in marriage,

Of which I am expert in all mine age,

175   (This is to say, myself has been the whip)

Then may'st thou choose whether thou wilt sip

Of thilke tunne, that I shall abroach.   *that cask / tap*

Beware of it, ere thou too nigh approach,   *too near*

For I shall tell examples more than ten.

180   Whoso that n'ill beware by other men   *Whoever will not*

By him shall other men corrected be.

These same wordes writeth Ptolemy;   *P. the astronomer*

Read in his Almagest, and take it there."   *A = a book on astronomy*

"Dame, I would pray you, if your will it were,"   *Ma'am*

185   Said this Pardoner, "as you began,

Tell forth your tale, and spareth for no man,

And teacheth us young men of your practice."   *know-how*

"Don't take too seriously what I am going to say," she advises

"Gladly," quod she, "since that it may you like.   *may please you*

But that I pray to all this company,

190   If that I speak after my fantasy,   *fancy*

As taketh not a-grief of what I say,   *offence*

For my intent is not but for to play.

---

[1] 166-8: "I had rather not marry this year." If the reader remembers the description of the Pardoner from the General Prologue, it will be obvious that he could never be interested in women or marriage, a fact that leaves one free to speculate about why he should make this remark to the Wife, whom he addresses as *Dame,* a polite, not a slang, usage.

Now, sir, then will I tell you forth my tale.
As ever may I drinken wine or ale
195 I shall say sooth: the husbands that I had
As three of them were good, and two were bad.
The three men were good and rich and old.
Unnethe mighten they the statute hold   *Barely keep t. (sexual) contract*
In which that they were bounden unto me.
200 You wot well what I mean of this, pardee.   *You know / by God*
As God me help, I laughe when I think,
How piteously a-night I made them swink.   *work*

How to control husbands: with relentless nagging

But by my fay, I told of it no store: *faith, I didn't care*
They had me given their land and their treasure,
205 Me needed not do longer diligence [1]
To win their love, or do them reverence.   *respect*
They loved me so well, by God above,
That I ne told no dainty of their love.   *I didn't value*
A wise woman will busy her ever in one   *e. in one = always*
210 To get her love, yea, where as she has none,
But since I had them wholly in my hand,
And since that they had given me all their land,
What should I taken keep them for to please   *take care*
But it were for my profit, or mine ease?   *Unless it were*
215 I set them so a-worke, by my fay,   *faith*
That many a night they sungen 'Welaway!'   *'Alas'*
The bacon was not fetched for them, I trow,   *I guess*
That some men have in Essex at Dunmow.[2]
I governed them so well after my law,   *according to*
220 That each of them full blissful was and faw   *glad*
To bringe me gay thinges from the fair.   *pretty*

---

[1] 205. "I no longer needed to take pains" (lit. "It was no longer necessary to me").

[2] 218: The Dunmow Flitch of bacon, awarded every year to the couple who had not quarreled all year or regretted their marriage.

They were full glad when I spoke to them fair,   *nicely*
For God it wot, I chid them spitously.   *G. knows I nagged t. mercilessly*
Now hearken how I bore me properly.   *behaved / usually?*

225   You wisè wivès that can understand,
Thus shall you speak and bear them wrong on hand,   *deceive them*
For half so boldèly can there no man
Swear and lie as a woman can.
(I say not this by wivès that be wise,

230   But if it be when they them misadvise).   *unless they misbehave*
A wisè wife, if that she can her good,   *if she knows*
Shall bearen him on hand the chough is wood,[1]   *t. crow is mad*
And takè witness of her ownè maid
Of her assent. But hearken how I said:

235   'Sir oldè kaynard, is this thine array?[2]   *You old fool*
Why is my neighèbourè's wife so gay?   *so well dressed*
She is honourèd overall there she goes.   *everywhere*
I sit at home; I have no thrifty clothes.   *pretty*
What dost thou at my neigèhbourè's house?

240   Is she so fair? Art thou so amorous?
What rown you with our maid, ben'dicitee?   *whisper*
Sir oldè lecher, let thy japès be.   *games*
And if I have a gossip or a friend   *a confidant*
Withouten guilt, thou chidest as a fiend   *you complain l. a devil*

245   If that I walk or play unto his house.   *enjoy myself at*
Thou comest home as drunken as a mouse
And preachest on thy bench—with evil preef!   *evil take you!*

---

[1] 231-34: " A woman who knows what is good for her will convince her husband that 'the crow is mad', and call her maid to witness for her." In a well-known folktale a talking bird (a chough or crow) sees a woman committing adultery, and tells her husband. But with the help of her maid, the wife is able to convince the husband that the bird is talking nonsense. The wife is less lucky in Chaucer's version of that story, *The Manciple's Tale.*

[2] 235: *thine array* means either "your way of behaving" or (more probably) "the clothes you let me have."

What husbands preach and complain about—marriage, mostly

	Thou sayst to me it is a great mischief	
	To wed a poorė woman for costáge.	*expense*
250	And if that she be rich, of high paráge,	*birth*
	Then sayst thou that it is a tormentry	
	To suffer her pride and her meláncholy.	
	And if that she be fair (Thou very knave!)	*if she's pretty, you wretch*
	Thou sayst that every holor will her have;	*lecher*
255	She may no while in chastity abide	
	That is assailėd upon each a side.	*every side*
	Thou sayst some folk desire us for richesse,[1]	*riches*
	Some for our shape and some for our fairness,	*beauty*
	And some for she can either sing or dance,	
260	And some for gentleness and dalliance,	*playfulness*
	Some for their handės and their armės small.	
	Thus goes all to the devil, by thy tale.	*account*
	Thou sayst men may not keep a castle wall	
	It may so long assailėd be overall.	*(If) it*
265	And if that she be foul, thou sayst that she	*ugly*
	Coveteth every man that she may see,	
	For as a spaniel she will on him leap	
	Till she may findė some man her to cheap.	*to buy her*
	Ne none so gray goose goes there in the lake,	
270	As, sayst thou, that will be without a make,	*mate*
	And sayst it is a hard thing for to yield	*give away*
	A thing that no man will, his thankės, held.[2]	*gladly take*
	Thus sayst thou, lorel, when thou goest to bed,	*old fool*
	And that no wise man needeth for to wed,	
275	Nor no man that intendeth unto heaven.	*who hopes to go*

---

[1] 256: For the 25 lines or so following 256 notice the array of pronouns the Wife uses interchangeably: *us, she, I, their*. She also has a disconcerting habit of switching from *they* to *he* and back when speaking of her husbands.

[2] 271-2: A difficult couplet, meaning, perhaps "It is hard to give away a thing that no man will gladly take."

With wildė thunder dint and fiery leven   *thunderbolt & f. lightning*
May thy welkėd neckė be tobroke!   *wrinkled n. be broken*
Thou sayst that dripping houses and eke smoke   *leaky*
And chiding wivės maken men to flee   *nagging*

280 Out of their ownė house. Ah, ben'citee!   *bless us!*
What aileth such an old man for to chide!
Thou sayst we wivės will our vices hide
Till we be fast, and then we will them show.   *married*
Well may that be the proverb of a shrew.   *wretch*

285 Thou sayst that oxen, asses, horses, hounds,
They be assayėd at divérse stounds.   *tested at various times*
Basins, lavers, ere that men them buy,   *bowls*
Spoonės and stools, and all such husbandry,   *utensils*
And so be pots, clothės, and array;   *& equipment*

290 But folk of wivės maken no assay,   *no test*
Till they be wedded. (Oldė dotard shrew!)   *senile old fool!*
And then, sayst thou, we will our vices show.

I accused my husbands of jealousy, possessiveness and cheapness

Thou sayst also, that it displeaseth me,
But if that thou wilt praisen my beauty,   *Unless*
295 And but thou pore always upon my face,   *look*
And clepe me fairė dame in every place,   *call / lady*
And but thou make a feast on thilkė day   *(birthday)*
That I was born, and make me fresh and gay,   *buy me new clothes*
And but thou do unto my nurse honoúr,

300 And to my chamberer within my bower,   *my lady's maid*
And to my father's folk, and mine allies.   *my relatives*
Thus sayest thou, old barrel full of lies!

My vehement counter-claims and challenge

And yet of our apprenticė Jankin,
For his crisp hair, shining as gold so fine,
305 And for he squireth me both up and down,   *because he*
Yet hast thou caught a false suspicïon:
I will him not, though thou were dead to-morrow. *I wouldn't have him*

But tell me this, why hidest thou—with sorrow!— *bad luck to you!*
The keyės of thy chest away from me?

310 It is my good as well as thine, pardee. *my property / by God*
What, ween'st thou make an idiot of our dame?[1]
Now by that lord that callėd is Saint Jame,
Thou shalt not bothė—though that thou were wood— *mad*
Be master of my body and my good;

315 That one thou shalt forego maugre thine eyen. *in spite of y. eyes*
What helpeth it of me inquire and spyen? *about me*
I trow thou wouldest lock me in thy chest. *I guess*
Thou shouldest say: 'Fair wife, go where thee lest; *you please*
Take your disport; I will not 'lieve no talės; *Have fun / believe*

320 I know you for a truė wife, Dame Alice.'
We love no man, that taketh keep or charge *takes notice or account*
Where that we go; we will be at our large. *we want freedom*
Of allė men y-blessėd may he be
The wise astrologer Daun Ptolemy,

325 That says this proverb in his Almagest:
'Of allė men his wisdom is the highest,
That recketh not who has the world in hand.' *cares not who rules*
By this provérb thou shalt well understand:
Have thou enough, what thar thee reck or care *What need you?*

330 How merrily that other folkės fare?[2]
For certės, oldė dotard, by your leave, *certainly, old fool*
You shall have quaintė right enough at eve. *sex / evening*
He is too great a niggard that will wern *miser / refuse*
A man to light a candle at his lantern;[3]

335 He shall have never the lessė light, pardee. *by God*

---

[1] 311: "Do you think (*weenest thou*) that you can make an idiot of this lady?" (herself).

[2] 329-30: "If you have enough, why do you care how well other people do?"

[3] 333-4: "He is too great a miser who will refuse a man a light from his lantern." This is the Wife's interesting metaphor for sexual freedom. The word *quaint* is a vulgarism or a euphemism for the female sexual organ. See also later *quoniam* and *belle chose* (literally "beautiful thing").

Have thou enough, thee thar not 'plain thee.   *need not complain*

I attacked complaints about expensive clothes, and I claimed my freedom

Thou sayst also, if that we make us gay   *attractive*
With clothing and with precïous array,   *ornaments*
That it is peril of our chastity.
340 And yet—With sorrow!—thou must enforcë thee[1]
And sayst these words in the apostle's name:
'In habit made with chastity and shame   *clothing / modesty*
You women shall apparel you,' quod he,
'And not in tressëd hair, and gay perree,   *jewelry*
345 As pearls, nor with gold, nor clothës rich.'
After thy text, nor after thy rubric   *By your book / rule*
I will not work as muchel as a gnat.
Thou saidest this, that I was like a cat;
For whoso that would singe a cat's skin,   *If anyone*
350 Then would the cat well dwellen in its inn;   *home*
And if the cat's skin be sleek and gay,
She will not dwell in housë half a day,
But forth she will ere any day be dawed,   *dawned*
To show her skin and go a caterwawed.   *caterwauling*
355 This is to say, if I be gay, sir shrew,   *well dressed*
I will run out, my borel for to show.   *clothing*
Sir oldë fool, what helpeth thee to spy?
Though thou pray Argus with his hundred eyes
To be my wardëcorps, as he can best,   *bodyguard*
360 In faith he shall not keep me but me lest;   *unless I want*
Yet could I make his beard, so may I thee.[2]

I nagged him about his (imaginary) nagging

Thou saidest eke, that there be thingës three,   *said also*
The which things greatly trouble all this earth,

---

[1] 340: "And yet, blast you, you have to reinforce your opinion" (by quoting
the Bible).

[2] 361: "Still I could deceive him, I promise you." If *thee* is the verb "to prosper" rather than a pronoun, *so may I thee* means "So may I prosper,"

	And that no wightė may endure the fourth.	*no person*
365	O leve sir shrewė, Jesus short thy life!	*O dear / shorten*
	Yet preachest thou and sayst a hateful wife	
	Y-reckoned is for one of these mischances.	*Is counted*
	Be there no other manner résembláncesⁱ	*Are there no o. kinds?*
	That you may liken your parables to	
370	But if a silly wife be one of tho'?	*poor wife / those*
	Thou likenest ekė woman's love to hell,	
	To barren land, where water may not dwell.	
	Thou likenest it also to wildė fire;	
	The more it burns, the more it has desire	
375	To cónsume everything that burnt will be.	
	Thou sayest: 'Right as wormės shend a tree,	*destroy*
	Right so a wife destroyeth her husband;	
	This knowen they that be to wivės bound.'	

An admission

	Lordings, right thus, as you have understand,	
380	Bore I stiffly mine old husbands on hand	*boldly deceived*
	That thus they saiden in their drunkenness;	
	And all was false, but as I took witness	
	On Jankin and upon my niece also.²	
	O Lord, the pain I did them and the woe	
385	Full guiltėless, by Godė's sweetė pine!	*suffering*
	For as a horse, I couldė bite and whine;	
	I couldė 'plain and I was in the guilt,	*complain even when*
	Or elsė often time I had been spilt.	*ruined*
	Whoso that first to millė comes, first grint.	*The one / grinds*
390	I 'plainėd first, so was our war y-stint.³	*over*

ⁱ 368: Are there no other kinds of comparison?

² 382-3: "I called Jankin and my niece as witnesses, although it was all a lie," i.e. her accusations were a fabrication; she was putting words into the mouths of her husbands which they had never spoken.

³ 389-90: "The first one to the mill is the first to get the corn ground. I complained first, and so the battle was over." Whoever strikes first, wins.

	They were full glad to excusen them full blive[1]	*quickly*
	Of things of which they never a-guilt their lives.	*in their lives*
	Of wenches would I bearen them on hand,	*accuse falsely*
	When that for sick they might unnethe stand,	*sickness / barely*
395	Yet tickled I his hearte for that he	
	Wend that I had of him so great charity.[2]	*thought / love*

I had a trick for getting out of the house: a false but flattering accusation

	I swore that all my walking out by night	
	Was for to spy on wenches that he dight.	*girls he slept with*
	Under that color had I many a mirth.	
400	For all such wit is given us in our birth:	
	Deceit, weeping, spinning, God has give	
	To women kindly, while that they may live.	*by nature*
	And thus of one thing I avaunte me,	*I boast*
	At th'end I had the better in each degree,	*in every way*
405	By sleight or force or by some manner thing,	*By trickery*
	As by continual murmur or grouching;	*grumbling*

Sexual refusal as a weapon

	Namely a-bed, there hadden they mischance,	*Especially / bad luck*
	There would I chide, and do them no pleasance.	
	I would no longer in the bed abide,	
410	If that I felt his arm over my side,	
	Till he had made his ransom unto me;	
	Then would I suffer him to do his nicety.	*allow him*
	And therefore every man this tale I tell:	
	Win whoso may, for all is for to sell.	*whoever can*
415	With empty hand men may no hawkes lure.	

---

[1] 391-4: "They were glad to be excused quickly from things they had never been guilty of in their lives. I would accuse them of having girls *(wenches)* when they were so sick they could barely stand."

[2] 395-6: "I tickled his vanity by making him think I loved him so." Note again the slippage of pronouns from *they, them to his, him* in the preceding lines and below. The same thing happens with *I, us, women* in the following lines, a feature of the Wife's style.

For winning would I all his lust endure,
And makė me a feignėd appetite,   *desire*
And yet in bacon had I never delight.   *cured (old) meat*
That madė me that ever I would them chide.

Relentless nagging

420   For though the Pope had sitten them beside,
       I would not spare them at their ownė board.   *table*
       For by my truth I quit them word for word.
       As help me very God omnipotent,
       Though I right now should make my testament,   *my will*
425   I owe them not a word that it n'is quit.   *isn't repaid*
       I brought it so aboutė by my wit
       That they must give it up, as for the best,
       Or elsė had we never been in rest.
       For though he lookėd as a wood lion,   *angry*
430   Yet should he fail of his conclusïon.

Another tactic: I would ask him to be reasonable and yield

       Then would I say: 'Now, goodė leve, take keep,   *my dear, look*
       How meekly looketh Willikins our sheep!   *W = husband*
       Come near, my spouse, and let me ba thy cheek.   *kiss*
       You should be allė patïent and meek,
435   And have a sweetė spicėd conscïence.   *easy, forgiving*
       Since you so preach of Job's patïence,
       Suffereth always, since you so well can preach,   *Put up with things*
       And but you do, certain we shall you teach   *unless you do*
       That it is fair to have a wife in peace.   *is good*
440   One of us two must bowė doubtėless,
       And since a man is morė reasonable
       Than woman is, you mustė be sufferable.   *tolerant, forbearing*
       What aileth you to grouchė thus and groan?   *grumble*
       Is it for you would have my quaint alone?[1] *my body for yourself*

---

[1] 444: "Is it because you want my body sexually for yourself alone?" See earlier note on *quaint*.

445	Why, take it all. Lo, have it every deal.	*every bit*
	Peter, I shrew you, but you love it well.[1]	*By St. Peter*
	For if I wouldė sell my *belle chose*,	*my body*
	I couldė walk as fresh as is a rose,	
	But I will keep it for your ownė tooth.	*just for you*
450	You be to blame, by God, I say you sooth.'	*truth*
	Such manner wordės haddė we in hand.	*together*

My fourth husband played the field, but I got even

	Now will I speaken of my fourth husband.	
	My fourthė husband was a reveller;	
	This is to say, he had a paramour,	*lover*
455	And I was young and full of ragery,	*passion*
	Stubborn and strong, and jolly as a pie.	*magpie*
	How I could dancė to a harpė small!	
	And sing, y-wis, as any nightingale	*indeed*
	When I had drunk a draught of sweetė wine.	
460	Metellius, the foulė churl, the swine,	
	That with a staff bereft his wife her life	*robbed*
	For she drank wine, though I had been his wife,	*Because / if I*
	Ne should he not have daunted me from drink.	*scared*
	And after wine, of Venus most I think,	
465	For all so siker as cold engenders hail,	*surely / produces*
	A likerous mouth must have a likerous tail.[2]	
	In woman vinolent is no defense,	*full of wine*
	This knowen lechers by experience.	

A parenthesis: the pleasure of nostalgia—and the regret

	But, Lord Christ, when that it remembereth me	*when I remember*
470	Upon my youth, and on my jollity,	
	It tickleth me about my heartė's root.	
	Unto this day it does my heartė boot	*good*

---

[1] 446: "By St. Peter, I declare that you really love it very much."

[2] 466: Probably a pun on *liquorous* (liquored) and *likerous* (lecherous), as well as on *tail*.

That I have had my world as in my time.
But age, alas! that all will envenime,   *envenom, poison*
475 Hath me bereft my beauty and my pith.   *robbed me / vigor*
Let go! Farewell! The devil go therewith!
The flour is gone; there is no more to tell.
The bran, as I best can, now must I sell.
But yet to be right merry will I fond.   *try*
480 Now will I tellen of my fourth husband.

My revenge

I say I had in hearté great despite,   *jealousy*
That he of any other had delight;   *other (woman)*
But he was quit, by God and by Saint Joce: *repaid*
I made him of the samé wood a cross,
485 Not of my body in no foul mannér,
But certainly I madé folk such cheer,[1]
That in his owné grease I made him fry
For anger and for very jealousy.
By God, in earth I was his purgatory,
490 For which I hope his soulé be in glory.
For, God it wot, he sat full oft and sung,   *God knows*
When that his shoe full bitterly him wrung.[2]
There was no wight, save God and he, that wist   *that knew*
In many wise how sorely I him twist.   *ways / tortured*
495   He died when I came from Jerusalem,
And lies y-grave under the roodé-beam,   *buried u. t. church cross*
All is his tombé not so curious   *Although / so elaborate*
As was the sepulchre of him, Darius,   *tomb*
Which that Apelles wroughté subtlely.   *made*
500 It is but waste to bury them preciously.   *expensively*
Let him farewell, God give his soulé rest.
He is now in his grave and in his chest.   *coffin*

---

[1] 486: "I was so pleasant to folk (men) ....," that is, she was a great flirt.

[2] 492: "... when his shoe pinched him severely." He often had to put on a good face when in fact he was hurting badly.

I married my fifth husband for love. **He** *managed* **me**.

	Now of my fifthe husband will I tell.	
	God let his soule never come in Hell.	
505	And yet was he to me the moste shrew;	*roughest*
	That feel I on my ribbes all by row,	
	And ever shall, unto mine ending day.	
	But in our bed he was so fresh and gay,	
	And therewithal he could so well me glose,	*sweet-talk me*
510	When that he would have my *belle chose*,	*body*
	That, though he had me beat in every bone,	
	He coulde win again my love anon.	*promptly*
	I trow, I loved him beste for that he	*I guess / because he*
	Was of his love daungerous to me.	*sparing, cool*

515	We woman have, if that I shall not lie,	
	In this matter a quainte fantasy.	*odd caprice*
	Wait what thing we may not lightly have,	*Watch whatever*
	Thereafter will we cry all day and crave.	*For that*
	Forbid us thing, and that desiren we;	
520	Press on us fast, and thenne will we flee.	
	With daunger outen we all our chaffare;[1]	*bring out our goods*
	Great press at market maketh dearer ware,	*great demand / goods*
	And too great cheap is held at little price.	*market supply*
	This knoweth every woman that is wise.	

525	My fifthe husband, God his soule bless,	
	Which that I took for love and not richesse,	
	He sometime was a clerk of Oxenford,	*was once a student*
	And had left school, and went at home to board	*to lodge*
	With my gossip, dwelling in our town.	*my confidant*

---

[1] 521-523: "When there is reluctance (*daunger*) to buy, then we bring out all our merchandise (*chaffare*). Great market demand makes things more expensive (*dearer*); too great a supply (*cheap*) reduces the price." If her *wares* are much in demand, then the customer has to pay heavily; if the customer shows small interest, she has to seduce him to buy.

530 God have her soul, her name was Alison.
    She knew my heart and all my privity,   *secrets*
    Bet than our parish priest, so may I thee.   *Better / thrive*
    To her bewrayèd I my counsel all;   *confided*
    For, had my husband pissèd on a wall,
535 Or done a thing that should have cost his life,
    To her and to another worthy wife
    And to my niece which that I lovèd well,   *whom*
    I would have told his counsel every deal,
    And so I did full often, God it wot,   *God knows*
540 That made his facè often red and hot
    For very shame, and blamed himself for he
    Had told to me so great a privity.   *secret*

How I wooed Jankin, who became my fifth husband

    And so befell that oncè in a Lent,
    (So often times I to my gossip went,
545 For ever yet I lovèd to be gay,   *well dressed*
    And for to walk in March, April, and May
    From house to house, to hearen sundry talès)
    That Jankin Clerk, and my gossip, Dame Alice,   *my confidant*
    And I myself, into the fieldès went.
550 My husband was at London all that Lent;
    I had the better leisure for to play,
    And for to see, and eke for to be seen   *also*
    Of lusty folk. What wist I where my grace   *lively / did I know / fortune*
    Was shapen for to be, or in what place?[1]
555 Therefore made I my visitatïons
    To vigils, and to processïons,   *To evening services*
    To preachings eke, and to these pilgrimáges,
    To plays of miracles,[2] and to marriáges,
    And weared upon my gayè scarlet gites.   *And wore / gowns*

---

[1] 553-4: "How could I know what or where my fortune was destined to be?"

[2] 558: Miracle plays (also known as mystery plays) were short plays based on biblical events. Noah's wife in one of these was a forceful character rather like Alison.

560	These wormès nor these mothès nor these mites	
	(Upon my peril!) fret them never a deal.	*I assure you / ate*
	And wost thou why? For they were usèd well.	*know you why?*
	Now will I tellen forth what happened me:	
	I say, that in the fieldès walkèd we,	
565	Till truly we had such dalliance	*playful talk*
	This clerk and I, that of my purveyance	*foresight*
	I spoke to him, and said him how that he,	
	If I were widow, shouldè wedden me.	
	For certainly, I say for no bobbance,	*boasting*
570	Yet was I never without purveyance	*provision*
	Of marriage, nor of other thingès eke.	*also*
	I hold a mouse's heart not worth a leek,	
	That has but one hole for to start into,	*run to*
	And if that failè, then is all y-do.	*finished*
575	I borè him on hand he had enchanted me	*convinced him*
	(My damè taughtè me that subtlety);	*My mother*
	And eke I said, I mett of him all night,	*I dreamed*
	He would have slain me, as I lay upright,[1]	*face up*
	And all my bed was full of very blood;	
580	'But yet I hope that you shall do me good,	
	For blood betokens gold, as me was taught.'	
	And all was false, I dreamed of it right naught,	
	But I followèd aye my damè's lore,[2]	
	As well of that as of other thingès more.	*in other*
585	But now, sir, let me see, what shall I sayn?	
	Aha! by God, I have my tale again.	

At the funeral of my fourth husband my thoughts were not on the dead

	When that my fourthè husband was on bier,	
	I wept algate and madè sorry cheer,[3]	*indeed / acted sad*
	As wivès mustè, for it is uságe,	*custom*

---

[1] 577-79: The sexual implication of her pretend dreamwork is fairly obvious.

[2] 583: "I followed always my mother's teaching."

[3] 588: "I wept indeed, and put on a sad appearance."

590 And with my kerchief covered my viságe;   *face*
     But, for that I was purveyed of a make,[1]   *provided w. a mate*
     I wept but small, and that I undertake.   *I promise you*
     To churché was my husband borne a-morrow   *in morning*
     With neighébours that for him madé sorrow,
595 And Jankin, ouré clerk, was one of tho'.   *those*
     As help me God, when that I saw him go
     After the bier, methought he had a pair
     Of leggés and of feet so clean and fair
     That all my heart I gave unto his hold.
600 He was, I trowé, twenty winters old   *I guess, 20 years*
     And I was forty, if I shall say sooth,   *truth*
     But yet I had always a colté's tooth.   *youthful taste*

My attractions

     Gat-toothed I was, and that became me well: *gap-toothed*
     I had the print of Sainté Venus' seal.[2]
605 As help me God, I was a lusty one,
     And fair, and rich, and young, and well begone;   *well endowed*
     And truly, as mine husbands toldé me,
     I had the besté *quoniam* might be,   *"chamber of Venus"*
     For certés I am all Venerian
610 In feeling, and my heart is Martian;
     Venus me gave my lust and likerousness,   *sexual desire*
     And Mars gave me my sturdy hardiness.
     Mine áscendent was Taur, and Mars therein.   *sign was Taurus*

I loved sex

     Alas! alas! that ever love was sin!
615 I followed aye mine inclinatïon   *always*

---

[1] 591: "Because I was assured of (or provided with) a husband."

[2] 604: She was gap-toothed, a mark of Venus, the goddess and planet under whose influence she was born. Being gap-toothed was regarded in the Middle Ages as a sign of a strongly-sexed nature, making one a disciple of Venus, the patron saint (!) of Love. *Venerian* (below) is the adjective from Venus as *Martian* is from Mars, the god of war and the lover of Venus. Lines 609- 12 and 619-26 are not in Hgw MS.

By virtue of my constellatïon[1]
That madė me that I could not withdraw
My chamber of Venus from a good fellow.
Yet have I Mars's mark upon my face,
620 And also in another privy place.   *private*
For God so wise be my salvatïon,
I lovėd never by no discretïon,   *calculation*
But ever followėd mine appetite   *desire*
All were he short or long or black or white.   *Whether he was*
625 I took no keep, so that he likėd me,
How poor he was, nor eke of what degree.[2]   *social rank*

Within a month I married Jankin and gave him control of my property (alas), but not of my movements

What should I say? but at the monthė's end
This jolly clerk Jankin, that was so hend,   *charming*
Has wedded me with great solemnity,
630 And to him gave I all the land and fee   *money*
That ever was me given therebefore,
But afterward repented me full sore.
He woudė suffer nothing of my list.[3]   *allow / my wishes*
By God, he smote me once upon the list,   *struck / ear*
635 For that I rent out of his book a leaf,   *Because I tore*
That of the stroke mine earė waxed all deaf.   *grew*
Stubborn I was, as is a lioness,
And of my tongue a very jangleress,   *chatterer*
And walk I would as I had done beforn
640 From house to house, although he had it sworn;   *forbidden*

He would quote "authorities" against women gallivanting about.

For which he oftentimės wouldė preach,

---

[1] 616: "Given to me by the disposition of the stars at my birth."

[2] 625-6: " So long as he pleased me, I did not care about his poverty or social rank." ...*he liked me* almost certainly means "... he pleased me."

[3] 633: "He would allow none of my wishes."

	And me of oldė Roman gestės teach	*stories*
	How he, Simplicius Gallus, left his wife,	*How a man (named)*
	And her forsook for term of all his life,	
645	Not but for open-headed he her saw	*bareheaded*
	Looking out at his door upon a day.[1]	
	Another Roman told he me by name,	
	That, for his wife was at a summer game	*because*
	Without his witting, he forsook her eke.	*knowledge / also*
650	And then would he upon his Bible seek	*he = Jankin*
	That ilkė proverb of Ecclesiast	*Ecclesiasticus 25:25*
	Where he commandeth and forbiddeth fast:	*firmly*
	'Man shall not suffer his wife go roll about.'	*allow / roam*
	Then would he say right thus withouten doubt:	
655	'Whoso that buildeth his house all of sallows,	*willows*
	And pricketh his blind horse over the fallows,	*spurs / fields*
	And suffereth his wife go seeken hallows,	*allows / shrines*
	Is worthy to be hangėd on the gallows.'	
	But all for nought, I settė not an haw	*straw*
660	Of his provérbs, nor of his oldė saw;	*old sayings*
	Nor I would not of him corrected be.	*by him*
	I hate them that my vices tellen me,	
	And so do more (God wot) of us than I.	*God knows*
	This made him wood with me all utterly;	*angry*
665	I wouldė not forbear him in no case.[2]	
	Now will I say you sooth, by Saint Thomas,	*truth*
	Why that I rent out of his book a leaf,	*tore*
	For which he smote me, so that I was deaf.	*struck*

His favorite reading was an anti-feminist book

	He had a book, that gladly night and day	
670	For his desport he would it read alway,	*amusement*

---

[1] 645-6: "For nothing more than that he saw her one day looking out the door of the house with her head uncovered."

[2] 665: "I would not restrain myself for him under any circumstances".

He clepèd it Valere, and Theophrast,[1]
At whichè book he laughed always full fast.
And eke there was sometime a clerk at Rome,   *scholar*
A cardinal that hightè Saint Jerome   *was called*
675   That made a book against Jovinian,
In which book eke there was Tertullian,
Chrysippus, Trotula, and Eloise,
That was abbessè not far from Paris,
And eke the Parables of Solomon,
680   Ovid's Art, and bookès many a one;
And allè these were bound in one volume.[2]
And every night and day was his custom
(When he had leisure and vacatïon
From other worldly occupatïon)
685   To readen in this book of wicked wives.
He knew of them more legendès and lives
Than be of goodè wivès in the Bible.
For trusteth well, it is an impossible,
That any clerk will speaken good of wives,   *cleric*
690   (But if it be of holy saintès' lives)   *Unless*
Nor of no other woman never the mo'.

Who writes these books?

Who painted the lion, tell me, who?[3]
By God, if women haddè written stories

---

[1] 671: Two anti-feminist tracts: the *Epistola Valerii* of Walter Map, and the *Liber de Nuptiis* of Theophrastus known only from the large quotations from it that St.Jerome used in his argument against Jovinian.

[2] 681: A very odd anthology, with the Proverbs of Solomon and the work of the ascetic Jerome and Tertullian side by side with Ovid's pagan and sensual "Art of Love," and the sensual, sad but not pagan story of the love of Heloise and Abelard. Presumably the anthologist concentrated on those bits that were derogatory to women, especially married women.

[3] 692: A man and a lion see a representation of a man overpowering a lion. The lion questions the truth and accuracy of this picture: clearly a man and not a lion had produced it, he said; if lions could paint or sculpt, the representation would be totally reversed.

	As clerkès have within their oratories,	*cloisters*
695	They would have writ of men more wickedness	
	Than all the mark of Adam may redress.	*race of A, i.e. men*
	The children of Mercury and of Venus	
	Be in their working full contrarious.	*opposed*
	Mercury loveth wisdom and sciénce,	*knowledge*
700	And Venus loveth riot and dispense.	*parties & extravagance*
	And for their diverse dispositïon	
	Each fails in other's exaltatïon.	*domination*
	As thus, God wot, Mercury is desolate	
	In Pisces, where Venus is exaltate,	
705	And Venus fails where Mercury is raised.[1]	
	Therefore no woman of no clerk is praised;	
	The clerk when he is old, and may naught do	*nothing*
	Of Venus' workès worth his oldè shoe,	*sexual activity*
	Then sits he down, and writes in his dotáge,	*senility*
710	That women cannot keep their marrïáge.	

From Jankin's Book of Wicked Wives: Biblical examples

	But now to purpose, why I toldè thee,	
	That I was beaten for a book, pardee.	*by God*
	Upon a night, Jankin that was our sire,	*man of house*
	Read in his book, as he sat by the fire,	
715	Of Eva first, that for her wickedness	*because of*
	Was all mankindè brought to wretchedness,[2]	

---

[1] 697-705: The fancy astrological detail makes the simple point that people of such opposite tastes and temperaments do not get on well together and do not present flattering pictures of each other. Professional celibates had a higher opinion of themselves than of married people, let alone of enthusiasts for sensuality like Alison of Bath. For an elaborate discussion of the Wife's horoscope see J.D. North, *Chaucer's Universe*, pp. 289 ff.

[2] 715 -20: Eve, the first woman, ate the fruit of the Forbidden Tree in the Garden of Eden. In turn, she induced her husband Adam to eat of the fruit against God's commandment, and as a result they and all their descendants were excluded from Paradise. This human sin against God could only be atoned for by a God-man; hence the human race had to be redeemed by the death of Jesus Christ who was God become man.

For which that Jesus Christ himself was slain,
That bought us with his heartë's blood again.   *redeemed us*
Lo here, express of woman may you find,
720 That woman was the loss of all mankind.
Then read he me how Samson lost his hairs:[1]   *Judges XVI, 15-20*
Sleeping, his lemman cut them with her shears,   *lover*
Through whichë treason lost he both his eyen.

Classical examples

Then read he me, if that I shall not lien,
725 Of Hercules, and of his Dianire,
That causëd him to set himself a-fire.[2]
Nothing forgot he the sorrow and the woe,
That Socrates had with his wivës two;
How Xantippë cast piss upon his head.[3]
730 This silly man sat still, as he were dead.   *poor man*
He wiped his head; no morë durst he sayn,   *dared he say*
But: 'Ere that thunder stints there comes a rain.' *Before the t. stops*
Of Pasiphae, that was the queen of Crete,
For shrewëdness him thought the talë sweet.[4]   *nastiness*
735 Fie, speak no more! It is a grisly thing

---

[1] 721-3: Samson, a man of immense God-given strength, was seduced by his faithless lover, Dalilah, to tell her the secret of his strength which lay in his hair. While he was sleeping, the Philistines cut off his hair, blinded and enslaved him. He serves as another Biblical example of a strong man brought low by the wiles of a woman.

[2] 726: Dianira, the wife of Hercules, gave him the poisoned shirt of Nessus thinking that it had magical properties which would renew his affections for her. It poisoned him instead, and he burned himself with hot coals.

[3] 728-32: A version of a story told by St Jerome in his anti-marriage argument in the tract Against Jovinian: Socrates laughed at his two wives quarreling over a man as ugly as he was. Then one of them turned on him with the result mentioned. Socrates is an example of even a wise man's unhappy experience with women.

[4] 734-36: Pasiphae, wife of Minos of Crete, fell in love with the bull from the sea and hid herself in a cow constructed specially by Daedalus so that she could copulate with the bull. The result was the monster Minotaur.

Of her horrible lust and her liking. *(for a bull)*
Of Clytemnestra for her lechery,
That falsely made her husband for to die,[1] *(Agamemnon)*
He read it with full good devotïon.
740 He told me eke, for what occasïon *also / cause*
Amphiorax at Thebès lost his life.
My husband had a legend of his wife
Eriphilë, that for an ouche of gold, *brooch*
Has privily unto the Greekès told
745 Where that her husband hid him in a place, *"Thebaid,"Bk VII*
For which he had at Thebès sorry grace. *bad fortune*
Of Livia told he me, and of Lucy.
They bothè made their husbands for to die;
That one for love, that other was for hate.
750 Livia her husband on an evening late
Empoisoned has, for that she was his foe.
Lucia likerous loved her husband so *jealous*
That for he should always upon her think, *(So) that*
She gave him such a manner lovè-drink
755 That he was dead ere it were by the morrow;
And thus algatès husbandès have sorrow. *always*
Then told he me, how that one Latumius
Complained unto his fellow Arius,
That in his garden growèd such a tree
760 On which he said how that his wivès three
Hangèd themselves for heartès déspitous. *out of spite*
'O levè brother,' quod this Arius, *dear*
'Give me a plant of thilkè blessèd tree, *of that*
And in my garden planted shall it be.'
765 Of later date of wives had he read,
That some had slain their husbands in their bed,
And let their lecher dight them all the night *cover*

---

[1] 737-8: Clytemnestra, with her lover's help, murdered her husband Agamemnon on his return from the Trojan War. 740-6: Eryphele was bribed to get her husband to join the war against Thebes in which he was killed.

While that the corpse lay on the floor upright.   *face up*
And some have driven nails into their brain
770 While that they slept, and thus they have them slain.
Some have them given poison in their drink.
He spoke more harm than heartė may bethink.

Anti-feminist proverbs

And therewithal he knew of more provérbs,   *moreover*
Than in this world there growen grass or herbs.
775 'Bet is,' quod he, 'thine habitatïon   *It's better*
Be with a lion, or a foul dragon,   *Ecclesiasticus 15: 16*
Than with a woman using for to chide.'   *always scolding*
'Bet is,' quod he, 'high in the roof abide,   *Better*
Than with an angry wife down in the house.   *Prov. 21: 9*
780 They be so wicked and contrarious
They hatė what their husbands loven, aye.'   *always*
He said: 'A woman casts her shame away,
When she casts off her smock; and furthermore,   *her shift*
A fair woman, but she be chaste also,   *pretty / unless*
785 Is like a gold ring in a sowė's nose.'   *Proverbs 11: 22*

Tired of his anti-feminist readings and quotations, I acted.

Who couldė weenė, or who could suppose   *c. think or estimate*
The woe that in my heart was, and the pine!   *resentment*
And when I saw that he would never fine   *finish*
To readen on this cursėd book all night,
790 All suddenly three leavės have I plight   *plucked*
Out of his book, right as he read, and eke   *and also*
I with my fist so took him on the cheek   *punched*
That in our fire he fell backward adown.
And up he starts as does a wood lion,   *jumped / angry*
795 And with his fist he smote me on the head
That on the floor I lay as I were dead.   *so that*
And when he saw how stillė that I lay,
He was aghast, and would have fled his way,
Till at the last out of my swoon I braid: *I woke*

800 'Oh, hast thou slain me, false thief?' I said,
     'And for my land thus hast thou murdered me?
     Ere I be dead, yet will I kissen thee.'   *Before I die*
     And near he came, and kneeled fair adown,
     And saide: 'Deare sister Alison,

805 As help me God I shall thee never smite;   *strike*
     What I have done it is thyself to wite,   *blame*
     Forgive it me, and that I thee beseech.'
     And yet eftsoons I hit him on the cheek,   *promptly*
     And saide: 'Thief! thus much am I wreak.   *avenged*

810 Now will I die, I may no longer speak.'

My husband's surrender and our reconciliation

     But at the last, with muche care and woe
     We fell accorded by ourselves two.   *were reconciled*
     He gave me all the bridle in my hand
     To have the governance of house and land,

815 And of his tongue, and of his hand also,
     And made him burn his book anon right tho.   *promptly right there*
     And when that I had gotten unto me
     By mastery all the sovereignty,   *control*
     And that he said: 'Mine owne true wife,

820 Do as thee list the term of all thy life,   *as you please, the length*
     Keep thine honour, and keep eke mine estate'— [1]
     After that day we never had debate.   *argument*
     God help me so, I was to him as kind
     As any wife from Denmark unto Inde,   *India*

825 And also true, and so was he to me.
     I pray to God that sits in majesty
     So bless his soule, for His mercy dear.
     Now will I say my tale, if you will hear.

---

[1] 821: This line seems to mean something like "Keep your liberty and also control of my property" but that stretches the meaning of *honour*. It might mean: "Guard your chastity (or good name) and respect my position as your husband."

Interruption: A Quarrel between the Summoner and the Friar

The Friar laughed when he had heard all this.

830   "Now, Dame," quod he, "so have I joy or bliss,[1]

This is a long preamble of a tale."   *preface to*

And when the Summoner heard the Friar gale,   *spout*

"Lo," quod this Summoner, "Godė's armės two!

A friar will intermit him evermore.   *interpose himself always*

835   Lo, goodė men, a fly and eke a frere   *& also a friar*

Will fall in every dish and eke mattér.

What speak'st thou of preámbulaïon?

What! Amble or trot or peace or go sit down.   *be quiet*

Thou lettest our disport in this mannér."   *You spoil our fun*

840   "Yea, wilt thou so, Sir Summoner?" quod the Frere.

"Now by my faith I shall, ere that I go,

Tell of a Summoner such a tale or two,

That all the folk shall laughen in this place."

"Now elsė, Friar, I will beshrew thy face,"   *damn*

845   Quod this Summoner, "and I beshrewė me,   *I'll be damned*

But if I tellė talės two or three   *If I do not*

Of friars, ere I come to Sittingbourne,

That I shall make thy heartė for to mourn;

For well I wot thy patïence is gone."   *I know*

850   Our hostė criėd: "Peace, and that anon,"   *at once*

And saidė: "Let the woman tell her tale.

You fare as folk that drunken be of ale.

Do, Dame, tell forth your tale, and that is best."   *Go on, ma'am*

"All ready, sir," quod she, "right as you lest,   *please*

855   If I have licence of this worthy Frere."   *permission*

"Yes, Dame," quod he, "tell forth, and I will hear."[2]

---

[1] 830: "Now, Ma'am, as sure as I hope to be saved ..." As in line 164 above, "Dame" is polite usage, not slang.

[2] 856: The outbreak of hostilities between two pilgrims sets up two further tales which will fulfill these threats: the Friar later tells a rather good tale involving the iniquity of summoners. The Summoner, in turn, retorts with a rather rambling tale about a greedy friar.

The Wife of Bath's Tale

Fairies in King Arthur's Britain

In the olden days of King Arthúr,
Of which that Britons speaken great honoúr,
All was this land fulfillèd of faérie;
860 The Elf-Queen, with her jolly company,
Dancèd full oft in many a greenè mead.   *meadow*
This was the old opinion as I read.
I speak of many hundred years ago,
But now can no man see no elvès mo',   *anymore*
865 For now the greatè charity and prayers
Of limiters and other holy freres,[1]
That searchen every land and every stream,
As thick as motès in the sunnè-beam,
Blessing hallès, chambers, kitchens, bowers,   *bedrooms*
870 Cities, boroughs, castles, highè towers,
Thorps and barns, shippens and dairiès—   *Villages / sheep pens*
This maketh that there be no fairiès,
For there as wont to walken was an elf,   *used to*
There walketh now the limiter himself   *begging friar*
875 In undermeles and in mornings,   *early and later a.m.*
And says his matins and his holy things   *morning prayers*
As he goes in his limitatïon.   *rounds*
Women may go now safely up and down.
In every bush and under every tree,
880 There is no other incubus but he,   *impregnating spirit*
And he ne will not do them but dishonour.[2]

---

[1] 866: *limiters* were mendicant friars (*freres*) licensed to beg within a given limited district.

[2] 881. A difficult line. It appears to mean "He will only dishonor them." Commentators get some sense out of that by pointing out that the "real" incubus, a night spirit who "came upon" women, not only "dishonored" them but impregnated them so that they bore little devils. MS Cam reads "he will do him(self) no dishonour" which makes sense in a different way, but lacks the bite of the preceding lines.

Crime and punishment

And so befell it, that this king Arthúr
Had in his house a lusty bachelor,   *young knight*
That on a day came riding from the river
885 And happened, that, alone as she was born,
He saw a maiden walking him beforn,
Of whichė maid anon, maugre her head,   *against her will*
By very force he raft her maidenhead,   *robbed her virginity*
For which oppressïon was such clamoúr
890 And such pursuit unto the king Arthúr
That damnėd was this knight for to be dead   *condemned*
By course of law, and should have lost his head,
(Peráventure such was the statute tho),   *It seems / then*
But that the queen and other ladies mo'   *more*
895 So longė prayėden the king of grace   *for mercy*
Till he his life him granted in the place,
And gave him to the queen, all at her will,
To choose whether she will him save or spill.   *destroy*

The Queen will pardon the offender on one condition

The queen thankėd the king with all her might;
900 And after this thus spoke she to the knight
When that she saw her time upon a day:
'Thou standest yet,' quod she, 'in such array,   *position*
That of thy life yet hast thou no surety;
I grant thee life, if thou canst tellen me,
905 What thing is it that women most desiren.
Beware, and keep thy neckė-bone from iron.
And if thou canst not tell it me anon,   *at once*
Yet will I give thee leavė for to gon   *to go*
A twelvemonth and a day, to seek and lere   *learn*
910 An answer suffisant in this mattér.   *satisfactory*
And surety will I have, ere that thou pace,   *assurance / go*
Thy body for to yielden in this place.'   *surrender*
Woe was the knight, and sorrowfully he sigheth.

	But what? he may not do all as him liketh.	*as he pleases*
915	And at the last he chose him for to wend	*go away*
	And come again right at the yeare's end	
	With such answer as God would him purvey,	*provide*
	And takes his leave and wendeth forth his way.	
	He seeketh every house and every place,	
920	Where as he hopeth for to finden grace,	*good fortune*
	To learn what thinge women loven most.	

He gets various answers to the Queen's question. The Wife comments.

	But he ne could arriven in no coast,	*country*
	Where as he mighte find in this matter	
	Two creatures according in fere.	*agreeing together*
925	Some saide women loven best richesse,	
	Some said honour, some saide jolliness,	
	Some rich array, some saide lust a-bed,	*expensive clothes*
	And often times to be widow and wed.	
	Some saide that our hearte is most eased	
930	When that we be y-flattered and y-pleased.[1]	
	He goes full nigh the sooth, I will not lie;	*near the truth*
	A man shall win us best with flattery;	
	And with attendance and with busyness	*great attentiveness*
	Be we y-limed bothe more and less.	*caught, ensnared*
935	And some sayen that we loven best	
	For to be free, and do right as us lest,	*as we please*
	And that no man reprove us of our vice	
	But say that we be wise and nothing nice.	*silly*
	For truly there is none of us all,	
940	If any wight will claw us on the gall,	*person / sore spot*
	That we n'ill kick for that he says us sooth.[2]	*won't kick / truth*
	Assay, and he shall find it that so doth.	*Try*

---

[1] 925 ff: Note the characteristic slippage from *women* to *we / our* to *I* to *us*.

[2] 939-41: "There isn't one of us who will not strike out at someone who touches our sore spot by telling the truth."

> For be we never so vicïous within,[1]
> We will be holden wise and clean of sin.   *want to be thought*
> 945 And somė say that great delight have we
> For to be holden stable and eke secree,   *discreet with secrets*
> And in one purpose steadfastly to dwell,
> And not bewrayen things that men us tell.   *disclose*
> But that tale is not worth a rakė-stele.   *rake handle*
> 950 Pardee, we women cannė nothing hele.   *By God / can hold nothing in*
> Witness on Midas; will you hear the tale?

A classical anecdote to illustrate the point that women cannot keep secrets

> Ovid, amongst other thingės small,   *(the Latin poet)*
> Said Midas haddė under his long hairs
> Growing upon his head two ass's ears;
> 955 For whichė vice he hid, as he best might,   *this defect*
> Full subtlely from every mannė's sight,   *v. cleverly*
> That, save his wife, there wist of it no mo'.   *no one else knew*
> He loved her most, and trusted her also.
> He prayėd her, that to no creätúre
> 960 She should not tellen of his dísfigúre.   *disfigurement*
> She swore him: Nay, for all this world to win,   *to him*
> She would not do that villainy nor sin   *dishonor*
> To make her husband have so foul a name;
> She would not tell it for her ownė shame.
> 965 But natheless her thoughtė that she died   *would die*
> That she so longė should a counsel hide;   *secret*
> Her thought it swelled so sore about her heart   *It seemed to her*
> That needėly some word her must astart;[2]
> And since she durst not tell it to no man,   *dared*
> 970 Down to a marshė fastė by she ran.
> Till she came there, her heartė was afire,
> And as a bittern bumbleth in the mire,   *bird calls in t. mud*
> She laid her mouth unto the water down.

---

[1] 943: "No matter how vicious we are inside ..."

[2] 968: "That of necessity some word would have to escape her."

'Bewray me not, thou water, with thy sound,'   *Betray*
975 Quod she, 'To thee I tell it, and no mo',
Mine husband has long ass's eares two.
Now is mine heart all whole, now it is out.
I might no longer keep it, out of doubt.'   *without doubt*
Here may you see, though we a time abide,
980 Yet out it must, we can no counsel hide.
The remnant of the tale, if you will hear,
Read Ovid, and there you may it lere.[1]   *learn*

Back to the tale: the knight sets out for home without a good answer

This knight, of which my tale is specially,
When that he saw he might not come thereby,   *discover it*
985 (This is to say, what women loven most)
Within his breast full sorrowful was the ghost.   *spirit*
But home he goes, he mighte not sojourn,   *delay*
The day was come that homeward must he turn.
And on his way, it happened him to ride
990 In all this care, under a forest side,   *a forest's edge*
Whereas he saw upon a dance go   *Where*
Of ladies four-and-twenty and yet mo'.
Toward the whiche dance he drew full yern,   *eagerly*
In hope that some wisdom he should learn;
995 But certainly, ere he came fully there,
Vanished was this dance, he wist not where;   *knew*

He meets an ugly old woman

No creäture saw he that bore life,
Save on the green he saw sitting a wife—   *older woman*
A fouler wight there may no man devise.   *uglier creature / imagine*
1000 Against this knight this old wife gan arise,   *At the approach of*

---

[1] 982: *Metamorphoses* XI, 174-193, where you would learn that it was his
barber and not his wife who knew his secret and whispered it into a hole near the
water out of which later grew reeds that continually whispered in the wind:
"Midas has ass's ears."

And said: 'Sir Knight, here forth ne lies no way.[1]

Tell me what you seeken, by your fay.   *faith*

Peráventure it may the better be;   *Perhaps*

These oldė folk can muchel thing,' quod she.   *know a lot*

1005 'My levė mother,' quod this knight, 'certáin,   *My dear*

I n'am but dead, but if that I can sayn[2]

What thing it is that women most desire.

Could you me wiss, I would well quit your hire.'[3]

'Plight me thy truth here in mine hand,' quod she,   *Give your word*

1010 'The nextė thing that I require of thee

Thou shalt it do if it lie in thy might,

And I will tell it you ere it be night.'

'Have here my truthė,' quod the knight, 'I grant.'

'Then,' quod she, 'I dare me well avaunt   *boast*

1015 Thy life is safe, for I will stand thereby   *I guarantee*

Upon my life the queen will say as I.

Let's see, which is the proudest of them all

That weareth on a kerchief or a caul,   *women's headdresses*

That dare say nay of what I shall thee teach.   *contradict*

1020 Let us go forth withouten longer speech.'

The old woman gives him the answer to the Queen's question, and they
go to the royal court together

Then rownėd she a 'pistle in his ear,[4]   *whispered a message*

And bade him to be glad, and have no fear.

When they be comen to the court, this knight

Said he had held his day as he had hight,   *kept / promised*

1025 And ready was his answer as he said.

---

[1] 1001: At the approach of this Knight the old woman rose and said: "There is no way through here."

[2] 1006: "I am as good as dead unless I can say."

[3] 1008: "If you could inform me (*me wiss*), I would reward (*quit*) you well for your trouble."

[4] 1021: "'pistle" is short for "epistle" from L. "epistola" = letter, hence a message of some kind.

Full many a noble wife and many a maid
And many a widow (for that they be wise),
The queen herself sitting as justice,
Assembled be this answer for to hear,
1030 And afterward this knight was bid appear.
To every wight commanded was silence,   *every person*
And that the knight should tell in audience   *in public*
What thing that worldly women loven best.
This knight ne stood not still, as does a beast,
1035 But to this questïon anon answered   *promptly*
With manly voice, that all the court it heard: *so that*
'My liegë lady, generally,' quod he,   *My lady Queen*
'Women desiren to have sovereignty
As well over their husband as their love,
1040 And for to be in mastery him above.
This is your most desire, though you me kill.   *greatest*
Do as you list, I am here at your will.'   *wish*
In all the court ne was there wife nor maid
Nor widow, that contráried what he said,   *contradicted what*
1045 But said that he was worthy have his life.

The old woman demands her reward

And with that word up started that old wife
Which that the knight saw sitting on the green.
'Mercy,' quod she, 'my sovereign lady queen,   *Please*
Ere that your court depart, as do me right.   *Before*
1050 I taughtë this answer unto the knight,
For which he plighted me his truthë there,   *pledged his word*
The firstë thing I would of him require,
He would it do, if it lay in his might.
Before the court then pray I thee, Sir Knight,'
1055 Quod she, 'that thou me take unto thy wife,
For well thou wost, that I have kept thy life.   *know / saved*
If I say false, say nay, upon thy fay.'   *on your faith (word)*
This knight answered: 'Alas and welaway!
I wot right well that such was my behest.   *I know / promise*

1060 For Godė's love, as choose a new request.
     Take all my goods, and let my body go.'
     'Nay, then,' quod she, 'I shrew us bothė two,   *a curse on*
     For though that I be foul and old and poor,
     I n'ould for all the metal nor the ore,   *I would not*
1065 That under earth is grave, or lies above,   *buried*
     But if thy wife I were and eke thy love.'[1]   *unless I were*
     'My love?' quod he, 'nay, my damnatïon!
     Alas! that any of my natïon   *family*
     Should e'er so foulė disparáged be.'[2]   *degraded*

Unwillingly and ungraciously the knight keeps his promise

1070 But all for nought; the end is this, that he
     Constrainėd was; he needės must her wed,
     And taketh this old wife, and goes to bed.
     Now, wouldė some men say peráventure,
     That for my negligence I do no cure   *take no care*
1075 To tellen you the joy and all th'array   *splendor*
     That at the feastė was that ilkė day.   *same*
     To which thing shortly answeren I shall:
     I say there was no joy nor feast at all;
     There n'as but heaviness and muchel sorrow: *nothing but*
1080 For privily he wedded her a-morrow;   *privately / in the morning*
     And all day after hid him as an owl,
     So woe was him, his wifė looked so foul.   *So unhappy / ugly*
     Great was the woe the knight had in his thought
     When he was with his wife a-bed y-brought;
1085 He walloweth, and he turneth to and fro.   *tosses*
     This oldė wife lay smiling evermo',
     And said: 'O dearė husband, ben'citee,   *bless me!*

---

[1] 1064-66: "I would not (be satisfied) with all the (precious) metal and ore below ground and above unless I became your wife and your beloved." That is, "I want more than anything else to be your wife."

[2] 1069: *Disparaged* literally meant being forced to marry someone below one's rank.

Fares every knight thus with his wife as ye?[1]
Is this the law of king Arthoure's house?
1090 Is every knight of his thus daungerous?   *cool, distant*
I am your owne love, and eke your wife,   *also*
I am she that saved hath your life.
And certes yet did I you never unright.   *harm*
Why fare you thus with me this firste night?
1095 You faren like a man had lost his wit.   *You act*
What is my guilt?[2] For God's love tell me it,
And it shall be amended, if I may.'
'Amended!' quod this knight, 'alas! nay, nay.
It will not be amended never mo'.
1100 Thou art so loathly, and so old also,   *so ugly*
And thereto comen of so low a kind,   *also / a family*
That little wonder is though I wallow and wind;   *twist & turn*
So woulde God mine hearte woulde burst.'
'Is this,' quod she, 'the cause of your unrest?'
1105 'Yea, certainly,' quod he, 'no wonder is.'
'Now, Sir,' quod she, 'I could amend all this,
If that me list, ere it were dayes three,   *If it pleased me*
So well you mighte bear you unto me.[3]

The old wife answers the first objection to her: that she is not "gently" born

But for you speaken of such gentilesse,   *But because*
1110 As is descended out of old richesse,
That therefore shoulde you be gentlemen;[4]

---

[1] 1088-90: *Fares ...daungerous:* "Does every knight treat his wife this way? Is this some (peculiar) law in King Arthur's court? Is every knight as cold (as you)?"

[2] 1096: "What have I done wrong?"

[3] 1108: "If you were polite to me" or "So that you would be affectionate to me."

[4] 1111: The words "gentilesse," "gentle," "gentleman," "gentry" recur persistently in the passage that follows. The young knight gives them the aristocratic meaning: "gentle" birth is a matter of "genes." The wife insists on the moral meaning: no one is born "gentle," but must become so by his own efforts and God's grace. Likewise, "villains" and "churls," the opposites of "gentlemen," are not born but made—by their own vices. I have retained the original form "gentilesse" rather than "gentleness" for what I hope is greater clarity of meaning.

Such arrogancé is not worth a hen.
Look who that is most virtuous alway
Privy and apert, and most intendeth aye[1]   *(In) private & public*
1115 To do the gentle deedés that he can,
Take him for the greatest gentleman.
Christ wills we claim of Him our gentilesse,
Not of our elders for their old richesse.   *ancestors*
For though they gave us all their heritáge,
1120 For which we claim to be of high paráge,   *birth*
Yet may they not bequeathen, for no thing,   *in no way*
To none of us, their virtuous living,
That made them gentlemen y-callèd be,
And bade us follow them in such degree.[2]

Dante and others on heredity and gentilesse

1125 Well can the wisé poet of Florénce
That hightè Dante speak of this senténce.   *named D./ this idea*
Lo, in such manner rhyme is Dante's tale:
'Full seld uprises by his branches small   *seldom*
Prowess of man, for God of his goodness
1130 Wills that of Him we claim our gentilesse";[3]
For of our elders may we nothing claim   *ancestors*
But temporal thing, that may man hurt and maim.
Eke every wight wot this as well as I.   *person / knows*
If gentilesse were planted naturally   *by birth*
1135 Unto a certain lineage down the line,

---

[1] 1113-15: "Note who is most virtuous always, privately and publicly (*privy and apert*) and who always tries (*intendeth aye*) to do ...."

[2] 1121-4: *Yet may ... degree:* "There is no way they can leave to us the virtuous way of life which caused them to be called gentlemen and to urge us to follow in the same path." The triple negative *not, no, none* is perfectly good grammar for Chaucer's day.

[3] 1128-30: *Full ... man:* "Man's moral integrity seldom goes into the branches (descendants) from the main stock," i.e. moral quality is not inherited. *Prowess* = Dante's "probity." *Branches small* are the heirs of "gentle" stock. God wants us to ascribe our "gentility" to His grace.

Privy and apert then would they never fine	*cease*
To do of gentilesse the fair office;[1]	*good works*
They mighten do no villainy nor vice.	*could not do*
Take fire, and bear it in the darkest house	
1140 Betwixt this and the Mount of Caucasus,	
And let men shut the doorės, and go thence—	
Yet will the fire as fairė lie and burn	
As twenty thousand men might it behold;	*as if*
Its office natural aye will it hold,[2]	*Its nature*
1145 Up peril of my life, till that it die.	*= On peril = I swear*
Here may you see well, how that gentery	
Is not annexėd to possessïon,	
Since folk ne do their operatïon	
Always as does the fire, lo, in its kind.	*its nature*
1150 For God it wot, men may well often find	*God knows*
A lord's son do shame and villainy.	
And he that will have price of his gentry,	*wants respect for*
For he was born of a gentle house,	*(Just) Because*
And had his elders noble and virtuous,	*ancestors*
1155 And n'ill himselfė do no gentle deeds,	*n'ill = will not*
Nor follow his gentle ancestor, that dead is—	
He is not gentle, be he duke or earl,	
For villain's sinful deedės make a churl.	
Thy gentilessė is but renomee	*only the renown*
1160 Of thine ancestors, for their high bounty,	*fine qualities*
Which is a strangė thing to thy person.	*foreign to*
For gentilessė comes from God alone.[3]	
Then comes our very gentilesse of grace;	

---

[1] 1134 - 37: *If ... office:* "If *gentilesse* were a result of being born into a certain family, then both publicly (*apert*) and privately (*privy*) the members of that family (*lineage*) would never cease (*fine*) from doing the good that belongs to (the *office* of) 'gentilesse.'"

[2] 1144: "It will always (*aye*) function according to its nature."

[3] 1162: *Gentilesse* in line 1162 has *her* meaning—moral quality. In 1159 it has *his* meaning—"gentle" birth.

It was no thing bequeathed us with our place.   *rank*

1165 Thinketh how noble, as says Valerius,   *(Roman historian)*

Was thilkė Tullius Hostilius

That out of poverte rose to high noblesse.

Read Seneca, and readeth eke Boece,[1]   *Boethius also*

There shall you see express, that no dread is,   *without doubt*

1170 That he is gentle that does gentle deedės.

And therefore, leve husband, I thus conclude,   *dear husband*

All were it that mine ancestors were rude,   *Although / "lowborn"*

Yet may the highė God, and so hope I,

Grant me grace to liven virtuously.

1175 Then am I gentle when that I begin

To liven virtuously and waiven sin.   *give up*

The virtues of poverty

And there as you of poverte me repreeve,[2]

The highė God, in whom that we believe,

In willful poverte chose to live His life.

1180 And certės every man, maiden, or wife

May understand that Jesus, heaven's king,

Ne would not choose a vicïous living.

Glad poverte is an honest thing certáin.

This will Senec' and other clerkės sayn.   *Seneca & other writers*

1185 Whoso that holds him paid of his povérte,   *Whoever is happy in*

---

[1] 1168: Seneca: pagan Roman philosopher (d. 65 a.d.). Boethius: Roman philosopher (perhaps Christian, d. 525 a.d.) whose *Consolations of Philosophy* was highly regarded in the Middle Ages. Having the fairytale wife cite these "authorities" is decidedly odd. Here and in the following lines I have retained the original form *poverte,* which has two syllables and seems to be able to stress either; its modern form *poverty* inconveniently has three, with stress invariably on the first.

[2] 1177 ff: "And whereas you reprove me for my poverty, [I answer that] the high God in whom we believe, deliberately chose to live his life in poverty." She is referring, of course, to Jesus Christ. Here and in some other lines I have retained the original form *povert(e)* which has two syllables and seems to be able to stress either; its modern form poverty inconveniently has three, with stress invariably on the first.

I hold him rich, all had he not a shirt.[1]
He that covets is a poorė wight,   *creature*
For he would have what is not in his might.
But he that naught has, nor coveteth to have,
1190 Is rich, although men hold him but a knave.   *servant*
Very povértė singeth properly.[2]   *True p. / naturally*
Juvenal says of poverte merrily: *Satire X, 21*
'The poorė man when he goes by the way,   *along the road*
Before the thievės he may sing and play.'   *In front of*
1195 Povértė is hateful good; and, as I guess,
A full great bringer out of busyness;   *diligence*
A great amender eke of sapience   *improver / wisdom*
To him that taketh it in patïence.
Povértė's a thing, although it seem alenge,[3]   *unpleasant (?)*
1200 Possessïon that no wight will challenge.
Povértė full oftė, when a man is low,
Maketh himself and eke his God to know.
Povértė's a spectacle, as thinketh me,[4]   *glass / seems to me*
Through which he may his very friendės see.   *true friends*
1205 And, therefore, Sir, since that I not you grieve,
Of my povértė no morė me repreve.   *reprove*

Her age and ugliness

Now, Sir, of eld, that you repreven me: *old age*
And certės, Sir, though no authority   *written opinion*
Were in no book, you gentles of honoúr
1210 Say that men should an old wight do favoúr   *respect an old person*
And clepe him "father," for your gentilesse;   *call him f. / courtesy*

---

[1] 1185-6: "Whoever is contented in his poverty, him I consider rich even if he does not possess a shirt."

[2] 1191: "True (i.e. contented) poverty sings by its very nature."

[3] 1199: "Alenge," an uncommon word in Chaucer, is generally glossed "miserable" or "wearisome," which hardly fits this couplet.

[4] 1203: "Spectacle" refers to eye glasses or a magnifying glass, or less likely, a mirror.

And authors shall I finden, as I guess.[1]

Now, where you say that I am foul and old,   *ugly*

Then dread you not to be a cuckėwold.   *cuckold*

1215 For filth and eldė, also may I thee,   *age / I assure you*

Be greatė wardens upon chastity.[2]   *guardians of*

But natheless, since I know your delight,   *pleasure*

I shall fulfill your worldly appetite.   *sexual*

She offers him a choice between two things

Choose now,' quod she, 'one of these thingės tway: *two*

1220 To have me foul and old till that I die,

And be to you a true and humble wife,

And never you displease in all my life;

Or elsė you will have me young and fair,

And take your áventure of the repair   *chance / visiting*

1225 That shall be to your house because of me,

(Or in some other place it may well be).[3]

Now choose yourselfė whether that you liketh.   *which one pleases you*

This knight aviseth him, and sorė sigheth,   *thinks to himself*

But at the last he said in this mannér:

He lets her choose

1230 'My lady and my love, and wife so dear,

I put me in your wisė governance.

Choose yourself which may be most pleasánce

---

[1] 1208 - 1212: "Even if no respected authors had said so, you 'gentry' your-selves say that, out of courtesy, one should respect an old man and call him 'Father.' And I am sure I can find authors who say so."

[2] 1215-16: "Ugliness and age, I assure you, are great preservers of chastity." In *also may I thee* (as I hope to prosper), the last word, *thee*, is the verb *to prosper*.

[3] 1224-26: "And take your chances with the large number of visitors (*repair*) that will come to our house because of me—or perhaps to someplace else."

The alternatives that the wife poses to her husband constitute a *demande d'amour,* a favorite game of medieval writers, and of aristocratic medieval women, according to Andreas Capellanus. The Knight and the Franklin also propose *demandes* in their tales.

And most honoúr to you and me also;
I do no force the whether of the two.[1]   *I don't care*
1235 For as you liketh, it sufficeth me.'   *As you please*
'Then have I got of you mastery,' quod she,
'Since I may choose and govern as me lest?'   *as I please*
'Yea, certès, wife,' quod he, 'I hold it best.'
'Kiss me,' quod she, 'we be no longer wroth,   *angry*
1240 For by my truth I will be to you both,
This is to say, yea, bothè fair and good.   *pretty & faithful*
I pray to God that I may starven wood,   *die mad*
But I to you be all so good and true   *Unless*
As ever was wife, since that the world was new;
1245 And but I be to-morrow as fair to seen   *unless*
As any lady, empress or queen,
That is betwixt the East and eke the West,
Do with my life and death right as you lest.   *as you please*
Cast up the curtain, look how that it is.'

The happy result

1250 And when the knight saw verily all this,   *truly*
That she so fair was, and so young thereto,
For joy he hent her in his armès two: *he seized*
His heartè bathèd in a bath of bliss,
A thousand times a-row he gan her kiss;   *in a row*
1255 And she obeyèd him in every thing
That mightè do him pleasance or liking.
And thus they live unto their livès end
In perfect joy.

A prayer of sorts

And Jesus Christ us send   *(May) Christ send us*
Husbands meekè, young, and fresh a-bed,
1260 And grace to overbide them that we wed.   *to outlive*
And eke I prayè Jesus short their lives   *also / shorten*

---

[1] 1234: "I do not care which of the two."

That will not be governèd by their wives.
And old and angry niggards of dispense,   *tight spenders*
God send them soon a very pestilence.   *veritable plague*

THE CANTERBURY TALES

The Clerk of Oxford and His Tale

THE CLERK'S TALE

Introduction

This tale of patient Griselda was quite popular in the Middle Ages, a fact that may be puzzling for modern taste, which often finds the story grotesque for different reasons, even if we also find it fascinating. It first appeared in literary form in Italian, as the last tale in Boccaccio's *Decameron* (c. 1355), and was then retold by his contemporary and fellow-countryman, the poet Petrarch (c. 1373).

One thing to bear in mind is that one of the pilgrims, Harry Bailly, the Host, refers to it as a "legend," wishing that his wife had heard it (1212, below). A legend in the Middle Ages was not just an old or incredible story, though the story of Griselda's patience is incredible enough. Legend meant literally "something to be read," something edifying, that is, like a saint's life in, say, the great medieval hagiographical collection known as *The Golden Legend*. The stories in that book are often of incredible feats of endurance accomplished by virgins and martyrs for the faith. These saints are "patient," that is literally, "suffering, enduring." Christians were to look on them, if not as patterns to be directly imitated, at least as models to be admired, examples of what a real hero or heroine could do for God's sake; and ordinary Christians should try to follow in their own less perfect way.

The Clerk's Tale is similar and disturbingly different: it shows a saintly woman with the virtue of patience on the heroic scale, but the tortures inflicted upon her (mental not physical) are not inflicted by wicked men who are obviously the enemies of God and the faith, but by her husband who, in some way, seems to represent God!

The Wife of Bath had admitted that clerics *could* sometimes speak well about women even if only about those who qualified for a place in *The Golden Legend.* She may be right about this clerk, although having heard this tale, she might also have said that the Clerk is not speaking well of women, since this is an exemplary tale which (in spite of his final disclaimer) encourages women to be obedient to their husbands' whims and to participate in their own subjection; it is a man's fantasy of a wife eternally docile and forbearing, but told by a clerk, an unmarried clerical "authority" without any experience.

The Golden Legend, a collection put together by another clerk, Jacobus de Voragine, was not taken at face value by all. Indeed, it was dubbed the Leaden Legend by some, with its stories of the Seven Sleepers, St. Mary of Egypt, or St. James the Dismembered, and the like, which strained belief and were dubiously edifying. Similarly, even Petrarch, from whom Chaucer takes his tale, finds the story of Griselda both fascinating and grotesque, and to make it acceptable even to medieval tastes allegorizes it or turns it into an exemplary tale the details of which were not expected to be always plausible. Chaucer follows him, or purports to:

> This story is said not for that wivès should
> Follow Griseld as in humility,
> For it were importáble though they would,   (impossible)
> But for that every wight in his degree   (person)
> Should be constant in adversity

As was Griselda; therefore Petrarch writes
This story which with high style he endites.   *(composes)*

For since a woman was so patïent
Unto a mortal man, well more us ought
Receiven all in gree that God us sent   (1142 ff)   *(in patience)*

According to this reading Griselda represents the faithful soul which, like Job, patiently endures the hardships that God sends even when it least understands. One may, however, find it difficult to take the human, whim-driven, wifebaiting cruelty of Walter as something Godlike. Sympathizing with Griselda against "God" is almost impossible to avoid. At a number of points in the poem Chaucer uses his considerable power to evoke pathos on Griselda's behalf, as when Griselda's children are taken away, and when she herself is dismissed half naked and followed by a crowd back to the wretched cabin of her father, who tries to cover her nakedness with the old clothes that no longer fit. The closest she ever comes to complaint is at this point, with the words spoken more in sorrow than in anger, the whole passage from 815-896 including this:

O goodë God! How gentle and how kind
You seemèd by your speech and your viságe
The day that makèd was our marrïage
But sooth is said (algate I find it true) ...   *(certainly I)*
Love is not old as when that it is new.

* * * *

Let me not like a worm go by the way.
Remember you, mine ownë lord so dear,
I was your wife, though I unworthy were   (852 - 882)

The scriptural story of Job does not work in this emotional way. And after all, his sufferings are inflicted by the devil whom God has allowed to afflict him. Is Walter God's diabolical instrument? If so, who is God in the allegory or exemplum? A reader of the above passage may be tempted to treat "O good God" not only as an exclamation but as a direct address to the Deity by the suffering "sponsa Christi".

It has been pointed out that in the pre-marital agreement scene Walter is peculiarly scrupulous to make clear to Griselda the one crucial term on which the marriage is to take place: her total obedience to his wishes. In one sense she has no grounds for complaint; she has made what might under other circumstances be called a Rash Promise, and she must take the consequences. But did she really have any choice?

Those who argue that the allegory of Griselda as the patient soul fits the tale nearly as poorly as Griselda's old clothes, insist that it is an exemplary story, not to be read either as pure allegory or as a realistic novel; one suspends one's disbelief and does not ask questions like these: Do God and Walter exactly correspond? Do noblemen go out and marry peasant girls just like that? Does such an uncultivated girl suddenly blossom into a member of the aristocracy with all the diplomatic and social graces normally acquired by long training? Why do the people who were so pressing about an heir not do something about his sudden disappearance? Would any woman accept Walter's apparent murder of her child with such placidity? Would Walter's sister and her husband collaborate in Walter's enormity? And so on.

There is more than a touch of the folk tale here, where cruelties like those in "Cinderella" or "Hansel and Gretel" seem almost expected, and the story builds on the reader's hopes that all will come out right in the end. There is the same absence of any religious feeling at the core, in spite of the allusions to the Annunciation, the Nativity and Planctus Mariae that critics have found in the story, in spite of the reference to the Pope (who is there for convenience), and in spite of the occasional phrase like "By him that for us died." Perhaps the most striking evidence of this lack of religious center is the absence of a church service when Walter and Griselda get married, or of any wedding service for that matter. In spite of the Clerk's geographical introduction, one has very little feeling that the story is set in Christian Italy—or Christian England either. Instead, it is much the same indeterminate territory as one sees, for example, in many ballads or folktales, a bit preternatural, not quite human, not at all like the village beside Bath where the Wife, Alison Masterman lives.

Inevitably one is brought to wonder why Chaucer found the story worth re-doing after it had been treated by two major authors of his own century, Boccaccio and Petrarch. To be sure, he makes it fit neatly into the Marriage Debate as a response to the Wife of Bath's prologue and tale, to which it is a striking contrast in more ways than one: the Wife's domineering is never cruel or inhuman like Walter's; her desire for "husbands young, meek, and fresh a-bed" is readily, even amusingly comprehensible. Her short tale is about as unrealistic as the Clerk's, but the milieu of her long prologue is an English world of gossips and clerics, household squabbles and theological argument, flirting, coupling, playgoing, domestic rebellion and church marriage.

The Clerk's tale of Griselda is not at all like this. The coolness at its center is appropriate for a tale which may be, in fact, a questioning of the very Christian lesson it purports to inculcate. This version of the tale may be a cry as muffled as Job's is loud against the arbitrary cruelty of a world that is supposed to be ruled by a good and just God. *Is* God like Walter—cruel, arbitrary, whimsical, tyrannizing over the defenceless men and women whom He has raised from the dust of the earth only to humiliate and torture them? Do we have any more choice in accepting His terms than Griselda did Walter's? Remember the swift and terrible punishment inflicted for the breaking of an arbitrary prohibition in Eden. Remember the terrible demand made on Abraham to sacrifice his son, so graphically portrayed in some medieval miracle plays. Griselda was expected to sacrifice her children in the same way. A questioning critique comes directly from the narrator:

> *What needed it*
> *Her for to tempt, and always more and more*
> *Though some men praise it for a subtle wit?*
> *But as for me, I say that evil it sits*
> *To assay a wife when that it is no need*   *(to test)*
> *And putten her in anguish and in dread*   (457-62)
>
> *O needless was she tempted in assay*   (621)
>
> *But now of women would I asken fain*   *(I want to ask)*
> *If these assayès mightè not suffice?*   (696-7)   *(these tests)*

Chaucer put some similar questions in the mouth of pagan Palam-
on in *The Knight's Tale*, direct questions to the gods themselves:

> *What is mankind more unto you hold*
> *Than is the sheep that rouketh in the fold?*   *(huddles)*
> *What governance is in this prescience*
> *That guiltless tormenteth innocence?*   (Kn.T. 1307-14)
>
> *The answer to this let I to divines*   (Kn.T. 1323) *(theologians)*

The "happy" ending in the Clerk's tale is as arbitrary as in the
Knight's; and, to the difficult questions posed by his own tale, the
Clerk, like the good divine he is, gives the standard (but question-
able) answer : "This story is said ...," quoted above (1142 ff).
Griselda finally makes it to the heaven of Walter's bosom as all
humanity may hope to make it to Abraham's. What this version of
the tale invites one to question is the price exacted for both
rewards. Each reader must be his or her own divine and must provide his or her own answer.

At the end, the Clerk (or Chaucer) shrewdly turns from
"earnestful matter" to humor, jokingly encouraging all women to
embrace the philosophy of the Wife of Bath and take no bullying
from the would-be Walters of this world. Perhaps the very humor
intentionally explodes his explanation.

Some Linguistic Notes for the Clerk's Tale

Spelling of Names:

Griselda is the usual form here in accordance with the modern usage. The MSS spell it Grisild, Grisilde, Grisildis, varying between two syllables and three and usually with the emphasis on the second syllable. But Chaucer does not scruple to change the stress to the first syllable when his rhythmic system needs it as at lines 752 and 948 *(Gríseldis)* where it also rhymes with *this* and *is*. Similarly, the heroine's father is called Janicula or Janicle (404). The name of the town varies from Sáluces to Salúces to Salúce.

Word Stress:

Stress that differs from our normal usage is most common in words of French origin, many of them clearly taking the French stress rather than the modern English emphasis. This is commonest in words ending in *-ure* like *natúre, conjectúre, creätúre* (3 syllables); or *-age* like *couráge, messáge, viságe,* though it is clearly *vísage* in 1085. Similarly *pleasánce, patïent* (3 syllables). *Pity* (142) with second-syllable stress rhymes with *me* because it was originally *pitee* and stressed French-fashion in Chaucer's poetic dialect. In 407/9 the rhyme is *she / bount-é,* but in 415 *boúnty.* Line 692 demands stresses almost totally like those of a French line:

> *And of malíce or of cruél couráge*
>
> but
>
> *He of his crúel purpose* (734)

The rhymes in the opening stanza of Pt II are almost totally French in stress.

This variable stress seems to extend all too often to words with the distinctly English endings in *-ness* and *-ing,* where it has an unfortunate effect, at least in: *cunníngly* (1017) : *ring / amblíng* (386/8); *quakíng / willíng / likíng* (317-20). Line 320 seems to require a scansion impossible in a modern reading: *"Is as you will nor ágainst your* *liking."* The situation in the MS form does not improve matters much: *Is as ye wole, nor ayeynes youre likynge.* We have a different apparent stress in *tórmenting, nourishing, súpposing* (1038-41) most of which I have not marked except for the first because I think readers can easily adapt to whatever accent they think necessary. See also 1080-83.

Fairnéss rhymes with *richesse* (384-5) and shares its stress. Similarly *witnéss / mistréss* (821/823) seem to demand this stress though I have not marked them in the text.

At 1044 the rhyming word *patience* should strictly be metered *patïence* and *malíce* so marked in 1045, but here and elsewhere the reader can adapt these lines to our normal stress on these words, and so the stress mark seems especially out of place, as no doubt it sometimes does elsewhere in the text. Readers should ignore these stress marks if they find them of no help.

The problem is at its most insistent in the Envoy, Chaucer's variation on a very French poetic form, the double *ballade,* where he uses only three rhymes throughout 36 lines, and where 4 out of every 6 rhymes are on French-derived words with distinctly French stress. It is almost impossible to be consistent in using the modern equivalents in these circumstances since both rhyme and rhythm will be thrown off that way: *marvel* will not go well with *nail* and *entrail.* In my first edition I allowed *camel, battle,* and *counsel* to stand, but though they might rhyme reasonably well, the rhythm clearly demands stress on the second syllable; hence I have here reverted to the Chaucerian spelling: *camail, batail, co(u)nsail,* which may, however, require glosses. See also the note to the opening stanza of Part II.

Scansion:

1048: *"Continuing ever her innocence overall."* There is an *-e* at the end of each of the first three words in the original, but even not counting these *-e*'s there are thirteen syllables in this line, which argues strongly for slurring or elision which must have been common in many other cases also.

The Portrait, Prologue and Tale of the Clerk

The Portrait of the Clerk from the General Prologue

The Clerk is a deeply serious university man, more interested in study and books than in money, food, clothes or worldly position

	A CLERK there was of Oxenford also	*Oxford*
	That unto logic haddė long y-go.[1]	*gone*
	As leanė was his horse as is a rake,	
	And he was not right fat, I undertake,	*he=the Clerk*
	But lookėd hollow, and thereto soberly.	*gaunt & also*
290	Full threadbare was his overest courtepy,	*outer cloak*
	For he had gotten him yet no benefice	*parish*
	Nor was so worldly for to have office,	*secular job*
	For him was lever have at his bed's head	*For he would rather*
	Twenty bookės clad in black or red	*bound*
295	Of Aristotle and his philosophy	
	Than robės rich or fiddle or gay psalt'ry.	*stringed instrument*
	But albeit that he was a philosopher,	*although*
	Yet haddė he but little gold in coffer,[2]	*chest*
	But all that he might of his friendės hent	*get*
300	On bookės and on learning he it spent,	
	And busily gan for the soulės pray	*regulary prayed for*
	Of them that gave him wherewith to scholay.	*study*

---

[1] 285-6: He had long since set out to study logic, part of the trivium or lower section of the university syllabus (the other two parts were rhetoric and grammar); hence his early college years had long since passed. "y-go" (gone) is the past participle of "go." Clerk = cleric / student / scholar. Our Clerk is all of these.

[2] 298: A joke. Although he was a student of philosophy, he had not discovered the "philosopher's stone," which was supposed to turn base metals into gold. The two senses of "philosopher" played on here are: a) student of the work of Aristotle b) student of science ("natural philosophy"), a meaning which shaded off into "alchemist, magician." "Philosópher" was probably the stress here, French fashion, to rhyme with "coffer."

Of study took he most care and most heed.
Not one word spoke he morė than was need,
305   And that was spoke in form and reverence,
And short and quick and full of high senténce.   *lofty thought*
Sounding in moral virtue was his speech,
And gladly would he learn and gladly teach.

The Prologue to the Clerk's Tale

The Host asks the Clerk for a tale, and pokes a little fun at him. The Clerk takes it in a good spirit, and in scholarly and somewhat pedantic fashion he gives the source of the tale he is going to tell.

"Sir Clerk of Oxenford," our Hostė said,
You ride as coy and still as does a maid
Were new espousėd sitting at the board.   *newly married / table*
This day ne heard I of your tongue a word.
5   I trow you study about some sophime.   *I guess / logic problem*
But Solomon says: 'Everything hath time.'
For God's sake as be of better cheer;
It is no timė for to study here.
Tell us some merry thingė, by your fay,   *by your faith*
10   For what man that is entered in a play   *game*
He needs must unto the play assent.   *agree to the rules*
But preacheth not, as Friars do in Lent
To make us for our oldė sinnės weep.
Nor that thy talė make us not to sleep!
15   Tell us some merry thing of áventures.
Your termės, your coloúrs, and your figúres[1]—   *fancy rhetoric*
Keep them in store till so be you endite   *until you write*
High style, as when that men to kingės write.
Speaketh so plain at this time we you pray
20   That we may understanden what you say."
This worthy Clerk benignėly answerėd: *good humoredly*

---

[1] 16: Terms and tropes (of rhetoric), figures of speech.

	"Host," quod he, "I am under your yard.	*your rod i.e. authority*
	You have of us as now the governance,	
	And therefore will I do you obeisance	*obey you*
25	As far as reason asketh hardily.	*certainly*
	I will you tell a talė which that I	
	Learned at Padua of a worthy clerk	
	As provėd by his words and by his work.	
	He is now dead and nailėd in his chest.	*coffin*
30	I pray to God to give his soulė rest.	
	Francis Petrarch, the laureate poet[1]	
	Hightė this clerk, whose rhetoricė sweet	*this writer was called*
	Illumined all Itaille of poetry	*Italy*
	As Linian did of Philosophy,	*di Lignano*
35	Or law or other art particular.	*other study*
	But death, that will not suffer us dwellen here	*not allow*
	But as it were a twinkling of an eye,	*Only*
	Them both has slain. And allė shall we die.	*we shall all*
	But forth to tellen of this worthy man	
40	That taughtė me this tale, as I began,	
	I say first that with high style he enditeth,	
	(Ere he the body of his talė writeth)	
	A prohemie in which describeth he	*A preface*
	Piedmont, and of Saluces the country,	
45	And speaks of Apennines, the hillės high	
	That be the boundės of West Lombardy,	
	And of mount Vesulus in specïal	*Mt Viso*
	Where as the Po, out of a wellė small,	
	Taketh his firstė springing and his source	
50	That eastward aye increaseth in his course	
	To Emeliaward, to Ferrara and Venice,	
	The which a longė thing were to devise.	*to tell*
	And truly, as to my judgėment	

---

[1] 31: Chaucer gets his story from the Latin version of Petrarch, the great Italian poet who was crowned (with laurel) poet laureate in 1341.

Methinketh it a thing impertinent   *irrelevant*
55   Save that he will conveyen his matter.[1]
But this his talé, which that you shall hear.

The Clerk's Tale

Part One

The subjects of an Italian ruler want him to marry to ensure the succession. He agrees on condition that they accept and respect his choice of wife. A date is set.

There is, at the west side of Itaille,   *Italy*
Down at the root of Vesulus the cold,   *Mt Viso*
A lusty plain, abundant of vitaille,   *fertile w. crops*
60   Where many a tower and town thou mayst behold,
That founded were in time of fathers old,
And many another délitable sight,
And Sáluces this noble country hight.   *was called*

A marquis whilom lord was of that land,   *was once*
65   As were his worthy elders him before;
And obeisant, aye ready to his hand,   *obedient, always*
Were all his lieges, both less and more.   *subjects, b. high & low*
Thus in delight he lives, and has done yore,   *for long time*
Beloved and dread, through favor of Fortúne,   *Loved & feared*
70   Both of his lordés and of his commune.   *by his l. & common people*

Therewith he was, to speak as of lineage,   *ancestry*
The gentilest y-born of Lombardy,   *most nobly*
A fair person, and strong, and young of age,
And full of honor and of courtesy;
75   Discreet enough his country for to gye,   *guide (rule)*

---

[1] 54-55: "It is out of place unless it contributes to the story." So why was it not omitted here? Perhaps this is Chaucer's gentle poke at the pedantry of some scholars.

Save in some thingès that he was to blame;
And Walter was this youngè lordè's name.

I blame him thus, that he considered naught   *not at all*
In timè coming what might him betide,   *happen to him*
80   But on his lust presént was all his thought,   *desires of the moment*
As for to hawk and hunt on every side.
Well nigh all other curès let he slide,   *duties*
And eke he n'ould—and that was worst of all—   *would not*
Wed no wife, for naught that may befall.

85   Only that point his people bore so sore   *resented so much*
That flockmeal on a day they to him went,   *in a group*
And one of them that wisest was of lore,   *of learning*
Or elsè that the lord best would assent   *either because*
That he should tell him what his people meant
90   Or elsè could he show well such mattér,[1]   *knew best how to*
He to the marquis said as you shall hear:

"O noble marquis, your humanity
Assureth us and gives us hardiness,   *courage*
As oft as time is of necessity,
95   That we to you may tell our heaviness.   *problem*
Accepteth, lord, now of your gentleness   *Accepteth: polite plur*
What we with piteous heart unto you 'plain,   *complain*
And let your earès not my voice disdain.

"All have I naught to do in this matter   *Although / nothing*
100 More than another man has in this place,
Yet for as much as you, my lord so dear,
Have always showèd me favour and grace
I dare the better ask of you a space   *a moment*
Of audience, to showen our request,   *to present*
105 And you, my lord, to do right as you lest.   *as pleases you*

---

[1] 88-90: Either because the lord would agree to listen to *him* say what his people wanted; or because he was the best at presenting such cases.

"For certės, lord, so well us liketh you   *you please us*
And all your work, and ever have done, that we
Ne could we not ourselves devisen how
We mighten live in more felicity,
110   Save one thing, lordė, if it your will be,
That for to be a wedded man you lest;   *agree to marry*
Then were your people in sovereign heartės' rest.   *completely at ease*

"Boweth your neck under that blissfull yoke   *harness collar*
Of sovereignty, not of service,
115   Which that men clepe espousal or wedlock;   *men call*
And thinketh, lord, among your thoughtės wise
How that our dayės pass in sundry wise;
For though we sleep, or wake, or run, or ride,
Aye flees the time; it n'ill no man abide.   *Always / wait for*

120   "And though your greenė youthė flower as yet,
In creepeth age always, as still as stone,
And death menaces every age, and smites   *strikes*
In each estate, for there escapeth none;   *In every rank*
And all so certain as we know each one
125   That we shall die, as uncertain we all
Be of that day when death shall on us fall.

"Accepteth then of us the true intent,
That never yet refuseden thy hest,   *your orders*
And we will, lord, if that you will assent
130   Choose you a wife, in short time at the least,
Born of the gentilest and of the most   *noblest & highest*
Of all this land, so that it ought to seem
Honour to God and you, as we can deem.   *in our judgement*

"Deliver us out of all this busy dread,   *serious worry*
135   And take a wife, for highė Godė's sake!
For if it so befell, as God forbid,
That through your death your lineage should slake,   *die out*

And that a strangĕ súccessor should take
Your heritage, O, woe were us alive!   *God help us*
140 Wherefore we pray you hastily to wive."   *to marry*

Their meek prayer and their piteous cheer   *their sad looks*
Madĕ the marquis's heart to have pity.
"You will," quod he, "my ownĕ people dear,
To that I never erst thought strainĕ me.[1]
145 I me rejoicĕd of my liberty,
That seldom time is found in marrïage;   *rarely*
Where I was free, I must be in servage.   *servitude*

"But nathelees I see your true intent,
And trust upon your wit, and have done aye;   *judgement / always*
150 Wherefore of my free will I will assent
To weddĕ me, as soon as ever I may.   *To marry*
But there as you have proffered me to-day
To choosĕ me a wife, I you release
That choice, and pray you of that proffer cease.   *offer*

155 "For God it wot, that children often been   *God knows*
Unlike their worthy elders them before;
Bounty comes all of God, not of the strain   *goodness / stock*
Of which they been engendered and y-bore.[2]   *begotten & born*
I trust in Godĕ's bounty, and therefore
160 My marrïage and my estate and rest
I Him betake; He may do as Him lest.   *commend to Him / wishes*

"Let me alone in choosing of my wife;
That charge upon my back I will endure.   *burden*
But I you pray, and charge upon your life,   *demand*

---

[1] 143-4: "You will ... pressure me to do what I had never thought of doing."

[2] 155-58: These lines might have been spoken as part of the lecture on true nobility given by the hag in the *Wife of Bath's Tale*. And this tale of the Clerk proves her point. But with the preceding few lines they seem to be meant to hint at his unusual choice for a bride.

165	That what wife that I take, you me assure
	To worship her while that her life may dure,	*honor / last*
	In word and work, both here and everywhere,
	As she an emperourė's daughter were.	*As if*

"And furthermore, this shall you swear, that ye
170 Against my choice shall neither grouch nor strive;
  For since I shall forgo my liberty
  At your request, as ever may I thrive,   *as I hope to prosper*
  There as my heart is set, there will I wive;   *Wherever / marry*
  And but you will assent in such mannér,   *And unless*
175 I pray you, speak no more of this mattér."

With hearty will they swear and they assent
  To all this thing; there said no wightė nay,   *nobody said No*
  Beseeching him of grace, ere that they went,
  That he would granten them a certain day
180 Of his espousal, as soon as ever he may;   *wedding*
  For yet always the people somwhat dread,   *dreaded*
  Lest that the marquis no wife wouldė wed.

He granted them a day, such as him lest,   *he appointed / he pleased*
  On which he would be wedded sikerly,   *certainly*
185 And said he did all this at their request.
  And they, with humble intentė, buxomly,   *obediently*
  Kneeling upon their knees full reverently,
  Him thankėd all; and thus they have an end
  Of their intent, and home again they wend.   *they go*

190 And hereupon he to his officers
  Commandeth for the feastė to purvey,   *prepare*
  And to his privy knightės and his squires   *personal*
  Such chargė gave as him list on them lay;   *orders as he wished*
  And they to his commandėment obey,
195 And each of them does all his diligence   *his best*
  To do unto the feastė reverence.

Part Two

Wedding preparation are made, but nobody knows who the prospective bride is, not even the bride herself.

Not far from thilkė palace honorable,[1]
Where as this marquis shoop his marrïage,   *planned*
There stood a thorp, of sitė delitable,   *village / beautiful*
200 In which that poorė folk of that village
Hadden their beastės and their herbergage,   *homes*
And of their labour took their sustenance,
After that th'earthė gave them abundance.   *according as*

Amongst these poorė folk there dwelt a man
205 Which that was holden poorest of them all;   *regarded as*
But highė Godė sometimes senden can
His grace into a little ox's stall;
Janicula men of that thorp him call.   *village*
A daughter had he, fair enough to sight,
210 And Gríselda this youngė maiden hight.[2]   *was called*

But for to speak of virtuous beauty,
Then was she one the fairest under sun;
For poorly y-fostered up was she,   *reared in poverty*
No likerous lust was through her heart y-run.   *lecherous*
215 Well oftener of the well than of the tun   *(wine) cask*
She drank, and for she wouldė virtue please,   *and because / practise*
She knew well labour, but no idle ease.

---

[1] All the riming words in this stanza are of French derivation and probably in Chaucer's day bore French stress: honoráble, villáge, ábundánce, etc. Such heavy concentration of French words at line end makes it impossible to get full rime in normal modern English pronunciation. This is also notably true of the "Envoy" at the end of the poem. See Introduction to this tale.

[2] 208-210: The names of the father and daughter occur both here and in the manuscripts of the poem in different spellings. See the introduction.

But though this maiden tender was of age,   *was young*
Yet in the breast of her virginity
220   There was enclosèd ripe and sad couráge;   *mature & serious spirit*
And in great reverence and charity
Her oldè poorè father fostered she.   *cared for*
A few sheep, spinning, in field she kept;[1]
She wouldè not be idle till she slept.

225   And when she homeward came, she wouldè bring
Worts or other herbès timès oft,   *Cabbages*
The which she shred and seethed for their living,   *& boiled / meal*
And made her bed full hard and nothing soft;
And aye she kept her father's life on-loft   *always / going*
230   With every obeisance and diligence   *respect*
That child may do to father's reverence.

Upon Griselda, this poor creäture,
Full often sithe this marquis set his eye   *often times*
As he on hunting rode peráventure;   *by chance*
235   And when it fell that he might her espy,   *when it happened*
He not with wanton looking of folly[2]
His eyen cast on her, but in sad wise   *eyes / serious*
Upon her cheer he would him oft avise,   *face / look*

Commending in his heart her womanhood,
240   And eke her virtue, passing any wight   *surpassing / person*
Of so young age, as well in cheer as deed.   *in looks*
For though the people have no great insight
In virtue, he considerèd full right
Her bounty, and disposèd that he would   *her goodness & decided*
245   Wed her only, if ever he wed should.

---

[1] 223: She spun thread while she watched her sheep. The spinning was presumably not done with a wheel but with a distaff, a portable stick for making wool thread by hand.

[2] 236-7: "And not with foolish, lustful glances did he look at her."

The day of wedding came, but no wight can   *no one*
Tellė what woman that it shouldė be;
For whichė marvel wondered many a man,
And saidė when they were in privity: *in private*
250 "Will not our lord yet leave his vanity?   *his foolishness*
Will he not wed? Alas! Alas, the while!
Why will he thus himself and us beguile?"   *deceive*

But nathelees this marquis hath done make   *caused to be made*
Of gemmės set in gold and in azure,   *gems / blue enamel*
255 Brooches and ringės for Griselda's sake,
And of her clothing took he the measúre
Of a maiden like to her statúre,   *similar size*
And eke of other ornamentės all
That unto such a wedding should befall.   *be appropriate*

260 The time of undern of the samė day   *about 10 a.m.*
Approacheth that this wedding shouldė be;
And all the palace put was in array,
Both hall and chambers, each in its degree;
Houses of office stuffėd with plenty   *storehouses*
265 There mayst thou see, of dainteous vitaille   *delicious foods*
That may be found as far as last Itaille.   *furthest part of Italy*

This royal marquis richėly arrayed,   *dressed*
Lordės and ladies in his company,
The which that to the feastė were y-prayed,   *invited*
270 And of his retinue the bachelry,   *young knights*
With many a sound of sundry melody,
Unto the village of the which I told,
In this array the rightė way have hold.   *In this fashion*

Griseld of this, God wot, full innocent,   *unaware*
275 That for her shapen was all this array,   *was destined*
To fetchė water at a well is went,   *has gone*
And cometh home as soon as ever she may;

For well had she heard said that thilkė day   *that day*
The marquis shouldė wed, and if she might,
280   She wouldė fain have seen some of that sight.   *would like to see*

She thought, "I will with other maidens stand,
That be my fellows, in our door and see   *my friends*
The marquisess, and therefore will I fond   *try*
To do at home, as soon as it may be,
285   The labour which that longeth unto me;   *I have to do*
And then I may at leisure her behold,
If she this way unto the castle hold."   *comes*

*The marquis and his retinue arrive at Griselda's cottage; he asks for her
hand in marriage, and she promises to love, honor and obey, with special emphasis on* **obey.**

And as she would over her threshold go,
The marquis came, and gan her for to call;
290   And she set down her water pot anon,
Beside the threshold, in an ox's stall,
And down upon her knees she gan to fall,
And with sad countenancė kneeleth still   *serious*
Till she had heard what was the lordė's will.

295   This thoughtful marquis spoke unto this maid
Full soberly, and said in this mannér: *Very seriously*
"Where is your father, O Griseld?" he said.
And she with reverence, in humble cheer,   *manner*
Answered: "Lord, he is already here."
300   And in she goes withouten longer let,   *delay*
And to the marquis she her father fet.   *fetched*

He by the hand then took this oldė man,
And saidė thus, when he him had aside:
"Janicula, I neither may nor can
305   Longer the pleasance of my heartė hide.   *the desire*
If that thou vouchėsafe, what so betide,   *agree / happens*

Thy daughter will I take, ere that I wend,   *before I go*
As for my wife, unto my life's end.

"Thou lovest me, I wot it well certáin,   *I know*
310 And art my faithfull liegė man y-bore;   *loyal subject born*
And all that liketh me, I dare well sayn   *pleases me*
It liketh thee, and specially therefore
Tell me that point that I have said before,
If that thou wilt unto that purpose draw   *agree to this*
315 To takė me as for thy son-in-law."

The sudden case this man astonished so
That red he waxed; abashėd and all quaking   *flustered*
He stood; unnethės said he wordės mo'   *scarcely*
But only thus: "Lord," quod he, "my willing
320 Is as you will, nor against your liking
I will nothing. You be my lord so dear;
Right as you listė, governeth this mattér."   *as you wish, decide*

"Yet will I," quod this marquis softėly,   *I wish*
"That in thy chamber I and thou and she
325 Have a collatïon, and wost thou why?   *conference & know you why?*
For I will ask if it her willė be
To be my wife, and rule her after me.   *be ruled by me*
And all this shall be done in thy presénce;
I will not speak out of thine audience."   *hearing*

330 And in the chamber, while they were about
Their treaty, which as you shall after hear,   *agreement*
The people came unto the house without,
And wondered them in how honést mannér
And 'tentively she kept her father dear.   *attentively*
335 But utterly Griselda wonder might,
For never erst ne saw she such a sight.   *before*

No wonder is though that she were astoned   *astonished*
To see so great a guest come in that place;

She never was unto such guestės woned,   *accustomed*
340 For which she lookėd with full palė face.
But shortly forth this matter for to chase,   *to continue*
These are the wordės that the marquis said
To this benignė, very faithful maid.

"Griseld," he said, "you shall well understand
345 It liketh to your father and to me   *it pleases*
That I you wed, and eke it may so stand   *and also*
As I suppose, you will that it so be.
But these demandės ask I first," quod he,
"That, since it shall be done in hasty wise,
350 Will you assent, or else will you avise?[1]   *take counsel*

"I say this, be you ready with good heart
To all my lust; and that I freely may   *my wishes*
As me best thinketh, do you laugh or smart,[2]
And never you to grudge it, night nor day?   *complain*
355 And eke when I say 'Yea,' ne say not 'Nay,'   *And also*
Neither by word nor frowning countenance?
Swear this, and here I swear our álliance."

Wondering upon this word, quaking for dread,
She saidė, "Lord, undigne and unworthy   *undeserving*
360 Am I to thilk honoúr that you me bid,   *that honor / offer*
But as you will yourself, right so will I.
And here I swear that never willingly,
In work nor thought, I n'ill you disobey,
For to be dead, though me were loath to die."

---

[1] 350: Skeat and Riverside point out that the phrase "The king will take counsel " (*Le roy s'avisera*) was a formula for polite refusal. So the line means roughly: "Do you agree or not?"

[2] 351-3: "Are you ready with good will (to fulfill) all my wishes?" The rest is either "And (grant) that I may freely (do) as I think best, whether that causes you to laugh or to feel pain" or " And (grant) that I may freely cause you joy or pain, as I think best." There is a difference.

365   "This is enough, Griselda mine," quod he.

And forth he goes, with a full sober cheer,   *serious look*

Out at the door, and after that came she,

And to the people he said in this mannér:

"This is my wife," quod he, "that standeth here.

370   Honour her and loveth her, I pray,

Whoso me loves. There is no more to say."   *Whoever*

*With her change into princely clothing Griselda is transformed in every
way. In time a child is born.*

And for that nothing of her oldé gear   *clothes*

She shouldé bring into his house, he bade

That women should despoilen her right there;   *strip*

375   Of which these ladies weré not right glad

To handle her clothes wherein that she was clad.

But natheless, this maiden bright of hue

From foot to head they clothéd have all new.

Her hairés have they combed that lay untressed   *unbraided*

380   Full rudély, and with their fingers small   *loosely*

A coronet on her head they have y-dressed,   *tiara or garland / put*

And set her full of nowches great and small.   *brooches*

Of her array what should I make a tale?   *clothes / long story*

Unnethe the people her knew for her fairness,   *Scarcely / beauty*

385   When she transforméd was in such richesse.

This marquis hath her spouséd with a ring   *married*

Brought for the samé cause, and then her set *Brought for that purpose*

Upon a horse, snow-white and well ambling,   *slow paced*

And to his palace, ere he longer let,   *without delay*

390   With joyful people that her led and met,

Conveyéd her, and thus the day they spend

In revel, till the sun 'gan to descend.   *In celebration*

And shortly forth this talé for to chase,   *to tell the story*

I say that to this newé marquisess

395   God hath such favour sent her of his grace,

That it ne seemèd not by likeliness   *didn't seem possible*

That she was born and fed in rudèness,   *raised in poverty*

As in a cote or in an ox's stall,   *cottage*

But nourished in an emperourè's hall.   *reared*

400   To every wight she waxen is so dear   *To e. person she became*

And worshipfull that folk where she was born   *And honored*

And from her birthè knew her year by year,

Unnethè trowèd they, but durst have sworn   *Hardly believed / dared*

That to Janicle, of which I spoke before,

405   She daughter were, for as by cónjecture,

Them thought she was another creäture.   *It seemed to them*

For though that ever virtuous was she,

She was increasèd in such excellence

Of thewès good, y-set in high bounty,   *manners*

410   And so discreet and fair of eloquence,

So benign and so digne of reverence,   *worthy of*

And couldè so the people's heart embrace,   *win*

That each her loved that lookèd in her face.

Not only of Salúces in the town

415   Published was the bounty of her name,   *good reputation*

But eke beside in many a region,   *But also*

If one said well, another said the same;

So spread of her high bounty the fame   *great goodness*

That men and women, as well young as old,

420   Go to Saluce upon her to behold.   *to look at her*

Thus Walter lowly (nay, but royally!)

Wedded with fortunatè honesty,   *virtue*

In Godè's peace liveth full easily

At home, and outward grace enough had he;[1]

---

[1] 424: *outward* may mean "apparently, to all appearances," or it may contrast with "home" and mean "abroad, in foreign policy."

425 And for he saw that under low degree	*And because / rank*
Was often virtue hid, the people him held	*considered him*
A prudent man, and that is seen full seld.	*seldom*
Not only this Griselda through her wit	*wisdom*
Could all the feat of wifely homeliness,[1]	*Had all the skills*
430 But eke, when that the case requirèd it,	*But also*
The common profit couldè she redress.	*public good promote*
There n'as discórd, rancor, nor heaviness	*bitterness*
In all that land that she ne could appease	
And wisely bring them all in rest and ease.	
435 Though that her husband absent were anon,	
If gentlemen or others of her country	
Were wrath, she wouldè bringen them at one;	*Were angry / to agree*
So wise and ripè wordès haddè she,	*mature*
And judgèments of so great equity,	*fairness*
440 That she from heaven sent was, as men wend,	*thought*
People to save and every wrong t'amend.	
Not longè time after that this Griseld	
Was wedded, she a daughter has y-bore.	*borne*
All had her lever have had a knavè child,[2]	
445 Glad was the marquis and the folk therefore;	
For though a maidè child came all before,	*girl / first*
She may unto a knavè child attain	*boy child*
By likelihood, since she is not barrén.	*probability*

Part Three

The marquis inexplicably decides to test his wife's obedience in cruel fashion. She quietly submits.

There fell, as it befalleth timès more,	*It happened / often*
450 When that this child had suckèd but a throw,	*nursed a short while*

---

[1] 429: "Knew everything about managing a household."

[2] 444: "Although she would rather have had a boy" (to ensure the succession).

This marquis in his hearté longeth so
To tempt his wife, her sadness for to know,[1]
That he ne might out of his hearté throw
This marvellous desire his wife t'assay;   *to test*
455   Natheless, God wot, he thought her for t'affray.   *God knows / to frighten*

He had assayéd her enough before,   *tested*
And found her ever good; what needed it
Her for to tempt, and always more and more,   *to test*
Though some men praise it for a subtle wit?
460   But as for me, I say that evil it sit   *it is evil*
To assay a wife when that it is no need,   *To test*
And putten her in anguish and in dread.

For which this marquis wrought in this mannér: *acted*
He came alone a-night, there as she lay,   *at night*
465   With sterné face and with full troubled cheer,   *expression*
And saidé thus: "Griseld," quod he, "that day
That I you took out of your poor array,   *clothes*
And put you in estate of high noblesse,   *noble rank*
You have not that forgotten, as I guess?

470   "I say, Griseld, this present dignity,
In which that I have put you, as I trow,   *I hope*
Maketh you not forgetful for to be.
That I you took in poor estate full low,
For any weal, you must yourselfen know.[2]
475   Take heed of every word that I you say;
There is no wight that hears it but we tway.   *nobody / we two*

"You wot yourself well how that you came here   *You know*
Into this house, it is not long ago;

---

[1] 452: "To test his wife to find out her constancy."

[2] If 474 goes with 473, as my punctuation suggests, it might mean "in spite of any wealth you might have had" (i.e. nothing), or "You must know that I took you for richer for poorer," as the marriage ceremony put it. If it goes with what follows, it may mean "For your own good," "If you know what is good for you, take heed..."

And though to me that you be lief and dear, *you are beloved*
480 Unto my gentles you be nothing so. *nobles*
They say, to them it is great shame and woe
For to be subjects and be in serváge *owe allegiance*
To thee, that born art of a small villáge.

"And namely since thy daughter was y-bore *And especially / born*
485 These wordès have they spoken, doubtèless.
But I desire, as I have done before,
To live my life with them in rest and peace.
I may not in this casè be reckless;
I must do with thy daughter for the best,
490 Not as I would, but as my people lest. *Not as I wish / desire*

"And yet, God wot, this is full loath to me, *G. knows / distasteful*
But natheless withouten your witting *knowledge*
I will not do; but this will I," quod he,
"That you to me assent as in this thing.
495 Show now your patïence in your working
That you me hight and swore in your villáge *promised me*
That day that makèd was our marrïage."

When she had heard all this, she not a-moved *changed*
Neither in word, nor cheer, nor countenance; *manner*
500 For, as it seemèd, she was not aggrieved.
She saidè: "Lord, all lies in your pleasance. *pleasure*
My child and I, with hearty obeisance, *obedience*
Be yourès all, and you may save or spill *or destroy*
Your ownè thing; worketh after your will. *do as you please*

505 "There may no thing, God so my soulè save,
Liken to you that may displeasè me; *Please you*
Nor I desirè no thingè for to have,
Ne dreadè for to lose, save only ye.
This will is in mine heart, and aye shall be; *and ever*
510 No length of time or death may this deface,

Nor change my courage to another place."   *my determination*

Glad was this marquis of her answering,
But yet he feignèd as he were not so;   *he pretended*
All dreary was his cheer and his looking,   *manner and face*
515 When that he should out of the chamber go.
Soon after this, a furlong way or two,   *a few minutes*
He privily hath told all his intent   *secretly*
Unto a man, and to his wife him sent.

A manner sergeant was this privy man,   *A kind of / discreet man*
520 The which that faithful oft he founden had
In thingès great, and eke such folk well can
Do executïon in thingès bad.
The lord knew well that he him loved and dread;   *dreaded*
And when this sergeant wist his lordè's will,   *knew*
525 Into the chamber he stalkèd him full still.   *walked quietly*

"Madame," he said, "you must forgive it me,
Though I do thing to which I am constrained.
You be so wise that full well knowen ye
That lordès' hestès must not been y-feigned;   *commands / evaded*
530 They may well be bewailèd or complained,
But men must needs unto their lust obey,   *their desire*
And so will I; there is no more to say.

"This child I am commanded for to take";
And spoke no more, but out the child he hent   *pulled*
535 Despitously,[1] and gan a cheer to make   *Roughly*
As though he would have slain it ere he went.
Griselda must all suffer and all consent;
And as a lamb she sitteth meek and still,
And let this cruel sergeant do his will.

---

[1] 534-6: "He pulled the child away roughly and looked as if he would kill it before he went."

540	Suspicious was the défame of this man,
	Suspéct his face, suspéct his word also;
	Suspect the time in which he this began.
	Alas! her daughter that she lovéd so,
	She wend he would have slain it righté tho.
545	But natheless she neither wept nor sighed
	Conforming her to what the marquis liked.

540 *reputation*

544 *thought / right then*

546 *C. her(self)*

But at the last to speaken she began,
And meekély she to the sergeant prayed,
So as he was a worthy gentle man,   *Since he was ...*
550 That she might kiss her child ere that it died.
And in her barm this little child she laid   *lap*
With full sad face, and gan the child to bless,
And lulléd it, and after gan it kiss.[1]

And thus she said in her benigné voice,
555 "Farewell my child! I shall thee never see.
But since I thee have markéd with the cross
Of thilké Father—blesséd may he be,—
That for us died upon a cross of tree,   *wood*
Thy soul, my little child, I Him betake,   *commend to Him*
560 For this night shall thou dien for my sake."

I trow that to a nursé in this case   *I think*
It had been hard this ruthé for to see;   *this pitiful thing*
Well might a mother then have cried "Alas!"
But natheless so sad steadfast was she   *so constantly*
565 That she enduréd all adversity,
And to the sergeant meekély she said,
"Have here again your little youngé maid.

"Go now," quod she, "and do my lord's behest;   *orders*
But one thing will I pray you of your grace,

---

[1] 552-3: Both uses of *gan* here illustrate its use as a mere past tense marker used to manoeuver the infinitive words into rhyme position: *bless / kiss = blisse, kisse* in the MSS.

570   That, but my lord forbade you, at the least   *unless my lord*
      Bury this little body in some place
      That beastès nor no birdès it to-race."   *tear it apart*
      But he no word will to that purpose say,   *will promise*
      But took the child and went upon his way.

575   This sergeant came unto his lord again,
      And of Griselda's words and of her cheer   *behavior*
      He told him point for point, in short and plain,
      And him presented with his daughter dear.
      Somewhat this lord had ruth in his mannér,   *had pity*
580   But nathelees his purpose held he still,
      As lordès do, when they will have their will,

      And bade this sergeant that he privily   *secretly*
      Should this childè softly wind and wrap
      With allè circumstances tenderly,   *with all due care*
585   And carry it in a coffer or in a lap,   *box or blanket*
      But, upon pain his head off for to swap,   *of being beheaded*
      That no man should ne know of his intent,
      Not whence he came, nor whither that he went.

      But at Bologna to his sister dear,
590   That thilkè time of Panik was countess,   *at that time*
      He should it take, and show her this mattér,   *and explain to her*
      Beseeching her to do her busyness   *her best*
      This child to foster in all gentleness;   *to raise*
      And whose child that it was he bade her hide
595   From every wight, for aught that may betide.   *everyone / happen*

      The sergeant goes, and has fulfilled this thing;
      But to this marquis now returnè we.
      For now goes he full fast imagining
      If by his wifè's cheer he mightè see,   *behavior*
600   Or by her wordè áperceive that she
      Were changèd; but he never could her find

But ever in one alikè sad and kind. *always constant and*

As glad, as humble, as busy in service,
And eke in love as she was wont to be *accustomed*
605 Was she to him in every manner wise; *in every way*
Nor of her daughter not a word spoke she.
No accident, for no adversity, *No change (of demeanor)*
Was seen in her, ne never her daughter's name
Ne namèd she, in earnest nor in game. *or in jest*

Part Four

Griselda bears a son whom the marquis treats as he had treated the daughter. Again Griselda quietly submits.

610 In this estate there passèd been four years *In this fashion*
Ere she with childè was, but, as God willed, *became pregnant*
A knavè child she bore by this Walter, *boy child*
Full gracïous and fair for to behold. *charming & beautiful*
And when that folk it to his father told,
615 Not only he, but all his country, merry
Was for this child, and God they thank and hery. *praise*

When it was two years old, and from the breast
Departed of his nurse, upon a day
This marquis caughtè yet another lest *got another fancy*
620 To tempt his wife yet oftener, if he may. *To test*
O needless was she tempted in assay! *tested in trial*
But wedded men ne knowen no measúre,
When that they find a patient creätúre.

"Wife," quod this marquis, "you have heard ere this,
625 My people sickly bear our marrïage; *take it badly*
And namely since my son y-boren is, *especially / was born*
Now is it worse than ever in all our age.
The murmur slays my heart and my couráge, *complaints / spirit*
For to mine earès comes the voice so smart *rumor so bitter*

630   That it well nigh destroyèd has my heart.   *very nearly*

"Now say they thus: 'When Walter is agon,
Then shall the blood of Janicle succeed
And be our lord, for other have we none.'
Such wordès say my people, out of dread.   *without doubt*
635   Well ought I of such murmur taken heed;
For certainly I dreadè such senténce,   *opinion*
Though they not speak plain in mine audience.   *openly in my hearing*

"I wouldè live in peace, if that I might.
Wherefore I am disposèd utterly,
640   As I his sister servèd have by night,   *treated*
Right so think I to serve him privily.   *secretly*
This warn I you, that you not suddenly   *so that*
Out of yourself for no woe should outrey.   *make outburst*
Be patïent, and thereof I you pray."

645   "I have," quod she, "Said thus, and ever shall.
I will no thing, nor n'ill no thing, certain,
But as you list. Naught grieveth me at all,   *as you wish / Nothing*
Though that my daughter and my son be slain
At your commandèment, this is to sayn.
650   I have not had no part of children twain   *two children*
But first sickness, and after, woe and pain.

"You be our lord; do with your ownè thing
Right as you list; asketh no rede of me.   *no advice*
For as I left at home all my clothing,
655   When I first came to you, right so," quod she,
"Left I my will and all my liberty,
And took your clothing; wherefore I you pray,
Do your pleasánce, I will your lust obey.   *pleasure / your wish*

"And certès, if I haddè prescience   *certainly / foreknowledge*
660   Your will to know, ere you your lust me told,   *your desire*
I would it do withouten negligence;

But now I wot your lust, and what you would,[1]   *I know your desire*
All your pleasánce firm and stable I hold;
For wist I that my death would do you ease,   *If I knew*
665   Right gladly would I dien, you to please.

"Death may not maké no comparison
Unto your love." And when this marquis saw
The constance of his wife, he cast adown   *constancy*
His eyen two, and wondereth that she may   *eyes*
670   In patïencé suffer all this array;   *this torture*
And forth he goes with dreary countenance,
But to his heart it was full great pleasánce.

This ugly sergeant, in the samé wise
That he her daughter caughté, right so he,
675   Or worsé, if men worsé can devise,
Has hent her son, that full was of beauty.   *Has seized*
And ever in one so patïent was she   *And constantly*
That she no cheeré made of heaviness,   *no sign of grief*
But kissed her son, and after gan it bless.

680   Save this, she prayéd him that, if he might,
Her little son he would in earthé grave,   *bury*
His tender limbs, delicate to sight,
From fowlés and from beastés for to save.
But she no answer of him mighté have.
685   He went his way as him no thingé raught;   *cared nothing*
But to Bologna tenderly it brought.

This marquis wondered, ever longer the more,
Upon her patïence, and if that he
Ne haddé soothly knowen therebefore   *truly*
690   That perfectly her children lovéd she,
He would have wend that of some subtlety,   *thought / trickery*

---

[1] 662-3: "Now that I know your desire and your will, I hold firmly and steadily to your wishes."

And of malice, or of cruel courage,   *heart*
That she had suffered this with sad visage.   *unmoved expression*

But well he knew that next himself, certain,
695   She loved her children best in every wise.
But now of women would I asken fain   *like to ask*
If these assayès mighten not suffice?   *tests*
What could a sturdy husband more devise   *stern*
To prove her wifehood and her steadfastness,
700   And he continuing ever in sturdiness?

But there been folk of such conditïon
That when they have a certain purpose take,
They can not stint of their intentïon,   *stop*
But, right as they were bounden to a stake,   *as if tied*
705   They will not of that firstè purpose slake.   *desist from*
Right so this marquis fully hath proposed
To tempt his wife as he was first disposed.

He waiteth if by word or countenance
That she to him was changèd of couráge;   *in her heart*
710   But never could he findè variance.
She was aye one in heart and in viságe;   *always / face*
And aye the further that she was in áge,   *ever*
That morè true (if that it were possíble)
She was to him in love, and more peníble.   *ready to please*

715   For which it seemèd thus, that of them two
There was but one will; for, as Walter lest,   *desired*
The samè lust was her pleasánce also.   *desire / pleasure*
And, God be thankèd, all fell for the best.
She showèd well, for no worldly unrest
720   A wife as of herself ne nothing should   *(That) a wife should not*
Will in effect but as her husband would.   *Wish / wishes*

The slander of Walter often and widè spread,   *scandal*
That of a cruel heart he wickedly,

For he a poorė woman wedded had,   *Because he*
725 Has murdered both his children privily.   *secretly*
Such murmur was among them commonly.
No wonder is, for to the people's ear
There came no word, but that they murdered were.

For which, whereas his people therebefore
730 Had loved him well, the slander of his defame   *scandal of his crime*
Made them that they hated him therefore.
To be a murderer is a hateful name;
But natheless, for earnest nor for game,
He of his cruel purpose would not stent;   *desist*
735 To tempt his wife was set all his intent.   *To test*

The marquis makes the motions of divorce from Griselda

When that his daughter twelve years was of age,
He to the court of Rome, in subtle wise   *secretly*
Informėd of his will, sent his message,
Commanding them such bullės to devise   *papal documents*
740 As to his cruel purpose may suffice,
How that the pope, as for his people's rest,   *satisfaction*
Bade him to wed another, if him lest.   *if he wished*

I say, he bade they shouldė counterfeit
The popė's bullės, making mention   *documents*
745 That he has leave his firstė wife to let,   *permission to divorce*
As by the popė's dispensation
To stintė rancor and dissension   .   *to stop*
Bitwixt his people and him; thus said the bull,
The which they have published at the full.[1]

---

[1] 738-749: Walter goes to the extraordinary length of having documents forged, purporting to be from the Pope and saying that, in order to stop dissension among his nobles about the "baseborn" Griselda, he has a dispensation from the Pope to leave his wife and marry another woman. A "bull" is literally a seal, hence a document with the papal seal.

750   The rudė people, as it no wonder is,   *common*
       Wenden full well that it had been right so;   *Thought*
       But when these tidings came to Gríseldis,
       I deemė that her heart was full of woe.   *I judge*
       But she, alikė sad for evermo'   *steadfast always*
755   Disposėd was, this humble creäture,
       Th'adversity of Fortune all t'endure,

       Abiding ever his lust and his pleasánce,   *Enduring / desire*
       To whom that she was given heart and all,
       As to her very worldly suffisánce.   *As her whole world*
760   But shortly if this story I tell shall,
       This marquis written has in specïal
       A letter, in which he showeth his intent,
       And secretly he to Bologna sent.

       To the Earl of Panik, which that haddė tho   *who had then*
765   Wedded his sister, prayed he specially
       To bringen home again his children two
       In honorable estate all openly,   *In honorable fashion*
       But one thing he him prayėd utterly,
       That he to no wight, though men would enquire,   *to nobody*
770   Should not tell whose children that they were,

       But say the maiden should y-wedded be   *was to be married*
       Unto the Marquis of Saluce anon.   *Saluzzo*
       And as this earl was prayėd, so did he;   *was asked*
       For at the day set he on his way is gone   *appointed day*
775   Toward Saluce, and lordės many a one
       In rich array, this maiden for to guide,
       Her youngė brother riding her beside.

       Arrayėd was toward her marrïage   *Dressed for*
       This freshė maidė, full of gemmės clear;   *bright*
780   Her brother, which that seven years was of age,
       Arrayėd eke full fresh in his mannér.

And thus in great noblesse and with glad cheer,
Toward Salúces shaping their journey,
From day to day they riden on their way.

Part Five

Griselda is dismissed from the Marquis's household in humiliating circumstances. She submits with dignity.

785 Among all this, after his wick'd uságe,   *in his wicked fashion*
     This marquis, yet his wife to temptė more
     To th'utterestė proof of her couráge,   *supreme test / spirit*
     Fully to have experience and lore   *& knowledge*
     If that she were as steadfast as before,
790 He on a day, in open audience,   *in public*
     Full boistously hath said her this senténce: *loudly*

     "Certės, Griseld, I had enough pleasance
     To have you to my wife for your goodness,
     As for your truth and for your obeisance,
795 Not for your lineage, nor for your richesse;
     But now know I in very soothfastness   *in truth*
     That in great lordship, if I well avise,   *if I consider it*
     There is great servitude in sundry wise.   *various ways*

     "I may not do as every plowman may.
800 My people me constraineth for to take   *pressure me*
     Another wife, and crien day by day;
     And eke the popė, rancour for to slake,   *to calm anger*
     Consenteth it, that dare I undertake;   *I assure you*
     And truly thus much I will you say,
805 My newė wife is coming by the way.   *is on her way*

     "Be strong of heart, and void anon her place,   *vacate at once*
     And thilkė dowry that you brought to me,
     Take it again; I grant it of my grace.

Returneth to your father's house," quod he;

810   "No man may always have prosperity.

With even heart I rede you to endure   *W. calm heart I advise*

The stroke of Fortune or of áventure."   *of chance*

And she again answered in patïence,

"My lord," quod she, "I wot, and wist alway,   *know and knew*

815   How that bitwixen your magnificence

And my povertè no wight can nor may

Maken comparison, it is no nay.   *no question*

I ne held me never digne in no mannér   *considered myself worthy*

To be your wife, no, nor your chamberer.   *chamber maid*

820   "And in this house, where you me lady made—

The highè God take I for my witness,

And all so wisly he my soulè glad,[1]

I never held me lady nor mistress,   *considered myself*

But humble servant to your worthiness,

825   And ever shall, while that my life may dure,   *may last*

Aboven every worldly creäture.

"That you so long of your benignity   *kindness*

Have holden me in honour and nobley,   *& high rank*

Where as I was not worthy for to be,

830   That thank I God and you, to whom I pray

Foryield it you; there is no more to say.   *Reward you*

Unto my father gladly will I wend,   *go*

And with him dwell unto my life's end.

"Where I was fostered of a child full small,   *was reared*

835   Till I be dead my life there will I lead,

A widow clean in body, heart, and all;

For since I gave to you my maidenhead,   *virginity*

And am your truè wife, it is no dread,   *without question*

---

[1] 822: "As surely as I hope He will make my soul glad."

God shieldė such a lordė's wife to take   *God forbid*
840 Another man to husband or to make!   *mate*

"And of your newė wife God of his grace
So grantė you weal and prosperity!   *joy*
For I will gladly yielden her my place,
In which that I was blissfull wont to be.   *used to be*
845 For since it liketh you, my lord," quod she,   *it pleases you*
"That whilom weren all my heartė's rest,   *Who once were*
That I shall go, I will go when you lest.   *when you wish*

"But there as you me proffer such a dower   *offer / dowry*
As I first brought, it is well in my mind
850 It were my wretched clothės, nothing fair,   *It would be only*
The which to me were hard now for to find.
O goodė God! how gentle and how kind
You seemėd by your speech and your viságe   *manner*
The day that makėd was our marrïage!

855 "But sooth is said—algate I find it true,   *truth / certainly*
For in effect it provėd is on me—
Love is not old as when that it is new.
But certės, lord, for no adversity,
To dien in the case, it shall not be   *Even if I die*
860 That ever in word or work I shall repent
That I you gave my heart in whole intent.

"My lord, you wot that in my father's place   *you know*
You did me strip out of my poorė weed,   *poor clothes*
And richėly me cladden, of your grace.   *clothed me / goodness*
865 To you brought I naught elsė, out of dread,   *certainly*
But faith and nakedness and maidenhead;   *virginity*
And here again your clothing I restore,
And eke your wedding ring, for evermore.

"The remnant of your jewels ready be
870 Inwith your chamber, dare I safely sayn.   *Within*

Naked out of my father's house," quod she,
"I came, and naked must I turn again.
All your pleasánce will I follow fain;   *gladly*
But yet I hope it be not your intent
875   That I smockless out of your palace went.   *without a shift*

"You could not do so díshonest a thing,   *shameful*
That thilke womb in which your children lay   *the very womb*
Should before the people, in my walking,
Be seen all bare; wherefore I you pray,
880   Let me not like a worm go by the way.
Remember you, mine owne lord so dear,
I was your wife, though I unworthy were.

"Wherefore, in guerdon of my maidenhead,   *in return / virginity*
Which that I brought, and not again I bear,   *do not take back*
885   As vouchesafe to give me, to my meed,   *Be good enough / reward*
But such a smock as I was wont to wear,[1]
That I therewith may wry the womb of her   *may cover*
That was your wife. And here take I my leave
Of you, mine owne lord, lest I you grieve."

890   "The smock," quod he, "that thou hast on thy back,
Let it be still, and bear it forth with thee."
But well unnethes thilke word he spoke,   *could barely speak*
But went his way, for ruth and for pity.   *sorrow*
Before the folk herselfen strippeth she,
895   And in her smock, with head and foot all bare,
Toward her father's house forth is she fare.   *gone*

The folk her follow, weeping in her way,
And Fortune aye they cursen as they go;   *constantly curse*
But she from weeping kept her eyen dry,   *eyes*

---

[1] 885-6: "Be good enough *(vouchesafe)* to give me as my reward only such a shift as I used to wear."

900 Nor in this timė word ne spoke she none.	
Her father, that this tiding heard anon,	
Curseth the day and timė that Natúre	
Shope him to be a live creätúre.	*Made*
For out of doubt this oldė poorė man	
905 Was ever suspect of her marrïage;	*suspicious*
For ever he deemėd, since that it began,	*thought*
That when the lord fulfilled had his couráge,	*satisfied his desire*
Him would think it were a dísparáge	*dishonor*
To his estate so low for to alight,[1]	*rank / to stoop*
910 And voiden her as soon as ever he might.	*get rid of her*
Against his daughter hastily goes he,	*Towards*
For he by noise of folk knew her coming,	
And with her oldė coat, as it might be	*as well as possible*
He covered her, full sorrowfully weeping.	
915 But on her body might he not it bring,	*not fit it*
For rudė was the cloth, and more of age	*rough / older*
By dayės fele than at her marrïage.	*By many days*
Thus with her father, for a certain space,	
Dwelleth this flower of wifely patïence,	
920 That neither by her words nor by her face,	
Before the folk, nor eke in their absénce,	
Ne showėd she that her was done offence;	*to her*
Nor of her high estate no rémembrance	*high rank*
Ne haddė she, as by her countenance.	*by her manner*
925 No wonder is, for in her great estate	
Her ghost was ever in plain humility;	*her spirit, heart*
No tender mouth, no heartė delicate,	

---

[1] The father had always thought that when the marquis had satisfied his sexual infatuation with Griselda, it would seem to him a dishonor to have stooped so far below his rank, and he would get rid of her as soon as possible. *Him would think* is not bad grammar; it means literally: "It would seem to him."

No pompė, no semblánce of royalty,   *No love of show, no pretence*
But full of patïent benignity,   *goodness*
930   Discreet and prideless, aye honorable,   *always*
And to her husband ever meek and stable.   *faithful*

Men speak of Job, and most for his humblesse,   *humility*
As clerkės, when them list, can well endite
Namely of men, but as in soothfastness,[1]   *but in truth*
935   Though clerkės praisen women but a lite,   *but little*
There can no man in humblessė him acquit   *distinguish himself*
As woman can, nor can be half so true
As women been, but it be fall of new.

Part Six

*Griselda is brought back to prepare the household for the marquis's
new marriage*

From Bologna is this Earl of Panik come,
940   Of which the fame up sprang to more and less,   *rumor / to rich & poor*
And to the people's earės, all and some,   *one and all*
Was couth eke that a newė marquisess   *became known also*
He with him brought, in such pomp and richesse   *splendor & richness*
That never was there seen with mannė's eye
945   So noble array in all West Lombardy.

The marquis, which that shaped and knew all this, *who had planned*
Ere that this earl was come, sent his messáge
For thilkė silly poorė Gríseldis;   *that poor unfortunate G.*
And she with humble heart and glad viságe,
950   Not with no swollen thought in her couráge,[2]

---

[1] 933-8: "As scholars, when they please, can write, especially about men, but
in truth, though clerics praise women little, no man can distinguish himself for
humility the way a woman can, nor be as faithful as women, unless there is something totally new in the world." *when them list* means "when it pleases them."

[2] 950: "Not with a heart (*courage*) swollen with anger (or vanity?)."

Came at his hest, and on her knees her set, *at his command*
And reverently and wisely she him gret. *solemnly / greeted*

"Griseld," quod he, "my will is utterly, *absolutely*
This maiden, that shall wedded be to me,
955 Receivèd be to-morrow as royally *is to be received*
As it is possible in my house to be,[1]
And eke that every wight in his degree *also / person / rank*
Have his estate, in sitting and service *his (proper) place*
And high pleasánce, as I can best devise. *as far as I can*

960 "I have no women suffisant, certáin, *no women good enough*
The chambers for t'array in ordinance *arange properly*
After my lust, and therefore would I fain *As I wish / I want ...*
That thinè were all such manner governance. *...you to manage it all*
Thou knowest eke of old all my pleasánce;
965 Though thine array be bad and evil bisey,[2]
Do thou thy devoir at the leastè way." *thy duty*

"Not only, lord, that I am glad," quod she,
"To do your lust, but I desire also *your wish*
You for to serve and please in my degree
970 Withouten fainting, and shall evermo'; *slacking*
Ne never, for no wealè nor no woe, *neither joy nor*
Ne shall the ghost within my heartè stent *the spirit / cease*
To love you best with all my true intent."

And with that word she gan the house to dight, *get ready*
975 And tables for to set, and beds to make;
And painèd her to do all that she might, *took pains*
Praying the chamberers, for Godè's sake, *chamber maids*
To hasten them, and fastè sweep and shake;

---

[1] 954-9: The marquis gives orders that his bride-to-be is to be received with highest possible honor, and that every guest is to be assigned a place and servants appropriate to his rank to give him the greatest satisfaction.

[2] 965-6: "Even though your clothes are bad and look poor, do your best ..."

| | And she, the most serviceable of all, | *hard working* |
| 980 | Hath every chamber arrayèd and his hall. | *prepared* |

	Abouten undren gan this earl alight,	*About 10 a.m. / dismount*
	That with him brought these noble children tway,	*two*
	For which the people ran to see the sight	
	Of their array, so richély bisey;	*clothes so rich looking*
985	And then at erst amongèst them they say	*for the first time*
	That Walter was no fool, though that him lest	*though he chose*
	To change his wife, for it was for the best.	

	For she is fairer, as they deemen all,	*they all judge*
	Than is Griseld, and more tender of age,	
990	And fairer fruit between them shouldè fall,	*prettier offspring*
	And more pleasant, for her high lineage.	
	Her brother eke so fair was of viságe	*handsome*
	That them to see the people hath caught pleasánce,	*got pleasure*
	Commending now the marquis's governance.	*behavior*

	O stormy people! unsad and ever untrue!	*O fickle p. unfaithful*
	Aye indiscreet and changing as a fane!	*Always i. / weathervane*
	Delighting ever in rumble that is new,	*rumor*
	For like the moon aye waxè you and wane!	*you constantly grow & fade*
	Aye full of clapping, dear enough a jane!	*Always / chatter / a cent*
1000	Your doom is false, your constance evil preeveth;[1]	*judgement / constancy*
	A full great fool is he that on you 'lieveth.	*believes*

	Thus saiden saddè folk in that city,	*serious*
	When that the people gazèd up and down;	
	For they were glad, right for the novelty,	
1005	To have a newè lady of their town.	
	No more of this make I now mentïon,	
	But to Griseld again will I me dress,	*I'll turn*
	And tell her constancy and busyness.	

---

[1] 999-1000: "Forever full of chatter, not worth a cent. Your judgement is wrong and your constancy does not stand the test."

Full busy was Griseld in every thing
1010 That to the feastë was apertinent.   *appertained to*
Right not was she abashed of her clothing,   *not ashamed*
Though it were rude and somedeal eke to-rent;   *rough & somewhat torn*
But with glad cheerë to the gate she went
With other folk, to greet the marquisess,
1015 And after that does forth her busyness.   *her duties*

With so glad cheer his guestës she receiveth,
And so cunningly, ever each in his degree,   *tactfully / rank*
That no defaultë no man aperceiveth,
But aye they wonder what she mightë be   *all the time*
1020 That in so poor array was for to see,   *poor clothes*
And could such honour and such reverence,[1]   *knew*
And worthily they praisen her prudence.

In all this meanë whilë she ne stent   *did not cease*
This maid and eke her brother to commend
1025 With all her heart, in full benign intent,
So well that no man could her praise amend.
But at the last, when that these lordës wend   *went*
To sitten down to meat, he gan to call
Griseld, as she was busy in his hall.

1030 "Griseld," quod he, as it were in his play,   *as if in play*
"How liketh thee my wife and her beauty?"[2]
"Right well," quod she, "my lord; for, in good fay,   *faith*
A fairer saw I never none than she.
I pray to God give her prosperity;

---

[1] 1021: "And who knew so much about the right kind of honour and respect (to give to each guest)." The stanza expresses the understandable surprise of the aristocratic guests that they are being received by a woman dressed in rags who is nevertheless exquisitely tactful and perfectly courteous; nobody feels slighted because she knows exactly how each is to be treated according to rank.

[2] 1031: Again this is not poor grammar. The line means literally "How does my wife please thee?" i.e. What do you think of my wife?

1035 And so hope I that He will to you send
 Pleasance enough unto your livės' end.

 "One thing beseech I you, and warn also,
 That you ne prickė with no tórmenting   *torture*
 This tender maiden, as you have done mo';   *more (i.e. me)*
1040 For she is fostered in her nourishing   *reared / upbringing*
 More tenderly, and, to my supposing,
 She couldė not adversity endure
 As could a poorė fostered creäture."   *reared in poverty*

 And when this Walter saw her patience,
1045 Her gladė cheer, and no malice at all,
 And he so oft had done to her offence,
 And she aye sad and constant as a wall,   *ever firm*
 Continuing ever her innocence overall,
 This sturdy marquis gan his heartė dress   *harsh m. / dispose*
1050 To rue upon her wifely steadfastness.   *To have pity*

The marquis reveals the identity of the "bride" and her brother

 "This is enough, Griselda mine," quod he;
 "Be now no more aghast nor evil apaid.   *frightened nor angry*
 I have thy faith and thy benignity,   *goodness*
 As well as ever woman was, assayed,   *tested*
1055 In great estate and poorly arrayed.   *In high place & low*
 Now know I, dearė wife, thy steadfastness,"
 And her in arms he took and gan her kiss.

 And she for wonder took of it no keep;   *didn't notice*
 She heardė not what thing he to her said;
1060 She fared as she had start out of a sleep,   *suddenly woken*
 Till she out of her mazėdness abreyd.   *awoke*
 "Griseld," quod he, "by God, that for us died,
 Thou art my wife, nor no other I have,
 Ne never had, as God my soulė save!

1065   "This is thy daughter, which thou hast supposed
      To be my wife; that other faithfully   *t. other = their son*
      Shall be mine heir, as I have aye disposed;   *always intended*
      Thou bore him in thy body truly.
      At Bologna have I kept them privily;   *secretly*
1070   Take them again, for now mayst thou not say
      That thou hast lorn none of thy children tway.[1]   *lost*

      "And folk that otherwise have said of me,
      I warn them well that I have done this deed
      For no malice, nor for no cruelty,
1075   But for t'assay in thee thy womanhood,   *to test*
      And not to slay my children. God forbid!
      But for to keep them privily and still,   *secretly & securely*
      Till I thy purpose knew and all thy will."

      When she this heard, a-swoonė down she falls
1080   For piteous joy, and after her swooning
      She both her youngė children to her calls,
      And in her armės, piteously weeping,
      Embraces them, and tenderly kissing
      Full like a mother, with her saltė tears
1085   She bathed both their visage and their hairs.   *face*

      O which a piteous thing it was to see
      Her swooning, and her humble voice to hear!
      "Gramércy, lord, God thank it you," quod she,   *Great thanks*
      "That you have savėd me my children dear!   *saved for me*
1090   Now reck I never to be dead right here;[2]

---

[1] 1070-71: The double negative is unfortunate. The sentence means what it would mean without the "not" in 1070: "You cannot say that you have lost either of your two children".

[2] 1090-92: "I do not care if I die right here. Since I am once more in your love and favor; death, the departure of my soul, does not matter now. Death, when my soul leaves my body, is unimportant"

Since I stand in your love and in your grace,
No force of death nor when my spirit pace!   *No matter / goes*

"O tender, O dear, O youngė children mine!
Your woeful mother wendė steadfastly   *thought for sure*
1095 That cruel houndės or some foul vermin   *rats*
Had eaten you; but God, of his mercy,
And your benignė father tenderly
Hath do you kept." And in that samė stound   *moment*
All suddenly she swapped down to the ground.   *she fell*

1100 And in her swoon so sadly holdeth she   *tightly*
Her children two, when she gan them t'embrace,
That with great sleight and great difficulty   *effort*
The children from her arm they gan arace.   *detach*
O many a tear on many a piteous face
1105 Down ran of them that stooden her beside;
Unneth abouten her might they abide.[1]

Walter her gladeth, and her sorrow slaketh;   *comforts her / subsides*
She riseth up, abaisėd, from her trance,   *dazed*
And every wight her joy and feastė maketh [2]
1110 Till she hath caught again her countenance.   *composure*
Walter her doth so faithfully pleasance [3]
That it was dainty for to see the cheer   *a pleasure / the joy*
Betwixt them two, now they be met y-fere.   *together*

These ladies, when that they their timė saw,
1115 Have taken her and into chamber gone,
And strippen her out of her rude array,   *rough clothes*
And in a cloth of gold that brightly shone,
With a coronet of many a richė stone

---

[1] 1106: "They could hardly *(unneth)* bear to stay near her" (they were so moved).

[2] 1109: "Everyone cheers her up and makes much of her."

[3] 1111: "Walter tries to please her so assiduously ..."

Upon her head, they into hall her brought,
1120   And there she was honoúrėd as her ought.

Thus hath this piteous day a blissfull end,
For every man and woman does his might   *his best*
This day in mirth and revel to dispend   *to spend*
Till in the welkin shone the starrės light.   *sky*
1125   For more solemn in every mannė's sight
This feastė was, and greater of costáge,   *expense*
Than was the revel of their marrïage.

Full many a year in high prosperity
Liven these two in concord and in rest,
1130   And richėly his daughter married he
Unto a lord, one of the worthiest
Of all Itaille; and then in peace and rest   *Italy*
His wifė's father in his court he keeps,
Till that the soul out of his body creeps.

1135   His son succeeded in his heritage   *His = Walter's*
In rest and peace, after his father's day,
And fortunate was eke in marrïage,   *was also*
All put he not his wife in great assay.   *Although / test*
This world is not so strong, it is no nay,   *no denying*
1140   As it has been in oldė timės yore,
And hearken what this author says therefore.   *author = Petrarch*

The Clerk's envoy: the moral of the story

This story is said, not for that wivės should
Follow Griseld as in humility,
For it were inportáble, though they would.[1]
1145   But for that every wight in his degree,   *person / own walk of life*
Should be constant in adversity
As was Griselda; therefore Petrarch writeth

---

[1] 1144: "It would be impossible (unendurable) even if they wanted to."

This story which with high style he enditeth.   *composes*

For since a woman was so patient
1150 Unto a mortal man, well more us ought
Receiven all in gree that God us sent,   *in patience*
For great skill is that He prove what He wrought
But He ne tempteth no man that He bought[1]   *has redeemed*
As says St. James, if you his 'pistle read.   *James 1: 13 / epistle*
1155 He proveth folk alday, it is no dread.[2]   *no question*

And suffers us, as for our exercise,[3]   *permits us / our good*
With sharpe scourges of adversity
Full often to be beat in sundry wise,   *different ways*
Not for to know our will, for certes He,
1160 Ere we were born, knew our frailty.
And for our best is all His governance.
Let us then live in virtuous sufferance.   *patience*

But one word, lordings, hearken ere I go   *ladies & g'men*
It were full hard to finde nowadays
1165 In all a town Griseldas three—or two,
For if that they were put in such assays   *trials*
The gold of them has now so bad allays   *alloys*
With brass, that though the coin be fair at eye,   *fine to see*
It woulde rather burst a-two than ply.   *than bend*

1170 For which here, for the Wife's love of Bath,   *for love of the W o B*
Whose life and all her sect may God maintain,   *all her kind*
In high mastery—(and else were it scath)   *would be a pity*

---

[1] 1152-53: "For it is very reasonable (or likely) (*great skill is*) that He should test (*prove*) what He has made (*wrought*), but He will not lead into temptation anyone that He has redeemed (*bought*)."   1151: *sent* is a contracted form of *sendeth*: sends.

[2] 1155: "He constantly tests people; there is no doubt about that."

[3] 1156-8: "and He allows (*suffers*) us, for our good, to be beaten often in various ways with the sharp whips (*scourges*) of adversity."

I will with lusty heartè, fresh and green
Say you a song to gladden you, I ween.   *I hope*
1175 And let us stint of earnestful mattér.   *stop / serious*
Hearken my song that says in this mannér: *Listen to*

Envoy de Chaucer

Griseld is dead, and eke her patïence,
And both at once are buried in Itaille
For which I cry in open audience   *publicly*
1180 No wedded man so hardy be t'assail
His wifè's patïence, in trust to find   *hoping to*
Griselda's, for in certain he shall fail.

O noble wivès, full of high prudénce,
Let no humility your tonguè nail
1185 Nor let no clerk have cause or diligence   *or good reason*
To write of you a story of such marvail
As of Griselda, patïent and kind,
Lest Chichevache you swallow in her entrail.[1]   *her gut*

Followeth Echo that holdeth no silence
1190 But ever answereth at the contretail.   *answers back*
Be not bedaffèd for your innocence   *fooled*
But sharply take on you the governail.   *mastery*
Imprinteth well this lesson in your mind
For common profit since it may avail.   *may be for common good*

1195 You archèwives, standeth at defence,
Since you be strong as is a great camail   *camel*
Ne suffer not that men you do offence.   *don't allow men*
And slender wivès, feeble as in batail,   *battle*
Be eager as a tiger yond in Inde.   *India*

---

[1] 1188: Chichevache: the name of the legendary cow which was eternally
skinny because it fed on patient wives, in contrast to the well-fed Bicorne who
grew fat on patient husbands.

1200	Aye clappeth as a mill, I you counsail.	*Chatter constantly*
	Nor dread them not; do them no reverence	
	For though thy husband armèd be in mail,	
	The arrows of thy crabbèd eloquence	*bitter*
	Shall pierce his breast and eke his aventail.	*neck armor*
1205	In jealousy I rede eke thou him bind	*I advise*
	And thou shalt make him couch as does a quail.	*cower / (bird)*
	If thou be fair, there folk be in presénce	*pretty / in public*
	Show thou thy visage and thine ápparail.	*face / clothes*
	If thou be foul, be free of thy dispense;	*ugly / spend freely*
1210	To get thee friendès aye do thy travail.	*always do your best*
	Be aye of cheer, as light as leaf on lind,	*always cheerful / linden*
	And let him care, and weep and wring and wail.	

* * * *

Behold the merry words of the Host [1]

1212 a	This worthy Clerk, when ended was his tale,	*(To) This*
	Our Hostè said, and swore: "By Godè's bones,	
	Me were lever than a barrel ale	*I'd prefer before*
	My wife at home had heard this legend once!	*this story*
	This is a gentle talè for the nonce,	
	As to my purpose, wistè you my will.	*If you know what I mean*
1212 g	But thing that will not be, let it be still."	

---

[1] This last stanza (ll. 1212 a - g) stands after the Envoy in many manuscripts. It is omitted or footnoted in some editions to keep the neat connection between the last line of the Clerk's own words (1212 above) and the beginning of the Merchant's prologue:

End of Clerk's: *And let him care and weep and wring and wail.*

Beginning of Merchant's: *Weeping and wailing, care and other sorrow.*

THE CANTERBURY TALES

The Merchant and His Tale

THE MERCHANT'S TALE

 Introduction

The opening words of *The Merchant's Tale* deliberately repeat some prominent words at the end of the Clerk's tale, to which it is clearly a sharp response:

Clerk:
Be aye of cheer as light as leaf on lind   (tree)
And let him care and weep and wring and wail.

Merchant:
Weeping and wailing, care and other sorrow
I know enough on even and a-morrow   (morning & evening)

Moreover, he makes a direct reference to the Clerk's story:

There is a long and large difference
Betwixt Griselda's greate patïence
And of my wife the passing cruelty

So the *Merchant's Tale* is very much a member of the "Marriage Group." It is a response, not only to that of the Clerk, but also to that of the Wife of Bath, and it contrasts with the tale of the Franklin which comes after it. Its Prologue shares some of the confessional quality of the Wife's tale, and critics have disputed how closely the Merchant's tale itself should be associated with the confessional narrator of its Prologue; he is quite unlike the secretive Merchant of the General Prologue (see the word-Portrait). Is the deluded husband of the tale the creature of the embittered mind of the confessional Merchant, a scathing version of himself? Or is he simply another *senex amans* in a Chaucerian fabliau, a foolish old man of comedy who marries a very young woman to his cost, like John the Carpenter of *The Miller's Tale* only several notches less funny? Since Chaucer did give this confessional prologue to the Merchant, it is fair to think that there is meant to be some connection between the prologue and the tale that follows it.

The tale has produced some of the strongest critical responses from readers over the years, who often use language as vigorous and pungent as that of the tale itself. January the husband is a "repulsive dotard" whose "old man's folly" shows "disgusting imbecility." One or more of the characters is "degraded" or "crass." The tale is "a sordid adulterous intrigue" with a "dirtily obscene atmosphere," a tale of "harsh cynicism," "mordant irony," "savage satire," in which the Merchant indulges in "self-lacerating rage," one of the "most savagely obscene, angrily embittered, pessimistic and unsmiling tales in our language."

Not many works of art have called down such an acid rain of language from critics, certainly no other work by the "genial" Chaucer. To be sure, a few have thought that the tale was "fundamentally comic," with a tone of "rich and mellow irony," a broad "comedy of humors." But these voices have been pretty well drowned out by the more strident ones just mentioned.

The tale is, to be sure, one in which it is hard to like any of the characters portrayed. It is strikingly unlike the Miller's yarn at the same time that it has a striking likeness to it. There is grotesque farce in it, as there is in the Miller's, but the tone is quite different, and one's response is different also. There are few hearty laughs in the Merchant's tale. But it is not, perhaps, as destructively negative as many critics contend.

One reason that January calls forth so much stronger distaste than John the Carpenter of the Miller's tale is the difference between Show and Tell. We are told simply and briefly that John has married a very young girl and keeps her cooped up at home for fear of being cuckolded. In the present tale, however, January is *shown* making his foolish, self-absorbed plans to marry a young woman, and we are given his deluded thinking at some considerable length. In addition we are shown his aged love-making in such fashion as to make it seem grotesque and repulsive. Moreover, the fact of his inevitable jealousy is not merely stated but portrayed in all its grasping unpleasantness.

All of this may make the reader sympathize with May, the young wife, but Chaucer also undermines any easy romanticism. When May surreptitiously reads a love-letter written to her by her husband's squire, Damian, she does not kiss it and replace it in her bosom next to her heart; more shrewdly but much less romantically, she tears it up

> *And in the privy softly she it cast*   (toilet)

We are not even allowed to hear Damian's romantic phrases, and are free to speculate that they were no more romantic than May's written response, which we also get in paraphrase, brief and to the point, with a nice play on the double meaning of "lust" (any pleasure / sexual desire):

> *Right of her hand a letter makèd she*
> *In which she granteth him her very grace.*
> *There lacketh nought but only day and place*
> *Where that she might unto his lust suffice.*

Here is not the long wooing of courtly love; one letter from the pining male, and May promptly capitulates, offers her body, and makes arrangements for consummation.

At the assignation, while she is making protestations of fidelity to January, she is making signs to Damian to get up the pear tree. This *could* be comic—in a Mozart opera, say. Here it is unpleasant or worse. There follows the consummation of the grand passion: a sexual coupling in a pear tree, about as charming as that in January's bed. "Romantic" young love, it appears, is not necessarily much more lovely to look upon than old lust. And when January finally realizes what is going on in the tree, May has an answer ready. She can write a quick letter, turn a fast trick, return a smart answer. Love courtly? Love curtly.

May's partner, Damian, a young man to whom his master January has been rather kind, is hardly characterized. He is simply The Lover without the love, perhaps a reincarnation of January as he was forty years before, who

| *followed aye his bodily delight* | *(always)* |
| *On women there as was his appetite.* | *(desire)* |

Forty years later he may still be January, with just about as much character. Some of the other personae are more allegorical than real, like the advisors Placebo the Yesman and Justinus the Just man. In fact, the tale is an odd mixture: the two lovemaking scenes are about as frankly "realistic" as one could well want, but even January and May have allegorical names, and Pluto and Proserpina are out of Roman mythology, though they *sound* like the Wife of Bath and one of her husbands exchanging insults and "authorities"—sacred scripture, no less. Somehow the mixture works, and potently.

In the long climactic scene in January's garden, May's expression of longing for the pears is sexually obvious, and her talk of honor is about as sincere as that of ladies of quality in any Restoration play. The inherent contradiction implied in a January garden with May in it, is, I think, Chaucer's serious wordplay.

This May who hints at the fruit of her womb, is unrelated to her namesake, the virgin queen of heaven, whom she invokes. May is pregnant (*if* she is) not by the Holy Ghost but by someone a good deal more earthly. It was inevitable that some scholars would see a possible ironic reference to the medieval "Cherry Tree Carol" which recounts the story of how the cherry tree bent down to give the fruit for which the pregnant Virgin Mary craved, and which her old husband had refused to get because he thought her unfaithful.

The narrator also specifically draws attention to the relationship between January's garden and that romantic epitome of all romantic gardens for the medieval world—the Garden in *The Romance of the Rose,* (from which, however, two of the items specifically excluded were old age and ugliness!). The romantic delicacies of Guillaume de Lorris, who wrote the beginning of that poem, become bluntly priapic in the section by Jean de Meung who wrote the greater part of it, relating the efforts of the Lover to achieve the Rose in spite of all obstacles. Eventually, at the end of a very long poem, the Lover does achieve his aim: he plucks the virginal rose, as Damian gets the fruit of the peartree.

The Garden of Eden, with its primordial Fall and serpent in the fruit tree, is not far off from the literary memory either. There are also strong echoes of the enclosed garden, the "hortus conclusus," that evocatively romantic image of the lover in the biblical *Song of Songs,* phrases from which are put in the mouth of January himself. The enclosed garden had been used by bible commentators as an image for the Virgin Mary, the heavenly Queen whose name May impiously invokes as she asks help in her unmaidenly business. May's prayer *is* answered, but from another quarter, first by January who gives her a hoist into the Tree of Knowledge, carnal knowledge; then by Proserpina, the Queen of Hell, who gives her the gift of the forked, beguiling tongue of the serpent.

This complex mixing of images and allusions has had a potent effect on the critics, some of whom seem offended by its result— an unsentimental picture in dark, powerful colors, of the workings of the basic human desire that subtends romantic love, and which sometimes subverts good sense and marital fidelity. (As we see it undermine brotherhood and fellowship in, say, the tales of the Knight and the Shipman). Lust, that indispensable part of our human loving, is here shown without its saving consort, love, and barely covered by the tattered rags of romantic convention. Priapus, god of gardens and of sexual rutting, is worshipped in the garden which is both January's *and* May's. But then, it is implied, he was worshipped in the Garden of *The Romance of the Rose* too. And, if some biblical commentators were right, in the Garden of Eden, where they thought *that* was the Original Sin. January and May, after contact with the King of the Underworld, like (and unlike) our first parents in *Paradise Lost*

> *hand in hand, with wandering steps and slow*
> *Through Eden took their solitary way.*

Some Linguistic Notes for the Merchant's Tale

Stress and Rhythm:

Many of the remarks about word stress in the Clerk's Tale apply here also. Chaucer clearly felt free to vary the stress on many words from one syllable to another, for poetic reasons. This is especially true of words of French origin like *pity, miracle, counsel* but is not confined to them. Word stress and line rhythm are, of course, intimately connected.

Sometimes I have marked words stressed in ways that are unusual for us but sometimes not. *Purpose* (1571) and *mercury* (1735), for example, seem to have the stress on the second syllable, but marking them thus seems somehow excessive. Similarly for *obstacle / miracle* which were probably stressed as *obstácle /mirácle* 1659/60. But even quintessentially English words like *womán, womén*, it would seem, could sometimes be stressed thus on the second syllable (2279).

Among words that have alternating stress and that I have marked are: *cértain / certáin*; *Plácebo* and *Placébo*; *Jánuary* has 3 syllables at 2023 and sometimes elsewhere; otherwise it has four as in 1695 where it rhymes with *tarry*; *Cóunsel* 1480-85-90, but *That his counsél should pass his lordė's wit* (1504). I have not felt it necessary to adopt the Chaucerian spelling *c(o)unsail* as the word does not occur in rhyming position as it does in the Clerk's Tale.

pity / pitý:	But natheless yet had he great pitý	
	That thilkė night offenden her must he	(1755, and 1995)
but		
	Lo, pity runneth soon in gentle heart.	(1986)
Similarly:	On Ashuer, so meek a look has she.	
	I may you not devise all her beautý,	(1745/6)

SLURRING: Here as elsewhere in Chaucer *evil apaid* is almost certainly pronounced *ill apaid*, paralled with *well apaid*.

Lines that are difficult to scan even with Middle English spelling and pronunciation: 1630, 1780, 1784, 2109, 2248, 2273.

The Portrait, Prologue and Tale of the Merchant

The Portrait of the Merchant from the General Prologue

A MERCHANT was there with a forkèd beard,
In motley,[1] and high on horse he sat,
Upon his head a Flandrish beaver hat,   *from Flanders*
His boots claspèd fair and fetisly.   *neatly*
His reasons he spoke full solémpnély,   *solemnly*
275   Sounding always the increase of his winning.   *profits*
He would the sea were kept for anything [2]   *He wished*
Betwixt Middleburgh and Orèwell.
Well could he in Exchangè shieldès sell.[3]   *sell currency*
This worthy man full well his wit beset—   *used his brains*
280   There wistè no wight that he was in debt,   *no person knew*
So stately was he of his governance   *astute in management*
With his bargains and with his chevissance.   *money dealings*
Forsooth he was a worthy man withal,   *Truly / indeed*
But sooth to say, I n'ot how men him call.   *truth / I don't know*

The Prologue to the Merchant's Tale

The Merchant, picking up on some words at the end of the Clerk's tale, vents his bitter personal disappointment in marriage

"Weeping and wailing, care and other sorrow
I know enough, on even and a-morrow!"   *p.m. & a.m.*

---

[1] 271: "(dressed in) motley": probably not the loud mixed colors of the jester, but possibly tweed.

[2] 276-7: "He wished above all that the stretch of sea between Middleburgh (in Flanders) and Orwell (in England) were guarded (*kept*) against pirates."

[3] 278: He knew the intricacies of foreign exchange. Scholars have charged the Merchant with gold smuggling or even coin clipping; but, although "shields" were units of money, they were neither gold nor coins.

1215 Quod the Merchant. "And so do others more	*many others*
That wedded be! I trow that it be so,	*I guess*
For well I wot it fareth so with me!	*I know it goes*
I have a wife, the worstè that may be;	
For though the fiend to her y-coupled were,	*the devil*
1220 She would him overmatch, I dare well swear.	
What should I you rehearse in specïal	*tell in detail*
Her high malice? She is a shrew at all!	*in every way*
There is a long and largè difference	
Betwixt Griselda's greatè patïence[1]	
1225 And of my wife the passing cruelty.	
Were I unbounden, also may I thee,	*single / I promise you*
I never would eft come into the snare.	*never again*
We wedded men live in sorrow and care;	
Assayè whoso will and he shall find	*Let anyone try*
1230 That I say sooth, by Saint Thomas of Inde,	*truth / India*
As for the more part—I say not all;	*majority*
God shieldè that it shouldè so befall!	*God forbid*
Ah, good sir Host, I have y-wedded be	*been married*
These monthès two, and morè not, pardee,	*by God*
1235 And yet, I trowè, he that all his life	*I think*
Wifeless has been, though that men would him rive	*stab*
Unto the heart, ne could in no mannér	
Tellen so muchè sorrow as I now here	
Could tellen of my wifè's cursedness."	
1240 "Now," quod our Host, "Merchant, so God you bless,	
Since you so muchè knowen of that art,	
Full heartily I pray you tell us part."	
"Gladly," quod he, "but of mine ownè sore	*pain*
For sorry heart I tellè may no more."	

---

[1] 1224: Griselda is the heroine of the immediately preceding tale told by the Clerk. She endures with incredible patience the trials inflicted by her husband.

The Merchant's Tale

An old lecher finally decides to get married

1245　Whilom there was dwelling in Lombardy	*Once upon a time*
A worthy knight that born was of Pavie,	*born in Pavia*
In which he lived in great prosperity;	
And sixty years a wifeless man was he,	
And followed aye his bodily delight	*always indulged*
1250　On women, there as was his appetite,	*wherever he liked*
As do these foolės that been secular.	*worldly*
And when that he was passėd sixty year—	
Were it for holiness or for dotáge	*senility*
I can not say—but such a great couráge	*desire*
1255　Had this knight to be a wedded man,	
That day and night he does all that he can	
T'espyen where he mightė wedded be,	*To see*
Praying our Lord to granten him that he	
Might oncė know of thilkė blissful life	*of that*
1260　That is betwixt a husband and his wife,	
And for to live under that holy bond	
With which that first God man and woman bound:	
"No other life," said he, "is worth a bean!	
For wedlock is so easy and so clean	
1265　That in this world it is a paradise."	
Thus said this oldė knight that was so wise.	

An extended passage in "praise" of marriage

And certainly, as sooth as God is king,	*As sure as*
To take a wife, it is a glorious thing,	
And namely when a man is old and hoar!	*white-haired*
1270　Then is a wife the fruit of his treasúre:	
Then should he take a young wife and a fair,	
On which he might engender him an heir,	*On whom / beget*
And lead his life in joy and in soláce,	
Whereas these bachelorė's sing "Alas!"	
1275　When that they finden any adversity	

Has but one heart in weal and in distress. *good times*

A wife! Ah, Saintė Mary, ben'citee! *bless us!*

How might a man have any adversity

That has a wife? Certės, I cannot say. *certainly*

1340 The blissė which that is betwixt them tway, *two*

There may no tonguė tell or heartė think.

If he be poor, she helpeth him to swink. *to work*

She keeps his goods and wasteth never a deal. *she looks after / a bit*

All that her husband lusts, her liketh well.[1]

1345 She says not oncė "Nay" when he says "Yea."

"Do this," says he. "All ready, sir," says she.

O blissful order of wedlock precious,

Thou art so merry and eke so virtuous, *& also*

And so commended and approvėd eke,

1350 That every man that holds him worth a leek *thinks himself*

Upon his barė knees ought all his life

Thanken his God that him has sent a wife,

Or elsė pray to God him for to send

A wife to last unto his lifė's end,

1355 For then his life is set in sikerness. *security*

He may not be deceivėd, as I guess,

So that he work after his wifė's redde: *Provided that / advice*

Then may he boldly keepen up his head.

They be so true and therewithal so wise,

1360 For which, if thou wilt worken as the wise,

Do always so as women will thee rede. *advise*

Biblical wives and classical authorities

Lo how that Jacob, as these clerkės read, *scholars*

By good counsel of his mother Rebekke *Genesis 27*

Bound the kiddė's skin about his neck,

1365 For which his father's benison he won. *blessing*

---

[1] 1344: "Everything that her husband desires pleases her completely." The Chaucerian meaning of "lust," verb or noun, is not confined to sexual desire.

Lo Judith, as the story eke tell can,
By good counsel she Godë's people kept,   *Judith xi-xiii*
And slew him Holofernes while he slept.
Lo Abigail, by good counsel how she   *I Kings (Samuel), 25*
1370 Saved her husband Nabal when that he
Should have been slain. And look Esther also   *Esther 7*
By good counsel delivered out of woe
The people of God, and made him Mardochee
Of Ashuer enhancëd for to be.[1]

1375 There is no thing in gree superlative,   *degree*
As says Senek, above a humble wife.
Suffer thy wifë's tongue, as Cato bit.   *Endure / bids*
She shall command and thou shalt suffer it,
And yet she will obey of courtesy.
1380 A wife is keeper of thine husbandry.   *household economy*
Well may the sickë man bewail and weep
Where as there is no wife the house to keep.

I warnë thee, if wisely thou wilt work,
Love well thy wife, as Christë loved his church.
1385 If thou lovest thyself thou lovest thy wife.
No man hates his flesh, but in his life
He fosters it; and therefore bid I thee,
Cherish thy wife or thou shalt never thee.   *thee (vb) = succeed*
Husband and wife, what so men jape or play,   *joking aside*
1390 Of worldly folk holden the siker way.   *non-clerical / surer*
They be so knit there may no harm betide—   *occur*
And namëly upon the wifë's side.   *especially*

Back to the tale of January, who asks his friends to help him find a
wife—a young one

For which this January of whom I told
Considered has inwith his dayës old   *in his old age*

---

[1] 1374 and preceding: All of these "commendable" actions by women
involved deceit or trickery of some kind.

1395 The lusty life, the virtuous quiet
      That is in marrïage honey sweet;
      And for his friendės on a day he sent
      To tellen them th'effect of his intent.   *the gist*
      With facė sad this tale he has them told: *serious face*
1400 He saidė, "Friendės, I am hoar and old,   *white-haired*
      And almost, God wot, on my pittė's brink.   *God knows / grave's*
      Upon my soulė somewhat must I think.
      I have my body folily dispended.   *wantonly used*
      Blessėd be God that it shall be amended!
1405 For I will be, certáin, a wedded man,
      And that anon, in all the haste I can,   *promptly*
      Unto some maiden fair and tender of age.
      I pray you shapeth for my marrïage   *make arrangements*
      All suddenly, for I will not abide;   *wait*
1410 And I will fond t'espyen on my side   *try to see*
      To whom I may be wedded hastily.
      But for as much as you been more than I,
      You shallė rather such a thing espy
      Than I, and where me best were to ally.   *best for me to marry*
1415 But one thing warn I you, my friendės dear:
      I will no old wife have in no mannér.
      She shall not passen twenty years certáin!
      Old fish and young flesh would I have full fain.   *very gladly*
      Bet is," quod he, "a pike than a pickerel,   *Better / young pike*
1420 And better than old beef is tender veal.
      I will no woman thirty years of age;
      It is but beanė-straw and great foráge.   *bean stalks & coarse fodder*
      And eke these oldė widows, God it wot,   *also / God knows*
      They can so muchel craft on Wadė's boat,[1]
1425 So muchel broken harm when that them lest,   *breach of peace?*
      That with them should I never live in rest.

---

[1] 1424: "They know (*can*) so much about Wade's boat ..." Nobody seems to
know quite what this refers to. The reader must guess from the context. Much the
same is true of *muchel broken harm*.

For sundry schoolės maken subtle clerkės;
Woman of many schoolės half a clerk is.[1]
But certainly, a young thing men may gie,   *guide, train*
1430 Right as men may warm wax with handės ply.   *mould*
Wherefore I say you plainly in a clause,   *in a phrase*
I will no old wife have right for this cause:
For if so were I haddė such mischance
That I in her ne could have no pleasánce,   *sexual pleasure*
1435 Then should I lead my life in avoutry,   *adultery*
And go straight to the devil when I die.
No children should I none upon her geten—   *beget*
Yet were me lever houndės had me eaten   *I had rather*
Than that my heritagė shouldė fall
1440 In strangė hands. And this I tell you all
(I dotė not) I wot the causė why   *(I'm not senile) I know*
Men shouldė wed, and furthermore wot I   *I know*
There speaketh many a man of marrïage
That wot no more of it than wot my page.   *knows*

He knows all the orthodox reasons for marriage

1445 For whichė causes should man take a wife?
If he ne may not livė chaste his life,   *celibate*
Take him a wife with great devotion   *Let him take*
Because of lawful procreation
Of children, to th'honoúr of God above,
1450 And not only for paramour or love;   *sexual pleasure*
And for they shouldė lechery eschew,   *And because / avoid*
And yield their debtė when that it is due;[2]
Or for that each of them should helpen other
In mischief, as a sister shall the brother,   *In trouble*

---

[1] 1427-8: "Attendance at different schools makes sharper scholars; a woman who has studied many husbands is half a scholar."

[2] 1452: Each partner of the marriage owes sexual relief to the other when he or she demands it; this is the "debt" that is due from one to the other, so that married people should be more readily able to "eschew lechery," i.e. avoid adultery.

1455 And live in chastity full holily,
　　But sirs, by your leave, that am not I.[1]

He feels he is still quite virile

　　For God be thanked, I daré make avaunt,　　　　　*boast*
　　I feel my limbs stark and suffissaunt　　　*strong & able*
　　To do all that a man belongeth to.　　　*belongs to a man*
1460 I wot myselfé best what I may do.　　　　　　*I know*
　　Though I be hoar, I fare as does a tree　　*white haired*
　　That blossoms ere the fruit y-waxen be,　　　*is grown*
　　And blossomy tree is neither dry nor dead:
　　I feel me nowhere hoar but on my head.
1465 My heart and all my limbés be as green
　　As laurel through the year is for to seen.
　　And since that you have heard all my intent,
　　I pray you to my counsel you'll assent."

Different responses from different people

　　Divérse men divérsély him told　　　　　*Different(ly)*
1470 Of marrïagé many examples old.
　　Some blaméd it, some praiséd it, certáin.
　　But at the lasté, shortly for to sayn,
　　As alday falleth altercatïon　　　　*daily / quarrels*
　　Betwixté friends in disputatïon,
1475 There fell a strife betwixt his brethren two,
　　Of which that one was clepéd Plácebo,　　　*was called*
　　Justínus soothly calléd was that other.[2]　　　*truly*

Placebo tells January what he wants to hear

　　Placébo said: "O January, brother,

---

[1] 1445-56: For what causes should people marry? These lines list the accepted answers, the last of which seems to include the odd case, sometimes encountered in saints' lives, where the married partners agree to abstain from sex completely and live together like sister and brother. The speaker says he is definitely not one of those.

[2] 1476-7: The two "brothers" (two aspects of his mind?) have appropriately allegorical names: "Placebo" ("I will please," the Yesman) and Justinus (the Just man).

Full little need had you, my lord so dear,
1480 Counsel to ask of any that is here,
But that you be so full of sapience   *wisdom*
That you ne liketh, for your high prudénce,   *are not likely*
To waiven from the word of Solomon.   *to depart*
This word said he unto us everyone:
1485 'Work allé thing by counsel,' thus said he,   *by advice*
'And then shalt thou not repenten thee.'
But though that Solomon spoke such a word,
My owné dearé brother and my lord,
So wisly God my soulé bring at rest,[1]   *As surely as*
1490 I hold your owné counsel is the best.
For brother mine, of me take this motive: *for a fact*
I have now been a court-man all my life,
And God it wot, though I unworthy be,   *God knows*
I have stonden in full great degree   *high position*
1495 Abouten lordés in full high éstate,   *of great rank*
Yet had I ne'er with none of them debate.
I never them contráried truly.   *contradicted*
I wot well that my lord can more than I;   *knows more*
What that he says, I hold it firm and stable. *That which*
1500 I say the same, or elsé thing sembláble.   *similar*
A full great fool is any counsellor
That serveth any lord of high honour
That dare presume or elsé thinken it
That his counsél should pass his lordé's wit. *wisdom*
1505 Nay, lordés be no foolés, by my fay.   *by my faith*
You have yourselfé showéd here today
So high senténce so holily and well,   *such good sense*
That I consent and cónfirm everydeal   *completely*
Your wordés all and your opinïon.
1510 By God, there is no man in all this town
Nor in Itaille could better have y-said.

---

[1] 1489: "As surely as (I hope) God will bring my soul to His peace."

Christ holds him of this counsel well apaid.   *will be pleased*

And truly it is a high couráge   *spirit*

Of any man that stapen is in age   *advanced*

1515 To take a young wife. By my father's kin

Your heartë hangeth on a jolly pin!   *is well tuned*

Do now in this mattér right as you lest,   *as you please*

For, finally, I hold it for the best."

Justinus tells him some of the more unpleasant truths about marriage

Justínus that aye stillë sat and heard,   *all the time*

1520 Right in this wise he Plácebo answéred:

"Now, brother mine, be patïent I pray,

Since you have said, and hearken what I say.

Seneca, among other wordës wise,   *(Roman philosopher)*

Says that a man ought him right well avise   *consider carefully*

1525 To whom he gives his land or his chattél   *property*

And since I ought avisen me right well

To whom I give my goods away from me,

Well muchel more I ought avisëd be

To whom I give my body for always.

1530 I warn you well, it is no childë's play

To take a wife without avisëment.   *consideration*

Men must enquirë—this is mine assent—

Whe'r she be wise, or sober, or drunkelew,   *Whether / alcoholic*

Or proud, or elsë other ways a shrew,

1535 A chidester, or waster of thy good,   *A nag*

Or rich, or poor, or elsë mannish wood.   *crazy for men*

Albeit so that no man finden shall   *Although*

None in this world that trotteth whole in all,   *is perfect*

Nor man nor beast such as men could devise,   *imagine*

1540 But natheless, it ought enough suffice

With any wife, if so were that she had

More goodë thewës than her vices bad.   *good points*

And all this asketh leisure for t'enquire.

For God it wot, I have wept many a tear   *God knows*

1545	Full privily since that I had a wife:	*privately*
	Praise whoso will a wedded manne's life,	
	Certain I find in it but cost and care,	*expense & trouble*
	And observánces of all blisses bare.	*thankless tasks*
	And yet, God wot, my neighebours about,	
1550	And namely of women many a rout,	*in large numbers*
	Say that I have the moste steadfast wife,	
	And eke the meekest one that beareth life,	*And also*
	But I wot best where wringeth me my shoe.	*I know*
	You may, for me, right as you liketh do.[1]	
1555	Aviseth you—you be a man of age—	*Beware*
	How that you enter into marrïage,	
	And namely with a young wife and a fair.	*and pretty one*
	By him that made water, earth, and air,	
	The youngest man that is in all this rout	*in this group*
1560	Is busy enough to bringen it about	
	To have his wife alone. Trusteth me,	*to himself*
	You shall not pleasen her fully yeares three;	
	This is to say, to do her full pleasánce.	*total satisfaction*
	A wife asks full many an óbservance.	*much attention*
1565	I pray you that you be not evil apaid."	*angry*

Placebo confirms January in what he wants to hear

	"Well," quod this January, "and hast thou said?	*finished*
	Straw for thy Seneca, and thy provérbs!	
	I counte not a panier full of herbs	*basket of weeds*
	Of schoole-terms. Wiser men than thou,	*scholars' talk*
1570	As thou hast heard, assenteden right now	*have agreed*
	To my purpose. Placebo, what say ye?"	
	"I say it is a cursed man," said he,	
	"That letteth matrimony, sikerly."	*hinders / certainly*
	And with that word they risen suddenly,	
1575	And been assented fully that he should	
	Be wedded when him list and where he would.	*he pleased & wanted*

---

[1] 1554: "You may do as you please, as far as I am concerned."

January fantasizes about brides beautiful, young, and wise. He makes his choice.

	High fantasy and curious busyness	*Beautiful & fanciful thoughts*
	From day to day gan in the soul impress	*ran in the mind*
	Of January about his marrïage.	
1580	Many fair shapes and many a fair viságe	*a beautiful face*
	There passeth through his hearté night by night;	
	As whoso took a mirror polished bright,	*whoever*
	And set it in a common market place,	
	Then should he see full many a figure pace	
1585	By his mirroúr; and in the samé wise	
	Gan January inwith his thought devise	*within / think*
	Of maidens which that dwelten him beside.	*lived near*
	He wisté not where that he might abide.	*knew / settle on*
	For if that one has beauty in her face,	
1590	Another stands so in the people's grace	
	For her sadness and her benignity,	*seriousness & goodness*
	That of the people greatest voice had she;	
	And some were rich and had a baddé name.	
	But natheless, between earnest and game,	*to tell the truth*
1595	He at the last appointed him on one	*decided on*
	And let all others from his hearté gone,	
	And chose her of his own authority,	*initiative*
	For Love is blind alday, and may not see.	*always*
	And when that he was in his bed y-brought,	
1600	He portrayed in his heart and in his thought	
	Her freshé beauty and her agé tender,	
	Her middle small, her armés long and slender,	
	Her wisé governance, her gentleness,	
	Her womanly bearing and her sadness.	
1605	And when that he on her was condescended,	*maturity*
	Him thought his choicé might not be amended.	*settled*
	For when that he himself concluded had,	*improved*
	Him thought each other manné's wit so bad	*had decided*
	That impossíble it were to reply	*every o. m's advice*

1610 Against his choice. This was his fantasy.

He announces his choice to his friends

  His friendės sent he to at his instánce,   *request*
  And prayėd them to do him that pleasánce
  That hastily they would unto him come.
  He would abridge their labour, all and some: *one & all*
1615 Needeth no more for them to go nor ride;
  He was appointed where he would abide.[1] *had decided*
  Placebo came and eke his friendės soon,
  And alderfirst he bade them all a boon: *first he asked a favor*
  That none of them no argumentės make
1620 Against the purpose which that he has take, *decision he had made*
  Which purpose was pleasánt to God, said he,
  And very ground of his prosperity. *basis*
  He said there was a maiden in the town
  Which that of beauty haddė great renown.
1625 All were it so she were of small degree, *Although / low rank*
  Sufficeth him her youth and her beauty.
  Which maid he said he would have to his wife,
  To lead in ease and holiness his life,
  And thankėd God that he might have her all,
1630 That no wight his blissė parten shall; *nobody could share*
  And prayėd them to labour in this need,
  And shapen that he failė not to speed, *arrange / to succeed*
  For then, he said, his spirit was at ease.

One problem: since marriage is such a paradise on earth, how will he ever get to heaven?

  "Then is," quod he, "nothing may me displease.
1635 Save one thing pricketh in my conscïence,
  The which I will rehearse in your presénce: *I'll mention*
  I have," quod he, "heard said full yore ago
  There may no man have perfect blisses two,

---

[1] 1616: "He had decided whom he would settle on."

This is to say, on earth and eke in heaven.	*also*
1640 For though he keep him from the sinnès seven,	
And eke from every branch of thilkè tree,[1]	*also / of that*
Yet is there so perféct felicity	*happiness*
And so great ease and lust in marrïage,	*& pleasure*
That ever I am aghast now in mine age	*afraid*
1645 That I shall leadè now so merry a life,	
So delicate, withouten woe and strife,	*So delicious*
That I shall have my heaven on earthè here.	
For since that very heaven is bought so dear	*heaven itself*
With tribulation and with great penánce,	
1650 How should I then, that live in such pleasánce	
As allè wedded men do with their wivès,	
Come to the bliss where Christ etern alive is?	
This is my dread. And you, my brethren tway,	*two*
Assoileth me this question, I you pray."	*Answer*

*Justinus assures him that marriage will provide him with quite enough
purgatory on earth*

1655 Justinus, which that hated his folly,	*which that = who*
Answered anonright in his japery.	*promptly / sarcasm*
And for he would his longè tale abridge,	*shorten*
He wouldè no authority allege	*quote no authors*
But saidè: "Sir, so there be no obstacle	*if there's no*
1660 Other than this, God of his high miracle	
And of his mercy may so for you work	
That ere you have your rites of holy church,[2]	*last rites*
You may repent of wedded mannè's life	
In which you say there is no woe nor strife.	
1665 And elsè God forbid but if he sent	
A wedded man him gracè to repent	

---

[1] 1640-41: The 7 Deadly Sins were: Pride, Covetousness, Lust, Anger, Gluttony, Envy, and Sloth. From these all other sins grew, and they were often portrayed as branches and leaves on the tree of vice.

[2] 1662: "Before you have the last rites of the church," (i.e. before you die).

Well often rather than a single man.[1]

And therefore, sir, the best rede that I can: *advice I know*

Despair you not, but have in your memóry,

1670 Paraunter she may be your purgatory;   *Perhaps*

She may be Godè's means and Godè's whip!

Then shall your soulè up to heaven skip

Swifter than does an arrow out of a bow!

I hope to God hereafter shall you know

1675 That there is not so great felicity

In marrïage, ne never more shall be,

That shall you let of your salvation,   *prevent your*

So that you use, as skill is and reason,   *Provided / right*

The lustès of your wife attemprely,[2]   *moderately*

1680 And that you please her not too amorously,

And that you keep you eke from other sin.   *keep yourself also*

My tale is donè, for my wit is thin.   *my wisdom*

Be not aghast hereof, my brother dear,   *amazed*

But let us waden out of this mattér.   *get out of*

1685 The Wife of Bath, if you have understand,

Of marrïagè which we have on hand

Declarèd has full well in little space.[3]

Fareth now well. God have you in His grace."

The marriage contract is drawn up, and the ceremony takes place

And with that word this Justin and his brother

---

[1] 1667: "God forbid that a married man should not have the grace (reason?) to repent even oftener than a single man."

[2] 1678-9: "Provided that you satisfy your wife's lust in moderation (*attremprely*), as is right and proper." The sarcasm is obvious.

[3] 1685-7: The literary impropriety of having one pilgrim (the Wife of Bath) mentioned by a character (Justinus) in one of the tales told by another pilgrim has often been remarked. It would be different if the <u>Merchant</u> had mentioned her, as he refers to a character within the Clerk's Tale. If lines 1685-87 could be regarded as a parenthesis by the Merchant, some of the awkwardness might be avoided. Or, of course, it might be Chaucer's little literary joke.

1690 Have take their leave and each of them of other.

And when they saw that it must needës be,

They wroughten so by sly and wise treaty   *arranged / agreement*

That she, this maiden, which that Mayus hight,   *was called May*

As hastily as ever that she might,

1695 Shall wedded be unto this January.

I trow it were too longë you to tarry[1]   *to delay you*

If I you told of every script and bond   *title deed*

By which that she was feoffëd in his land;[2]   *endowed with*

Or for to hearken of her rich array.   *clothes?*

1700 But finally y-comen is that day

That to the churchë bothë be they went

For to receive the holy sacrament.   *s. (of matrimony)*

Forth comes the priest with stole about his neck,

And bade her be like Sarah and Rebekke   *prayed her to*

1705 In wisdom and in truth of marrïage,

And said his orisons as is uságe,   *prayers / customary*

And croucheth them, and bade God should them bless,   *blesses*

And made all siker enough with holiness.   *secure*

Thus been they wedded with solemnity.

1710 And at the feastë sitteth he and she

With other worthy folk upon the daïs.

The marriage feast: classical and biblical analogues

All full of joy and blissë is the palace,

And full of instruments and of vitaille,   *victuals, food*

The mostë dainteous of all Itaille.   *Italy*

1715 Before them stood instruments of such sound

That Orpheus, ne of Thebës Amphion,

---

[1] 1696: "I think it would hold you up too long if ..."

[2] 1692-98: His friends conduct the negotiations for the marriage and draw up a formal marriage treaty by which, among other things, May is "enfeoffed," i.e. entitled to some or all of January's property.

Ne maden never such a melody.[1]
At every course then came loud minstrelcy,
That never trumpèd Joab for to hear,   *David's trumpeter*
1720 Ne he Theodamas yet half so clear
At Thebès when the city was in doubt.
Bacchus the wine them shenketh all about,   *pours for them*
And Venus laugheth upon every wight,
For January was become her knight,   *her = Venus*
1725 And wouldè both assayen his couráge   *prove his sexual power*
In liberty and eke in marrïage,[2]
And with her firebrand in her hand about
Danceth before the bride and all the rout.   *company*
And certainly, I dare right well say this:
1730 Hymeneus, that god of wedding is,
Saw never his life so merry a wedded man!
Hold thou thy peace, thou poet Martian,   *Martianus Capella*
That writest us that ilkè wedding merry   *that the*
Of her Philology and him Mercury,
1735 And of the songè that the Muses sung:
Too small is both thy pen and eke thy tongue
For to describen of this marrïage
When tender youth has wedded stooping age:
There is such mirth that it may not be written.[3]
1740 Assayeth it yourself; then may you witen   *try it / may know*
If that I lie or no in this mattér.

---

[1] 1716-21: Orpheus, the harpist of classical story, almost rescued his wife Eurydice from the underworld by the beauty of his music. Amphion built the walls of Thebes by moving the very stones into place by the music of his lyre. Joab was the trumpeter of David in the Old Testament. Theodamas was a trumpeter augur of Thebes.

[2] 1725-6: "And wished to demonstrate his sexual prowess both as a bachelor (in the past) and as a married man now."

[3] 1723-39: The mirth of the company and the laughter of Venus are presumably not just the usual wedding merriment but partly the laughter of derision at this particular marriage.

Mayus, that sits with so benign a cheer   *pleasant an expression*
Her to behold it seemėd faiėrie.   *enchanting*
Queen Esther lookėd never with such an eye
1745 On Ashuer, so meek a look has she.
I may you not devise all her beauty,   *describe*
But thus much of her beauty tell I may,
That she was like the brightė morrow of May,   *morning*
Fulfillėd of all beauty and pleasánce!

More fantasy

1750 This January is ravished in a trance
At every time he lookėd on her face!
But in his heart he gan her to menace
That he that night in armės would her strain
Harder than ever Paris did Elaine.   *Helen of Troy*
1755 But natheless yet had he great pity
That thilkė night offenden her must he,   *That this*
And thought: "Alas! O tender creäture,
Now wouldė God you mightė well endure
All my couráge, it is so sharp and keen.   *sexual power*
1760 I am aghast you shall it not sustain;   *I'm afraid*
But God forbid that I did all my might!
Now wouldė God that it were waxen night,   *that it was night*
And that the night would lasten evermo'.
I would that all this people were ago."   *wish / were gone*
1765 And finally he does all his laboúr,
As he best might, saving his honoúr,
To haste them from the meat in subtle wise.   *meal*
The timė came that reason was to rise,
And after that men dance and drinken fast,
1770 And spices all about the house they cast.

An unexpected if predictable reality intrudes

And full of joy and bliss is every man—
All but a squire that hightė Damian,   *was called*
Which carved before the knight full many a day: *Which = Who*

He was so ravished on his lady May

1775 That for the very pain he was nigh wood;   *nearly mad*

Almost he swelt and swoonèd there he stood,   *Almost fainted*

So sore has Venus hurt him with her brand,   *torch*

As that she bore it dancing in her hand.   *When*

And to his bed he went him hastily.

1780 No more of him at this time speak I,

But there I let him weep enough and 'plain   *complain*

Till freshè May will rue upon his pain.   *take pity on*

O perilous fire that in the bedstraw breedeth!

O familiar foe that his service biddeth!   *offers*

1785 O servant traitor, falsè homely hew,   *disloyal domestic servant*

Like to the adder in bosom, sly, untrue!

God shield us allè from your ácquaintance!

O January, drunken in pleasánce

In marrïage, see how thy Damian,

1790 Thine ownè squire and thy bornè man,

Intendeth for to do thee villainy!

God grantè thee thy homely foe t'espy,   *domestic enemy*

For in this world is no worse pestilence

Than homely foe alday in thy presénce!   *every day*

January gets ready for the wedding night

1795 Performèd has the sun his arc diurn;   *his daily round*

No longer may the body of him sojourn   *stay*

On th'orisont as in that latitude.   *Above horizon*

Night with his mantle that is dark and rude   *rough*

Gan overspread the hemisphere about,

1800 For which departed is this lusty rout,   *lively group*

From January with thanks on every side.

Home to their houses lustily they ride,

Where as they do their thingès as them lest,   *as they please*

And when they saw their timè, go to rest.

1805 Soon after that this hasty January

Will go to bed; he will no longer tarry.   *Wishes to go*

He drinketh ipocras, claret, and vernáge,   *(aphrodisiacs)*

Of spices hot t'encreasen his couráge,	*potency*
And many a letuary had he full fine,	*drug*

1810 Such as the cursed monk Daun Constantine
Has written in his book "De Coitu." [1]
To eat them all he was no thing eschew.   *not reluctant*
And to his privy friendès thus said he: *close*
"For Godè's love, as soon as it may be,

1815 Let voiden all this house in courteous wise."   *Clear the house*
And they have done right as he will devise.   *as he wished*
Men drinken, and the traverse draw anon;   *curtain*
The bride was brought a-bed as still as stone;
And when the bed was with the priest y-blessed,

1820 Out of the chamber has every wight him dressed.   *everyone went*

The wedding night

And January has fast in armès take
His freshè May, his paradise, his make.   *mate*
He lulleth her, he kisseth her full oft
With thickè bristles of his beard unsoft

1825 Like to the skin of houndfish, sharp as briar
For he was shaved all new (in his mannér).
He rubbeth her about her tender face,
And saidè thus: "Alas, I must trespass
To you, my spouse, and you greatly offend

1830 Ere timè come that I will down descend.
But natheless, consider this," quod he,
"There is no workman, whatsoe'er he be,
That may both workè well and hastily.
This will be done at leisure perfectly.

1835 It is no force how longè that we play.   *It doesn't matter*

---

[1] 1810-11: Constantine says that big wine drinkers will have plenty of desire and semen. His recipes for aphrodisiacs generally call for many different kinds of seed, including rape seed. Another requires the brains of thirty male sparrows and the grease surrounding the kidneys of a freshly-killed he-goat. For Paul Delany's translation of "De Coitu" ("On Copulation") by Constantinus Africanus see *Chaucer Review* IV, (1970), 55-66.

In truė wedlock coupled be we tway,   *two*
And blessėd be the yoke that we be in!   *bond*
For in our actės we may do no sin.
A man may do no sinnė with his wife,
1840   Nor hurt himselfen with his ownė knife,
For we have leave to play us by the law."[1]

Thus labours he till that the day gan dawn;
And then he takes a sop in fine claree,   *piece of bread in f. wine*
And upright in his bed then sitteth he,
1845   And after that he sang full loud and clear,
And kissed his wife and madė wanton cheer.   *merry talk*
He was all coltish, full of ragery,   *"gallantry"*
And full of jargon as a fleckėd pie: *old talk / magpie*
The slackė skin about his neckė shaketh
1850   While that he sang, so chanteth he and cracketh.   *croaks*
But God wot what that May thought in her heart   *God knows*
When she him saw up-sitting in his shirt,
In his night-cap and with his neckė lean;
She praiseth not his playing worth a bean.
1855   Then said he thus: "My restė will I take.
Now day is come. I may no longer wake."

And down he laid his head and slept till prime.   *about 9 a.m.*
And afterwards, when that he saw his time,
Up riseth January. But freshė May
1860   Held her chamber unto the fourthė day,
As usage is of wivės for the best.
For every labourer some time must have rest,
Or elsė longė may he not endure,
This is to say, no live creäture
1865   Be it of fish or bird or beast or man.

Laid low by lovesickness, squire Damian laments his love-lorn state in poetry

Now will I speak of woeful Damian

---

[1] 1841: "We have the right to enjoy ourselves legally."

That languisheth for love, as you shall hear.
Therefore I speak to him in this mannér:
I say: "O silly Damian, alas,
1870 Answer to my demand as in this case:
How shalt thou to thy lady freshė May
Tellė thy woe? She will always say nay.
Eke if thou speak, she will thy woe bewray.   *expose*
God be thy help, I can no better say."
1875 This sickė Damian in Venus' fire
So burneth that he dieth for desire,
For which he put his life in áventure.   *danger*
No longer might he in this wise endure,
But privily a penner gan he borrow,   *writing case*
1880 And in a letter wrote he all his sorrow,
In manner of a complaint or a lay[1]   *poems*
Unto his fairė freshė lady May.
And in a purse of silk hung on his shirt
He has it put and laid it at his heart.

January notices his squire's absence

1885 The moonė, that at noon was thilkė day   *that day*
That January has wedded freshė May
In two of Taur, was into Cancer gliden.[2]   *Taurus*
So long has May in her chamber abiden,
As custom is unto these nobles all.
1890 A bridė shall not eaten in the hall
Till dayės four, or three days at the least
Y-passėd been. Than let her go to feast.
    The fourthė day complete from noon to noon,
When that the highė massė was y-done,
1895 In hallė sit this January and May,

---

[1] 1881: Kinds of love poems.

[2] 1886-7: A roundabout astronomical way, dear to Chaucer, of saying apparently, that three or four days had passed.

As fresh as is the brightė summer's day.
And so befell how that this goodė man
Remembered him upon this Damian,
And saidė: "Saint Marie! how may it be
1900 That Damian attendeth not to me?
Is he aye sick, or how may this betide?" [1]
His squires which that stooden there beside
Excusėd him because of his sickness,
Which letted him to do his busyness—   *prevented from*
1905 No other causė mightė make him tarry.
"That me forthinketh," quod this January.   *grieves me*
"He is a gentle squire, by my truth.
If that he diėd, it were harm and ruth.   *pity*
He is as wise, discreet, and eke secree   *& also trustworthy*
1910 As any man I wot of his degree,   *I know of his rank*
And thereto manly and eke serviceable,
And for to be a thrifty man right able.   *successful*
But after meat as soon as ever I may,   *meal*
I will myselfė visit him, and eke May,
1915 To do him all the comfórt that I can."
And for that word him blessėd every man
That of his bounty and his gentleness
He wouldė so comfort in his sickness
His squire, for it was a gentle deed.

January instructs his wife to go visit the sick man

1920 "Dame," quod this January, "take good heed,   *Madame*
At after-meat you with your women all,   *after dinner*
When you have been in chamber out of this hall,
That all you go to see this Damian.
Do him desport—he is a gentle man;   *Cheer him up*
1925 And telleth him that I will him visit,
Have I no thing but rested me a lite;   *After I have / little*
And speed you fastė, for I will abide   *Hurry / wait*

---

[1] 1901: "Is he sick, or what is the matter?

Till that you sleepė fastė by my side,"
And, with that word, he gan to him to call
1930 A squire that was marshall of his hall,
And told him certain thingės that he would.   *he wanted*

May obeys her husband. The unintended result.

This freshė May has straight her way y-hold
With all her women unto Damian.
Down by his beddė's sidė sits she then,
1935 Comforting him as goodly as she may.
This Damian, when that his time he saw,
In secret wise his purse and eke his bill,   *fashion / letter*
In which that he y-written had his will,   *his wishes*
Has put into her hand withouten more,   *without delay*
1940 Save that he sigheth wonder deep and sore,
And softėly to her right thus said he:
"Mercy! and that you not discover me;   *Please do not betray*
For I am dead if that this thing be kid."   *known*
This purse has she inwith her bosom hid
1945 And went her way. You get no more of me.
But unto January y-come is she,
That on his beddė's sidė sits full soft,
And taketh her, and kisseth her full oft,
And laid him down to sleep and that anon.
1950 She feignėd her as that she mustė gon   *pretended she had to go*
There as you wot that every wight must need,[1]   *you know / has to*
And when she of this bill has taken heed,   *read this letter*
She rent it all to cloutės at the last,   *tore in bits*
And in the privy softly she it cast.
1955 Who studieth now but fairė freshė May?
Adown by oldė January she lay,
That slept till that the cough has him awakėd
Anon he prayed her strippen her all naked.

---

[1] 1950-51: "She pretended she had to go where, as you know, everyone has to" (i.e. the toilet).

He would of her, he said, have some pleasánce;
1960 He said her clothés did him éncumbránce;
And she obeyeth, be her lief or loth.   *like it or not*
But lest that precious folk be with me wroth,   *sensitive / angry*
How that he wrought I dare not to you tell,   *performed*
Or whether she thought it paradise or hell.
1965 But here I let them worken in their wise
Till evensongé rang, and they must rise.   *vespers*

May's positive response revives Damian

Were it by destiny or áventúre,   *or chance*
Were it by influence or by natúre [1]   *Influence of planets?*
Or constellation, that in such estate   *in the stars*
1970 The heavens stooden that time fortunate
As for to put a bill of Venus' works   *love-letter*
(For allé thing hath time, as say these clerks)   *scholars*
To any woman for to get her love,
I cannot say. But greaté God above,
1975 That knoweth that no act is causéless,
He deem of all, for I will hold my peace.   *Let Him judge*
But sooth is this: how that this freshé May
Has taken such impressïon that day
Of pity on this sické Damian
1980 That from her hearté she ne drivé can
The rémembrancé for to do him ease!   *intention*
"Certain," thought she, "whom that this thing displease
I recké not. For here I him assure   *I don't care*
To love him best of any creäture,
1985 Though he no moré haddé than his shirt."

Lo, pity runneth soon in gentle heart!
Here may you see how excellent franchise   *generosity*

---

[1] 1967-74: "Whether it was destiny or pure chance (*aventure*) or the position of the stars and planets that made it a good time to write a letter to gain a woman's love ... I do not know."

In women is when they them narrow avise.   *think deeply*
Some tyrant is, as there be many a one
1990   That has a heart as hard as any stone,
Which would have let him starven in the place   *let him die*
Well rather than have granted him her grace,   *favor*
And her rejoicen in her cruel pride,
And reckėd not to be a homicide.[1]

1995   This gentle May, fulfillėd of pitý,   *filled with*
Right of her hand a letter makėd she,   *with her hand*
In which she granteth him her very grace.
There lacketh nought, but only day and place
Where that she might unto his lust suffice;   *satisfy his wish*
2000   For it shall be right as he will devise.
And when she saw her time upon a day,
To visiten this Damian goes May,
And subtly this letter down she thrust
Under his pillow. Read it if him lest.   *if he wishes*
2005   She takes him by the hand and hard him twists,
So secretly that no wight of it wist   *nobody knew*
And bade him be all whole, and forth she went   *to get well*
To January, when that he for her sent.

Up riseth Damian the nextė morrow;
2010   All passėd was his sickness and his sorrow.
He combeth him, he preeneth him and piketh,   *& primps*
And does all that his lady lusts and liketh.   *desires and*
And eke to January he goes as low   *also*
As ever did a doggė for the bow.
2015   He is so pleasant unto every man
(For craft is all, whoso that do it can)   *cleverness / whoever*
That every wight is fain to speak him good;   *everyone is glad to*

---

[1] 1989-1994: The meaning of this ironic speech, is that many a woman would have played the tyrant and not granted him her favor, taking pleasure in her cruelty, and would not care if this killed him.

And fully in his lady's grace he stood.   *favor*

January makes a walled pleasure-garden for private use

     Thus let I Damian about his need,   *his business*
2020 And in my talė forth I will proceed.
     Some clerkės holden that felicity   *scholars / happiness*
     Stands in delight, and therefore certain, he,   *consists in*
     This noble January, with all his might
     In honest wise as 'longeth to a knight,   *as becomes*
2025 Shope him to liven full deliciously: *Arranged*
     His housing, his array, as honestly   *clothes, as appropriate*
     To his degree was makėd as a king's.   *To his rank*
     Amongėst other of his honest things,
     He made a garden wallėd all with stone.
2030 So fair a garden wot I nowhere none.   *know I*
     For out of doubt I verily suppose
     That he that wrote "The Romance of the Rose"
     Ne could of it the beauty well devise;[1]   *describe*
     Nor Priapus ne mightė not suffice,
2035 Though he be god of gardens, for to tell
     The beauty of the garden, and the well
     That stood under a laurel always green.[2]
     Full often time he Pluto and his Queen   *Pluto himself*
     Prosérpina and all her faérie   *fairy band*
2040 Desporten them and maken melody   *amuse themselves*
     About that well, and dancėd, as men told.
     This noble knight, this January the old,
     Such dainty has in it to walk and play   *delight*

---

[1] 2032-3: *The Romance of the Rose* was a thirteenth-century French poem by Guillaume de Lorris and Jean de Meun which influenced Chaucer profoundly; he may even have done the English version of it that often appears in complete editions of his work. For the ironic relationship of the garden and the characters of *The Romance* to old January, lusty Damian and May see introduction to this tale.

[2] 2034ff: Priapus was god of gardens but also of male sexual desire. He figures in one legend as being embarrassed when he is caught just about to rape a sleeping nymph.

That he will no wight suffer bear the key,   *allow nobody*
2045 Save he himself: for of the small wicket   *gate*
He bore always of silver a clicket,   *key*
With which, when that him lest, he it unshut.   *when he pleased*
And when that he would pay his wife her debt
In summer season, thither would he go,   *there*
2050 And May his wife, and no wight but they two.   *nobody*
And thingès which that were not done a-bed,
He in the garden performed them and sped.   *with success*
And in this wisè many a merry day
Lived this January and freshè May.

Fortune is fickle

2055 But worldly joy may not always endure
To January, nor to no creäture.
O sudden hap! O thou Fortúne unstable,   *Chance*
Like to the scorpion so deceivable,
That flatterest with thine head when thou wilt sting,
2060 Thy tail is death through thine envenoming!   *poisoning*
O brittle joy! O sweetè venom quaint!   *seductive poison*
O monster, that so subtly canst paint
Thy giftès under hue of steadfastness,   *under color*
That thou deceivest bothè more and less!   *rich & poor*
2065 Why hast thou January thus deceived,
That haddest him for thy full friend received?
And now, thou hast bereft him both his eyes,
For sorrow of which desireth he to die.

Physical affliction makes January even more jealously possessive

Alas! this noble January free,   *carefree*
2070 Amid his lust and his prosperity,
Is waxen blind, and that all suddenly.   *Has become*
He weepeth and he waileth piteously.
And therewithal the fire of jealousy,
Lest that his wife should fall in some folly,
2075 So burned his heartè that he wouldè fain   *he really wished*

That some man bothė her and him had slain.
For neither after his death nor in his life,
Ne would he that she were love nor wife,   *lover*
But ever live as widow in clothės black,
2080 Sole as the turtle that has lost her mak.[1]   *Alone / mate*
But at the last, after a month or tway,   *two*
His sorrow gan assuagė, sooth to say: *slacken, truth to*
For when he wist it may no other be,   *he realized*
He patiently took his adversity,
2085 Save, out of doubtė, he may not forgon   *Except / can't help*
That he n'as jealous evermore in one.[2]
Which jealousy it was so outrageous
That neither in hall nor in no other house,
Nor in no other placė neverthemo'   *either*
2090 He would not suffer her to ride or go,   *allow her to go anywhere*
But if that he had hand on her alway.   *Unless*
For which full oftė weepeth freshė May
That loveth Damian so benignly
That she must either dien suddenly
2095 Or else she mustė have him as her lest.   *as she wishes*
She waiteth when her heartė wouldė burst.   *She thought her ...*
       Upon that other sidė Damian
Becomen is the sorrowfullestė man
That ever was; for neither night nor day
2095 Ne might he speak a word to freshė May,
As to his purpose of no such mattér,
But if that January must it hear,   *without J. hearing*
That had a hand upon her evermo'.

Love finds a way to outwit Jealousy

But natheless, by writing to and fro,

---

[1] 2077-80: "He did not want her to have a lover while he lived nor become a wife after his death but live as a widow dressed in black, alone, like a turtledove who has lost her mate." The turtledove was a symbol of marital fidelity.

[2] 2085-6: "Except that he cannot stop being jealous constantly" *(evermore in one)*.

2100   And privy signės, wist he what she meant;   *secret / he knew*
       And she knew eke the fine of his intent.   *the point*
       O January! what might it thee avail
       Though thou mightst see as far as shippės sail?
       For as good is blind deceivėd be,[1]
2110   As be deceivėd when a man may see.
       Lo Argus, which that had a hundred eyes,
       For all that ever he could pore or pry
       Yet was he blent, and God wot so been mo' *hoodwinked, & God knows*
       That weenen wisly that it be not so.   *Who think indeed*
2115   Pass over is an ease; I say no more.[2]

       This freshė May that I spoke of so yore,   *earlier*
       In warm wax has imprinted the clicket   *key*
       That January bore of the small wicket,   *gate*
       By which into his garden oft he went.
2120   And Damian that knew all her intent
       The clicket counterfeited privily.   *secretly*
       There is no more to say, but hastily
       Some wonder by this clicket shall betide,
       Which you shall hearen if you will abide.
2125   O noble Ovid! sooth sayst thou, God wot,   *truth / God knows*
       What sleight is it, though it be long and hot,   *strategy*
       That he n'ill find it out in some manner![3]   *he = Love*
       By Pyramus and Thisbe may men lere: *learn*
       Though they were kept full long strict overall, *in every way*
2130   They been accorded rouning through a wall,   *whispering*

---

[1] 2109-10: "One might as well be blind and deceived as seeing and deceived." 2111-13: Argus of the hundred eyes was put to sleep by Hermes with music and storytelling, then killed.

[2] 2115: *Pass over is an ease* = "To pass this over is a comfort" or "It is easy to overlook things," or "There is comfort in not seeing some things."

[3] 2125 ff: "What you say is true, God knows. There is no strategy, however long and hard (may be the effort), that Love will not eventually work out." Ovid wrote the story of the lovers Pyramus and Thisbe in *Metamorphoses* 4.

Where no wight could have found out such a sleight. *nobody / trick*

But now to purpose: ere that dayės eight   *To get on with story: before ...*
Were passėd, of the month of June, befell   *...June 8*
That January hath caught so great a will,
2135 Through egging of his wife, him for to play   *urging / enjoy himself*
In his garden, and no wight but they tway,   *nobody but they two*
That in a morrow unto his May says he: *one morning*
"Rise up, my wife, my love, my lady free.
The turtle's voice is heard, my dovė sweet!   *turtle dove's*
2140 The winter is gone with all his rains wet.[1]   *its rains*
Come forth now with thine eyen columbine.   *dovelike eyes*
How fairer be thy breastės than is wine!
The garden is enclosėd all about.
Come forth, my whitė spousė, out of doubt,   *undoubtedly*
2145 Thou hast me wounded in mine heart! O wife,
No spot of thee ne knew I all my life!
Come forth and let us taken our desport;   *pleasure*
I chose thee for my wife and my comfort."
Such oldė lewėd wordės usėd he.
2150 On Damian a signė madė she
That he should go beforė with his clicket.   *key*
This Damian has opened then the wicket,
And in he starts, and that in such mannér
That no wight might it see, neither y-hear.   *nobody / nor hear*
2155 And still he sits under a bush anon.

January and May walk in his garden, and talk about love and fidelity

This January, as blind as is a stone,
With Mayus in his hand and no wight mo'   *no one else*
Into his freshė garden is ago,
And claptė to the wicket suddenly.   *closed*

---

[1] 2138 ff: This passage is full of phrases from the great biblical love poem "The Song of Songs." Referring to them as "old, lewd words" in line 2149 is therefore, meant to be especially ironic. "Lewd" here probably has the double meanings "stupid" and "lewd" in the modern sense.

2160 "Now wife," quod he, "here n'is but thou and I,
       That art the creäture that I best love.
       For by that Lord that sits in heaven above,
       Lever I had to dien on a knife   *I had rather*
       Than thee offend, truė dearė wife.
2165 For Godė's sakė, think how I thee chose,
       Not for no covetisė, doubtėless,
       But only for the love I had to thee.
       And though that I be old and may not see,
       Be to me true, and I will tell you why.
2170 Three thingės, certės, shall you win thereby:
       First, love of Christ; and to yourself honoúr;
       And all my heritagė, town and tower,
       I give it you—make charters as you lest.   *deeds as you wish*
       This shall be done tomorrow ere sun rest,
2175 So wisly God my soulė bring in bliss.   *As surely as*
       I pray you first in covenant you me kiss.   *in token*
       And though that I be jealous, wite me nought: *blame*
       You be so deep imprinted in my thought,
       That when that I consider your beauty,
2180 And therewithal the unlikely eld of me,   *age*
       I may not, certės, though I shouldė die,
       Forbear to be out of your company   *Cannot bear*
       For very love; this is without a doubt.
       Now kiss me, wife, and let us roam about."

2185 This freshė May, when she these wordės heard,
       Benignly to January answered,
       But first and foremost she began to weep.
       "I have," quod she, "a soulė for to keep
       As well as you, and also mine honoúr;
2190 And of my wifehood thilkė tender flower   *that*
       Which that I have assurėd in your hand   *sworn*
       When that the priest to you my body bound.
       Wherefore I will answer in this mannér,
       By the leave of you, my lord so dear:

2195	I pray to God that never dawn the day	
	That I ne starve as foul as woman may	*die*
	If ever I do unto my kin that shame,	*my family*
	Or elsė I impairė so my name	*soil*
	That I be false. And if I do that lack,	*unfaithful / sin*
2200	Do strip me, and put me in a sack,	*Have me stripped*
	And in the nextė river do me drench.	*have me drowned*
	I am a gentlewoman, and no wench!	*no trollop*
	Why speak you thus? But men be ever untrue,	*always unfaithful*
	And women have reproof of you aye new!	*ever new*
2205	You have no other countenance, I 'lieve,[1]	
	But speak to us of untrust and repreve!"	*reproof*

Damian, hiding in the garden, climbs up a pear tree at May's signal

	And with that word she saw where Damian	
	Sat in the bush, and coughen she began,	
	And with her finger signės madė she	
2210	That Damian should climb up on a tree	
	That chargėd was with fruit, and up he went;	*was loaded with*
	For verily he knew all her intent	
	And every signė that she couldė make	
	Well bet than January, her ownė make;	*better / mate*
2215	For in a letter she had told him all	
	Of this mattérė, how he worken shall.	*should operate*
	And thus I let him sit upon the perry,	*pear tree*
	And January and May roaming merry.	
	Bright was the day and blue the firmament.	*sky*
2220	Phoebus hath of gold his streams down sent	*P = The sun*
	To gladden every flower with his warmness.	
	He was that time in Gemini, as I guess,	
	But little from his declination	
	Of Cancer, Jovė's exaltation.	

---

[1] 2205-6: "You have no other way, I believe, to put a face on that but to accuse us of untrustworthiness."

The underworld deities Pluto and Proserpina, also living in the garden, engage in a vigorous verbal battle of the sexes, and take sides for and against January and May

2225	And so befell that brightė morrow-tide	*morning time*
	That in that garden, in the farther side,	
	Pluto, that is king of faėrie,[1]	
	And many a lady in his company,	
	Following his wife, the queen Prosėrpina,	
2230	Which that he ravishėd out of Etna	*snatched*
	While that she gathered flowers in the mead	*meadow*
	(In Claudian you may the story read	
	How in his grisly cartė he her fet).	*fetched*

Pluto

	This king of faerie then adown him set	
2235	Upon a bench of turvės fresh and green,	*bank of turf*
	And right anon thus said he to his queen:	
	"My wife," quod he, "there may no wightė say nay:	*nobody can deny*
	The experience so proveth every day	
	The treason which that woman does to man.	
2240	Ten hundred thousand talės tell I can	
	Notable of your untruth and brittleness.	
	O Solomon, wise and richest of richesse,	
	Fulfilled of sapience and wordly glory,	*full of wisdom*
	Full worthy been thy wordės to memóry	
2245	To every wight that wit and reason can.	*everyone / wisdom / knows*
	Thus praiseth he yet the bounty of man:	
	'Amongst a thousand men yet found I one,	
	But of women allė found I none'—	
	Thus says the king that knows your wickedness.	
2250	And Jesu filius Syrak, as I guess,	*Ecclesiasticus*

---

[1] 2227 ff: Pluto is not the king of fairyland but of the underworld. (One of his other names is Hades). He had snatched away the young and beautiful Proserpina (Persephone) while she had been gathering flowers in a meadow, to be his wife in the underworld from which she returned every year for spring and summer. The parallel between them and January/May is obvious.

Ne speaks of you but seldom reverence;[1]   *with respect*
A wildė fire and corrupt pestilence   *skin disease & rotting plague*
So fall upon your bodies yet tonight!
Ne see you not this honorable knight?
2255 Because, alas, that he is blind and old,
His ownė man shall make him a cuckold!
Lo where he sits, the lecher in the tree!
Now will I granten of my majesty
Unto this oldė, blindė, worthy knight
2260 That he shall have again his eyėsight,
When that his wife would do him villainy.   *wrong*
Then shall he knowen all her harlotry,
Both in reproof of her and others mo'."

Proserpine

"You shall?" quod Proserpínė. "Will you so?
2265 Now by my mother's sirė's soul I swear   *by Saturn's soul*
That I shall give her sufficïent answér!
And allė women after for her sake,
That though they be in any guilt y-take,   *taken (caught)*
With faces bold they shall themselves excuse,
2270 And bear them down that woulden them accuse.   *face down those*
For lack of answer none of them shall die!
All had man seen a thing with both his eyes,   *Even if*
Yet shall we women visage it hardily,   *brazen it out*
And weep, and swear, and chidė subtly,
2275 So that you men shall be as lewd as geese.   *stupid*
What recketh me of your authorities?
I wot well that this Jew, this Solomon,   *I know*
Found of us women foolės many a one,
But though that he ne found no good woman,

---

[1] 2242-51: Note the deliberate absurdity of a pagan god quoting the Bible, and later (2290-2300) Proserpina speaking of the "true god" and denouncing Solomon for having built a temple for false gods. 2250: Jesus, the supposed author of *Ecclesiasticus* (not Jesus Christ).

2280 Yet has there founden many another man	
Women full true, full good and virtuous.	
Witness on them that dwell in Christė's house:	*heaven?*
With martyrdom they provėd their constánce.	*constancy*
The Roman gestės eke make rémembránce	*stories*
2285 Of many a very truė wife also.	
But sir, ne be not wroth, albeit so,	*even if it is so*
Though that he said he found no good woman;	
I pray you, take the sentence of the man.	*general meaning*
He meantė thus: that in sovereign bounty	*total goodness*
2290 N'is none but God, but neither he nor she.	*man nor woman*
Eh! For very God that is but one,	*only true God*
What makė you so much of Solomon?	
What though he made a temple, Godė's house?	*So what if …*
What though he werė rich and glorious?	
2295 So made he eke a temple of falsė goddės!	*He also made*
How might he do a thing that more forbode is?	*forbidden*
Pardee, as fair as you his name emplaster,	*By God / paint*
He was a lecher and an idoláster,	*idolator*
And in his eld he very God forsook.	*old age / true God*
2300 And if God ne had, as says the book,	
Y-spared him for his father's sake, he should	*I Kings 11: 11-13*
Have lost his reignė rather than he would.	*throne / sooner / wished*
I set right nought, of all the villainy	*I care no more …*
That you of women write, a butterfly.	*…than a b.*
2305 I am a woman: needės must I speak,	
Or elsė swell until mine heartė break.	
For since he said that we be jangleresses,	*gossips*
As ever wholė may I brook my tresses,[1]	
I shall not sparė for no courtesy	*not cease*
2310 To speak him harm that would us villainy."	*wishes us ill*

---

[1] 2308: "As sure as I am proud of my (woman's long) hair uncut" (?), i.e. as long as I am proud to be a woman.

Truce

    "Dame," quod this Pluto, "be no longer wroth.   *Madame, / angry*
    I give it up. But since I swore mine oath
    That I would granten him his sight again,
    My word shall stand, I warnė you certain.
2315 I am a king; it sits me not to lie."   *It's not becoming*
    "And I," quod she, "a queen of faėrie.
    Her answer shall she have, I undertake.
    Let us no morė wordės hereof make.
    Forsooth, I will no longer you contráry."   *Indeed / contradict*

Back to the main narrative: May professes a craving for fruit, and asks for January's help

2320 Now let us turn again to January
    That in the garden with his fairė May
    Singeth full merrier than the popinjay: *parrot*
    "You love I best, and shall, and other none."
    So long about the alleys is he gone
2325 Till he was come against thilkė perry,   *that very peartree*
    Where as this Damian sits full merry
    On high among the freshė leavės green.
    This freshė May, that is so bright and sheen,   *shining*
    Gan for to sigh and said, "Alas, my side!   *Began to*
2330 Now sir," quod she, "for aught that may betide,
    I must have of the pearės that I see,
    Or I must die—so sorė longeth me   *I long to*
    To eaten of the smallė pearės green.
    Help, for her love that is of heaven queen!   *love of her who*
2335 I tell you well, a woman in my plight   *condition*
    May have to fruit so great an appetite
    That she may dien but she of it have."[1]   *unless*
    "Alas!" quod he, "that I n'ad here a knave   *I don't have a boy*

---

[1] 2335-7: Her clear implication is that she is pregnant, and has an unusually strong craving for fruit. The covert implication is less innocent.

That couldë climb! Alas, alas!" quod he,
2340 "For I am blind!" "Yea, sir, no force," quod she   *no matter*
"But would you vouchësafe, for Godë's sake,   *would you agree*
The perry inwith your armës for to take,   *peartree / within*
(For well I wot that you mistrustë me)   *I know*
Then should I climbë well enough," quod she,
2345 "So I my foot might set upon your back."   *If I could*
"Certës," quod he, "thereon shall be no lack;
Might I you helpen with mine hertë's blood." [1]
He stoopeth down, and on his back she stood,
And caught her by a twist, and up she goth.   *And seized a branch*

Damian and May get to know each other in the tree

2350 Ladies, I pray you that you be not wroth;
I cannot gloss, I am a rudë man,   *can't be delicate / uncultivated*
And suddenly anon this Damian
Gan pullen up the smock, and in he throng.   *the skirt / thrust*

Seeing what is going on, Pluto gives January a dubious gift

And when that Pluto saw this greatë wrong,
2355 To January he gave again his sight,
And made him see as well as ever he might.
And when that he had caught his sight again,
Ne was there never man of thing so fain;   *so glad*
But on his wife his thought was evermo'.
2360 Up to the tree he cast his eyen two,
And saw that Damian his wife had dressed   *had treated*
In such mannér it may not be expressed,
But if I wouldë speak uncourteously;   *Unless I were to*
And up he gave a roaring and a cry
2365 As does the mother when the child shall die:
"Out! Help! Alas! Harrow!" he gan to cry,
"O strongë lady store! What dost thou?"   *impudently brazen*

---

[1] 2346-7: "Certainly you shall not lack for that, even if I had to help you with my heart's blood."

Proserpine in turn gives May a plausible response

And she answéréd, "Sir, what aileth you?
Have patïence and reason in your mind.
2370 I have you helped in both your eyen blind.   *eyes*
On peril of my soul, I shall not lie,
As me was taught, to healé with your eye   *As I was told*
Was nothing better for to make you see   *(There) was*
Than struggle with a man upon a tree.
2375 God wot I did it in full good intent."   *God knows*
"Struggle!" quod he. "Yea! algate in it went!   *All the way*
God give you both on shamé's death to die!   *shameful death*
He swivéd thee! I saw it with mine eye,   *He penetrated*
And elsé be I hangéd by the hals."   *by the neck*
2380 "Then is," quod she, "my medicine all false!
For certainly, if that you mighté see,
You would not say these wordés unto me.
You have some glimpsing, and no perfect sight."
"I see," quod he, "as well as ever I might,
2385 Thankéd be God, with both mine eyen two;
And by my truth, me thought he did thee so."
"You mazé, mazé, goodé sir," quod she.   *You're dazed*
"This thanks have I for I have made you see!
Alas!" quod she, "that ever I was so kind!"

Another truce

2390 "Now dame," quod he, "let all pass out of mind.
Come down, my lief; and if I have mis-said,   *my love*
God help me so as I am evil apaid.   *I am sorry*
But by my father's soul, I wend have seen   *I thought I'd seen*
How that this Damian had by thee lain
2395 And that thy smock had lain upon his breast."
"Yea, sir," quod she, "you may ween as you lest!   *think as you like*
But sir, a man that wakes out of his sleep
He may not suddenly well take keep   *notice*
Upon a thing, nor see it perfectly

2400	Till that he be adawèd verily.	*fully awake*
	Right so a man that long hath blind y-be	*been*
	Ne may not suddenly so well y-see	
	First when his sight is newè come again,	
	As he that hath a day or two y-seen.	
2405	Till that your sight y-settled be awhile,	
	There may full many a sightè you beguile.	*deceive you*
	Beware, I pray you! For, by heaven's king,	
	Full many a man weeneth to see a thing	*thinks*
	And it is all another than it seemeth.	
2410	He that misconceiveth, he misdeemeth." [1]	

January chooses to stay comfortably sightless

And with that word she leaped down from the tree.
This January, who is glad but he?

	He kisseth her and clippeth her full oft,	*embraces*
	And on her womb he stroketh her full soft,	
2415	And to his palace home he has her led.	

Now, goodè men, I pray you to be glad.
Thus endeth here my tale of January.
God bless us and his mother, Saintè Mary.

The Host comments on the tale

	"Eh, Godès mercy!" said our Hostè tho	*then*
2420	"Now such a wife I pray God keep me fro.	*from*
	Lo, whichè sleightès and which subtleties	*See, what tricks*
	In women been. For aye as busy as bees	*For, always*
	Be they, us silly men for to deceive,	
	And from the soothè ever will they weive; [2]	*truth / veer*
2425	By this Merchantè's tale it proveth well.	
	But doubtèless, as true as any steel	
	I have a wife, though that she poorè be,	

---

[1] 2410: "He who misunderstands makes bad judgements."

[2] 2424: "They will always veer from the truth."

But of her tongue a labbing shrew is she
And yet she has a heap of vices mo'.
2430 Thereof no fors, let all such thinges go.   *Never mind*
But wit you what? In counsel be it said   *Do you know? / In confidence*
Me reweth sore I am unto her tied.   *I am v. sorry*
For an I shoulde reckon every vice   *if I should count*
Which that she hath, y-wis I were too nice.   *too foolish*
2435 And cause why? It shall reported be
And told to her of some of this meinie—   *this group*
Of whom, it needeth not for to declare
Since women cannen outen such chaffare[1]
And eke my wit sufficeth not thereto
To tellen all, wherefore my tale is do."   *finished*

---

[1] 2438: "Women like to reveal that sort of thing." Since *outen such chaffare* is a phrase of the Wife of Bath's, and since she openly admitted that women cannot keep secrets for long, it is likely that he is referring to her.

THE CANTERBURY TALES

The Franklin and His Tale

THE FRANKLIN'S TALE

 Introduction

The Franklin's Tale has been taken by many critics to be the final and admirable contribution to the Marriage Group of tales. The Wife's tale insists on female dominance, the Clerk's shows what can happen if male dominance becomes tyrannical, and the Merchant's is a tale of a marriage born in the stupidity and self-indulgence of one partner, and continued in the adultery and deceit of the other. The Franklin advocates tolerance and forebearance on both sides of marriage, a willingness to do each other's will, and to give up the hopeless notion that you can always make your will prevail. Even if you could, it would spell death to any hope of love:

> *When mastery comes, the God of love anon*
> *Beateth his wings, and farewell, he is gone*

But that is not the only trouble a marriage may have to face. The marriage partners in *The Franklin's Tale* have settled for mutual love and forebearance, but then the wife's truth to her marriage promise is tested by the persistence of a young squire who falls in love with her and gets a bad case of "hereos," an affliction that befalls young men who fall hopelessly in love. It includes an inability to talk to the beloved, as well as a strong tendency to write poetry and to take to bed for long periods at a time, sick with love longing. When the young man finally does approach the lady, she rejects his advances, but to soften the blow she lightly makes a rash promise to grant him his wish if he removes all the rocks around the coast which threaten the safe return of her husband. When he seems to accomplish this by magic, she now has to face the "truth," the answer to the question: Which shall she keep, the "troth" she has pledged to her husband in marriage or the troth she has so lightly pledged to Aurelius to breach that marriage? "Truth is the highest thing that man may keep," says her husband when she tells him her dilemma, and he sends her on her way to keep her rash promise to the love-sick squire. Just like that. The disturbing question as to which "troth / truth" takes precedence over which, is not discussed, but brushed aside by the narrator (1493-98).

When she meets the squire on her way to keep the tryst, her words unite three major topics of the tale: marriage, truth, submission. "Where are you going?" he asks:

> Unto the garden, as my husband bade,
> My truthė for to hold, alas! alas!

The squire, impressed by the fidelity of husband and wife to their word, releases her from her promise; the squire now has to keep truth with the magician to whom he has promised a sum that he cannot immediately pay. But in return for his generosity to the wife, he is forgiven his debt also.

For the Franklin, the generosity of all parties, and their fidelity to their word is a display of *gentilesse* or "gentleness," a topic on which Chaucer held forth through the mouth of the hag in *The Wife of Bath's Tale* and in his own ballade called *Gentilesse.* Indeed, *gentilesse* rivals *truth* for frequency of occurrence in this tale.

While all the "gentle" people display *gentilesse,* that is, the kind of magnanimous behavior that was supposed to go with being born into the gentry, the magician, who is not a born patrician, shows *gentilesse* also in a prominent way. He illustrates in his action what the old hag in the Wife's tale had insisted on: that *gentilesse* is not a matter of birth only, but of moral quality.

The Franklin, a country gentleman, is very concerned about being a gentleman, but he professes not to be well educated in Rhetoric, that is, in the art of speaking eloquently. He says he does not really know how to use the "colors" of rhetoric, the arts and tricks of presenting oneself in words: he only knows how to tell a plain, unadorned tale. This is Chaucer's little joke. *The Franklin's Tale* is told with as much skill as any other in the collection, and in fact displays a good many of the "colors" of rhetoric, which Chaucer knew very well how to use, even if his imaginary Franklin says *he* does not. For the Franklin's very protestation of literary incompetence was itself a rhetorical trope or "color" known as the "modesty topos." His little pun on color rhetorical and color literal is another "color." And so on throughout the tale: Dorigen's list of virtuous maidens and wives (1364 ff) is a very obvious rhetorical flourish, and is continued to such lengths as to make one feel that one is supposed to be amused. Chaucer is here probably mocking one aspect of rhetoric (the catalogue) as he does with another in *The Nun's Priest's Tale,* while showing that he knows very well indeed how to use it skilfully.

The story ends with another rhetorical trope, a *demande,* a question to the reader about love, somewhat like those in *The Knight's Tale* and *The Wife of Bath's Tale.* Here the *demande* is: Which of all the characters who kept a promise or forgave a debt was the most generous? Chaucer wisely leaves the answer to the reader.

Some Linguistic Notes for the Franklin's Tale

Word Stress:

It is fairly clear that some words were stressed in the original as we would no longer stress them: *sicknéss* to rhyme fully with *distress* (915-6). *philosópher* to rhyme with *coffer* (1570/1).

Sometimes indeed the same word occurs with different stress in different lines: *cólours, colóurs* (723-4-6); *pénance* (1238), *penánce* (1082); *cértain* and *certáin* (1568 / 719).

Rhyme:

This is sometimes closely related to word stress as the preceding section indicates. *Stable* rhymes with *unreasonable* (871-2), and *tables* with *delitables* (899-900) because they probably had a more French pronunciation than we give them. (See notes to the text). In this version of the tale some other rhymes do not work fully as they would have in the original Middle English as in lines 1145-50. And a rhyme between *yowthè* and *allowe thee* (675/6) may have been a stretch even in Chaucer's day. As *youth* and *allow thee* it does not even come close to rhyme in modern English.

Grammar:

So loath him was, how loath her was: we would now say "so loath he was, or she was." In Chaucer's day the phrases meant literally: "so hateful (to) him or her it was."

The Portrait, Prologue and Tale of the Franklin

The Portrait of the Franklin from the General Prologue

where he is shown as a generous man who enjoys the good things of life.
He travels in the company of a rich attorney, the Man of Law.

	A FRANKÈLIN was in his company.	*rich landowner*
	White was his beard as is the daisy.	
	Of his complexïon he was sanguine.[1]	*ruddy & cheerful*
	Well loved he by the morrow a sop in wine.	*in the a.m.*
335	To livèn in delight was ever his won,	*custom*
	For he was Epicurus's own son	
	That held opinïon that plain delight	*total pleasure*
	Was very felicity perfìte.[2]	*truly perfect happiness*
	A householder and that a great was he;	
340	Saint Julian he was in his country.[3]	
	His bread, his ale, was always after one.	*of one kind i.e. good*
	A better envinèd man was never none.	*with better wine cellar*
	Withouten bakèd meat was never his house	*food*
	Of fish and flesh, and that so plenteous	
345	It snowèd in his house of meat and drink	*food*
	Of allè dainties that men could bethink.	
	After the sundry seasons of the year	*according to*
	So changèd he his meat and his supper.	
	Full many a fat partridge had he in mew	*pen*
350	And many a bream and many a luce in stew.	*fish / in pond*
	Woe was his cook but if his saucè were	

---

[1] 333: *Complexion ... sanguine :* probably means (1) he had a ruddy face and (2) he was of "sanguine humor," i.e. outgoing and optimistic because of the predominance of blood in his system. See "Humors" in Endpapers.

[2] 336-8: Epicurus was supposed to have taught that utmost pleasure was the greatest good (hence "epicure").

[3] 340: St Julian was the patron saint of hospitality

	Poignant and sharp, and ready all his gear.[1]	*tangy*
	His table dormant in his hall alway	*set / always*
	Stood ready covered all the longe day.	
355	At sessïons there was he lord and sire.	*law sessions*
	Full often time he was knight of the shire.	*member of Parliament*
	An anlace and a gipser all of silk	*dagger / purse*
	Hung at his girdle white as morning milk.	
	A sherriff had he been, and a counter.	*tax overseer*
360	Was nowhere such a worthy vavasor.[2]	*gentleman*

The Link to the Tale of the Squire

The Franklin interrupts the tale of the Squire

	"In faith, Squire, thou hast thee well y-quit	*done well*
	And gentilly.[3] I praise well thy wit,"	*your intelligence*
675	Quod the Franklin. "Considering thy youth,	
	So feelingly thou speakest, sir, I allow thee,[4]	*I declare*
	As to my doom, there is none that is here	*In my judgement*
	Of eloquence that shall be thy peer,	
	If that thou live. God give thee good chance.	
680	And in virtue send thee continuance,	
	For of thy speeche I have great dainty.	*satisfaction*
	I have a son, and by the Trinity,	
	I had lever than twenty pound worth land,	*I had rather*
	Though it right now were fallen in my hand	
685	He were a man of such discretion	
	As that you be. Fie on possession,	*What use is wealth?*

---

[1] 351-2: His cook would regret it if his sauce was not sharp ....

[2] 359-60: *sherriff:* "shire reeve," King's representative in a shire, i.e. county. *counter:* overseer of taxes for the treasury. *vavasour:* wealthy gentleman, possibly also a family name.

[3] 673-4: "You have acquitted yourself well, like a gentleman." The *y-* on *y-quit* is a grammatical sign of the past participle. The meaning the same with or without the *y-*.

[4] 675-6: The original rhyme was *yowthe / allowe thee.*

But if a man be virtuous withall.	*Unless / as well*
I have my sonnĕ snibbĕd, and yet shall,	*rebuked*
For he to virtue listeth not intend,	*does not care*
690 But for to play at dice and to dispend	*spend*
And lose all that he hath, is his uságe.	*custom*
And he had lever talken with a page	*had rather*
Than to commune with any gentle wight	*converse / person*
Where he might learnĕ gentilesse aright." [1]	*to be a gentleman*

The Franklin in turn is interrupted by the Host

695 "Straw for thy gentilessĕ," quod our Host.	
"What! Frankelin, pardee sir, well thou wost	*you know well*
That each of you must tellen at the least	
A tale or two, or breaken his behest."	*his promise*
"That know I well, sir," quod the Franklin.	
700 "I pray you haveth me not in disdain,	
Though to this man I speak a word or two."	
"Tell on thy tale withouten wordĕs mo'." [2]	
"Gladly, sir Host," quod he, "I will obey	
Unto your will. Now hearken what I say.	
705 I will you not contráry in no wise,	*not oppose*
As far as that my wittĕs will suffice.	*as best I know how*
I pray to God that it may pleasen you.	
Then wot I well that it is good enow."	*I know / enough*

Prologue to the Franklin's Tale

These oldĕ gentle Bretons in their days	
710 Of diverse áventurĕs maden lays [3]	*stories / made poems*
Rimĕd in their oldĕ Breton tongue;	

---

[1] 694: For the concept of *gentle / gentil* and *gentleness / gentilesse,*" see Introduction above.

[2] 701: "Go on with your story without any more delay."

[3] 710: "They composed poems (*lays*) about various events (*aventures*)." Bretons were and are people of Brittany in France, sometimes called Armorica or Little Britain in contrast to Great Britain.

Which layės with their instruments they sung
Or elsė readen them for their pleasánce.
And one of them have I in rémembránce
715   Which I will say with good will as I can.

A modest disclaimer by the Franklin: I am not a polished speaker

But, sirs, because I am a burel man,   *simple*
At my beginning first I you beseech
Have me excusėd of my rudė speech.   *unpolished*
I learnėd never rhetoric certáin.[1]   *art of speaking*
720   Thing that I speak, it must be bare and plain.
I slept never on the Mount of Parnasso,   *[home of Muses]*
Nor learnėd Marcus Tullius Cicero.   *[Roman orator]*
Colours ne know I none, withouten dread,   *truthfully*
But such coloúrs as growen in the mead   *meadow*
725   Or elsė such as men dye or paint.
Colours of rhetoric be to me quaint.   *strange*
My spirits feeleth not of such mattér.   *I have no taste*
But if you list, my talė you shall hear.   *wish*

The Franklin's Tale

A Knight falls in love with a very highborn lady well above his rank
who nevertheless accepts him

In Armorik, that callėd is Britáin,   *Armorica, Brittany*
730   There was a knight that loved and did his pain   *took pains*
To serve a lady in his bestė wise.
And many a labour, many a great emprise   *enterprise, task*
He for his lady wrought, ere she were won;   *performed, before*
For she was one the fairest under sun,

---

[1] 719: Rhetoric, one of the Seven Liberal Arts, taught skill in writing and speaking. The "colors" of rhetoric were the stylistic "tricks" e.g. a modest disclaimer at the beginning (like the Franklin's), puns like that on "colors," rhetorical questions, exclamations, exempla, elaborate similes, etc. Many of the "colors" are displayed in this tale.

735 And eke thereto come of so high kindred [1]	*also / noble family*
That well unnethès durst this knight for dread	*scarcely dared*
Tell her his woe, his pain, and his distress.	
But at the last she for his worthiness,	
And namely for his meek obeïsance	*especially / humility*
740 Has such a pity caught of his penánce,	*pain*
That privily she fell of his accord	*secretly*
To take him for her husband and her lord,	
Of such lordship as men have o'er their wives.	

They make a special agreement

And for to lead the more in bliss their lives	
745 Of his free will he swore her as a knight	
That ne'er in all his life he day nor night	
Ne should upon him take no mastery [2]	
Against her will, nor kith her jealousy,	*show*
But her obey and follow her will in all,	
750 As any lover to his lady shall—	
Save that the *name* of sovereignty,	
That would he have, for shame of his degree.	*sake of his position*
She thankèd him, and with great humbleness	
She saidè: "Sir, since of your gentilesse	
755 You proffer me to have so large a rein,	*such wide freedom*
Ne wouldè never God bitwixt us twain, [3]	*between us two*
As in my guilt, were either war or strife.	*Through my fault*
Sir, I will be your humble, truè wife—	
Have here my truth—till that mine heartè burst."	
760 Thus been they both in quiet and in rest.	

---

[1] 734-7: "She was the most beautiful woman on earth, and of such an exalted family, that this knight hardly dared to tell her how he ached with love for her."

[2] 744-8: And to lead even happier lives, of his free will he swore to her, as a knight, that he would never throughout his life, day or night, try to be master against her will, or show jealousy. ...

[3] 756-7: "God forbid that there should ever be, through *my* fault, quarreling or fighting between us."

A comment on the qualities of genuine love & the need for patience

> For one thing, sirs, safely dare I say:
> That friendės ever each other must obey
> If they will longė holden company.
> Love will not be constrained by mastery.
765 When mastery comes, the God of Love anon
> Beateth his wings and farewell—he is gone!
> Love is a thing as any spirit free:
> Women of kind desiren liberty,   *by nature*
> And not to be constrainėd as a thrall—   *like a slave*
770 And so do men, if I sooth sayen shall.   *if I tell truth*
> Look who that is most patïent in love:
> He is at his advantage all above.   *above others*
> Patience is a high virtúe, certáin,
> For it vanquisheth (as these clerkės sayn)   *as clerics say*
775 Thingės that rigor never should attain.   *severity*
> For every word men may not chide or 'plain.   *(com)plain*
> Learneth to suffer, or else, so may I go,   *endure / I assure you*
> You shall it learn whether you will or no,
> For in this world, certain, there no wight is   *no person*
780 That he ne does or says sometime amiss.
> Ire, sickness, or constellatïon,   *Anger / the stars*
> Wine, woe, or changing of complexïon   *change of mood*
> Causeth full oft to do amiss or speaken.
> On every wrong a man may not be wreaken.   *avenged*
785 After the timė must be temperance
> To every wight that can on governance.[1]   *knows self control*
> And therefore has this wisė worthy knight
> To live in easė sufferance her behight,   *tolerance promised*
> And she to him full wisly 'gan to swear   *firmly*
790 That never should there be default in her.

---

[1] 785-6: "Everyone who knows anything about self control must show tolerance according to the occasion."

A paradox

> Here may men see a humble wise accord:　　　*agreement*
> Thus hath she take her servant and her lord—
> Servant in love and lord in marrïage.
> Then was he both in lordship and servàge.　　　*servitude*
> 795　Servàgè? Nay, but in lordship above,
> Since he has both his lady and his love—
> His lady, certès, and his wife also,　　　*i.e. his lady is his wife*
> The which that law of love accordeth to.[1]　　　*agrees with*

After some time, the husband goes off to seek knightly honor

> And when he was in this prosperity,
> 800　Home with his wife he goes to his country
> Not far from Pedmark, there his dwelling was,
> Where as he lives in bliss and in soláce.　　　*& comfort*
> Who couldè tell, but he had wedded be,　　　*unless he had*
> The joy, the ease and the prosperity
> 805　That is bitwixt a husband and his wife?
> A year and more lasted his blissful life
> Till that the knight of which I speak of thus—
> That of Kairrúd was cleped Arveragus—　　　*was called A. of K.*
> Shope him to go and dwell a year or twain　　　*Prepared / or two*
> 810　In Engeland that cleped was eke Britain　　　*was also called*
> To seek in armès worship and honoúr　　　*renown*
> (For all his lust he set in such laboúr)　　　*all his desire*
> And dwellèd there two years—the book says thus.

Lamenting the absence of her husband, Dorigen is comforted by her friends.

> Now will I stint of this Arveragus　　　*stop (speaking)*

---

[1] 791-798: Chaucer is here playing with another rhetorical color, the paradox. According to one medieval code of love (literary), a man's beloved was his "mistress," i.e. he did what she said, he was her servant—*in servage*. After marriage, he was her lord and she his lady. Legally he was "master," "lord." Since people often married partners chosen for them, a spouse might not be one's chosen "love." Dorigen and Arveragus are fortunate: they are spouses and lovers at once, an ideal arrangement according to another code of love—*the which that law of love accordeth to.*

815   And speak I will of Dorigen his wife,
That loves her husband as her heartë's life.
For his absénce weepeth she and sigheth
As do these noble wivës when them liketh.
She mourneth, waketh, waileth, fasteth, 'plaineth;   *(com)plains*
820   Desire of his presénce her so distraineth   *upsets*
That all this widë world she set at nought.
Her friendës, which that knew her heavy thought,
Comfort her in all that ever they may.
They preachen her, they tell her night and day
825   That causëless she slays herself, alas—
And every comfort possible in this case
They do to her with all their busyness—
All for to make her leave her heavyness.
By process, as you knowen everyone,   *By persistence*
830   Men may so longë graven in a stone   *carve*
Till some figúre therein emprinted be.
So long have they comfórted her, till she
Receivëd hath, by hope and by reason,
Th'emprinting of their consolatïon,
835   Through which her greatë sorrow 'gan assuage—
She may not always duren in such rage.   *endure such grief*
And eke Arveragus in all this care   *And, besides*
Has sent her letters home of his welfáre
And that he will come hastily again,
840   Or elsë had this sorrow her heartë slain.
Her friendës saw her sorrow 'gan to slake,   *slacken*
And prayëd her on knees, for Godë's sake,
To come and roamen in their company   *stroll*
Away to drive her darkë fantasy;   *gloomy thoughts*
845   And finally she granted that request,
For well she saw that it was for the best.
Now stood her castle fastë by the sea,
And often with her friendës walketh she
Her to disport upon the bank on high   *to relax*

850   Where as she many a ship and bargė saw

      Sailing their course where as them listė go,   *where they wished*

      But then was that a parcel of her woe,   *part*

      For to herself full oft, "Alas!" said she,

      "Is there no ship of so many as I see

855   Will bringen home my lord? Then were mine heart

      All warished of its bitter painės smart."   *cured*

Concerned about the safe return of her husband along the rocky coast,
Dorigen wonders why God creates such dangers

      Another time there would she sit and think

      And cast her eyen downward from the brink—

      But when she saw the grisly rockės black,

860   For very fear so would her heartė quake

      That on her feet she might her not sustain.

      Then would she sit adown upon the green

      And piteously into the sea behold,

      And say right thus, with sorrowful sighės cold:

865   "Eternal God, that through thy purveyance   *providence*

      Leadest the world by certain governance,

      In idle, as men say, you nothing make.   *In vain*

      But Lord, these grisly fiendly rockės black,   *devilish*

      That seemen rather a foul confusïon

870   Of work, than any fair creatïon

      Of such a perfect wisė God and a stable,

      Why have you wrought this work unreasonáble?[1]

      For by this work—south, north, nor west nor east—

      There n'is y-fostred man nor bird nor beast.   *is not nourished*

875   It doth no good, to my wit, but annoyeth.   *in my opinion*

      See you not, Lord, how mankind it destroyeth?

      A hundred thousand bodies of mankind

---

[1] 871-2: *stable / unreasonable:* the rhyme presupposes a somewhat French pronunciation for these words in Middle English with a stress on the last syllable of *unreasonáble*.

	Have rockės slain, all be they not in mind,	*though not*
	Which mankind is so fair part of thy work	*This mankind*
880	That thou it madest like to thine own mark.	*image*
	Then seemėd it you had great charity	*love*
	Toward mankind. But how then may it be	
	That you such meanės make it to destroy,	
	Which meanės do no good, but ever annoy?	
885	I wot well clerks will sayen as them lest	*I know / as they like to*
	By arguments that all is for the best,[1]	
	Though I ne can the causes not y-know,	*I don't know*
	But thilkė God that made the wind to blow,	*But (may) that God*
	As keep my lord! This my conclusïon.	*Protect my husband*
890	To clerks let I all disputatïon—	*To scholars*
	But wouldė God that all these rockės black	*I wish to God*
	Were sunken into hellė for his sake!	
	These rockės slay mine heartė for the fear!"	
	Thus would she say with many a piteous tear.	

Her friends take her to a dance in a lovely garden

895	Her friendės saw that it was no disport	*no recreation*
	To roamen by the sea, but díscomfòrt,	
	And shopen for to playen somewhere else.	*And planned to relax*
	They leaden her by rivers and by wells,	
	And eke in other places délitàbles;[2]	*delightful*
900	They dauncen and they play at chess and tables.	*checkers*
	So on a day, right in the morrowtide,	*morning*
	Unto a garden that was there beside	
	In which that they had made their ordinance	*given orders*
	Of vítaille, and of other purveyance,	*for food / necessities*
905	They go and play them all the longė day.	*amuse themselves*

---

[1] 885-6: "I know well that scholars will say, as they like to do, and produce arguments (to prove), that everything that happens is for the best."

[2] 899-900: *places delitables / tables:* Not only does the adjective *delitables* come after the noun *places,* but it is pluralized, French fashion. It is also stressed in French fashion: *délitàbles.*

And this was on the sixthe morrow of May,

Which May had painted with its softe showers   *This May*

This garden full of leaves and of flowers;

And craft of manne's hand so curiously   *skill / ingeniously*

910 Arrayed had this garden truly

That never was there garden of such price

But if it were the very Paradise.   *Unless / real Paradise*

The odour of flowers and the freshe sight

Would have maked any hearte light

915 That ever was born, but if too great sickness   *unless*

Or too great sorrow held it in distress,

So full it was of beauty with pleasánce.

At after-dinner they began to dance

And sing also, save Dorigen alone,

920 Which made always her cómplaint and her moan,   *Which = Who*

For she ne saw him on the dance go

That was her husband and her love also.

But natheless she must a time abide,   *wait a while*

And with good hope let her sorrow slide.

A young man falls secretly and painfully in love with Dorigen

925 Upon this dance, amongst other men,

Danced a squire before Dorigen

That fresher was and jollier of array,

As to my doom, than is the month of May.   *my judgement*

He singeth, danceth, passing any man   *surpassing*

930 That is or was since that the world began.

Therewith he was, if men him should describe,

One of the beste faring man alive.   *best looking*

Young, strong, right virtuous, and rich, and wise,   *very virile*

And well-beloved, and holden in great prize.   *highly regarded*

935 And shortly, if the sooth I tellen shall,   *truth*

Unwitting of this Dorigen at all,   *unknown to*

This lusty squire, servant to Venus—[1]   *lover*

---

[1] Venus is the goddess of love, hence a "servant of Venus" is a lover.

	Which that y-cleped was Aurelius—	*Who was called*
	Had loved her best of any creäture	
940	Two years and more, as was his áventure;	*destiny*
	But never durst he tellen her his grievance.	*never dared*
	Withouten cup he drank all his penance.[1]	
	He was despairèd—nothing durst he say,	*in despair / dared*
	Save in his songès somewhat would he wray	*display*
945	His woe, as in a general cómplaining.	
	He said he loved, and was beloved no thing,	
	Of whichè matter made he many lays,	*poems*
	Songs, complaints, roundels, virelays,	*(kinds of poem)*
	How that he durstè not his sorrow tell,	
950	But languished as a fury does in hell.	
	And die he must, he said, as did Echó	
	For Nárcissus that durst not tell her woe.	*Ovid, "Met," III, 370*
	In other manner than you hear me say	
	Ne durst he not to her his woe bewray,	*show, reveal*
955	Save that peráventure sometimes at dances	
	Where youngè folkè keep their observánces	
	It may well be he lookèd on her face	
	In such a wise as man that asketh grace—	*favor*
	But nothing wistè she of his intent.	*she knew nothing*

The lover finally makes his advance

960	Natheless, it happened ere they thencè went,	
	Becausè that he was her neighèboúr	
	And was a man of worship and honoúr,	
	And had y-knowèn him of timè yore,	*(she) had known*
	They fell in speech, and forthè more and more	*& ever closer*
965	Unto his purpose drew Aurelius,	

---

[1] 942: *Penance,* normally a word used in religious contexts, is a word frequently used in the Middle Ages for the pain of unsatisfied love. Hence the line seems to mean "He drank the pains of love to the dregs" (without a measuring cup). *Penánce / grievánce,* like some other words in Chaucer, probably had a French stress an the last syllable.

And when he saw his time he saidė thus:

"Madame," quod he, "by God that this world made,

So that I wist it might your heartė glad,[1]   *gladden*

I would that day that your Arveragus

970 Went o'er the sea that I, Aurelius,

Had went where never I should have come again!

For well I wot my service is in vain—   *I know*

My guerdon is but bursting of mine heart.   *reward*

Madame, rueth upon my painės smart,   *have pity*

975 For with a word you may me slay or save!

Here at your feet God would that I were grave!   *buried*

I have as now no leisure more to say—[2]

Have mercy, sweet, or you will do me die!"   *cause me to*

She gan to look upon Aurelius:

980 "Is this your will?" quod she, "and say you thus?

Never erst," quod she, "ne wist I what you meant.   *before / knew*

But now, Aurelius, I knowė your intent,

By thilkė God that gave me soul and life,   *that God*

Ne shall I never be an untrue wife

985 In word nor work. As far as I have wit,   *as I know how*

I will be his to whom that I am knit—

Take this for final answer as of me."

Dorigen makes a tactical error

But after that in playė thus said she: *in jest*

"Aurelius," quod she, "by highė God above,

990 Yet would I grantė you to be your love,

Since I you see so piteously complain.

Look what day that endalong Britáin   *whole length of*

You remove all the rockės, stone by stone,

That they ne lettė ship nor boat to gon—   *they do not hinder*

---

[1] 968-72: This passage makes much more sense without line 968, whether "So that" means "If" or "Since": "If (Since) I knew it might gladden your heart."

[2] 977: A very odd line with which to finish such a passionate outburst.

995   I say, when you have made the coast so clean
      Of rockės that there is no stone y-seen,
      Then will I love you best of any man—
      Have here my truth, in all that ever I can.
      For well I wot that it shall ne'er betide.   *I know / never occur*
1000 Let such follies out of your heartė slide!
      What dainty should a man have in his life   *satisfaction*
      For to go love another mannė's wife
      That hath her body when so that him liketh!"
      Aurelius full often sorė sigheth.
1005 "Is there no other grace in you?" quod he.   *favor*
      "No, by that Lord," quod she, "that maked me."[1]
      Woe was Aurelius when that he this heard,
      And with a sorrowful heart he thus answered.
      "Madame," quod he, "this were an impossíble!"
1010 Then must I die of sudden death horríble!"
      And with that word he turnėd him anon.
         Then came her other friendės many a one,
      And in the alleys roamėd up and down,
      And nothing wist of this conclusïon.   *knew / arrangement*
1015 But suddenly began the revel new
      Till that the brightė sun had lost his hue,   *his color*
      For the horizon had reft the sun his light—   *robbed*
      This is as much to say as it was night—
      And home they go in joy and in soláce,
1020 Save only wretch Aurelius, alas.   *wretched*
      He to his house is gone with sorrowful heart.
      He sees he may not from his death astart: *escape*
      Him seemėd that he felt his heartė cold.
      Up to the heavens he his hands 'gan hold,
1025 And on his barė knees he set him down
      And in his raving said his orisoun.   *prayer*
      For very woe out of his wit he braid.   *he was going mad*

---

[1] 1005-06: I follow Manly-Rickert's suggestion in putting these 2 lines here rather than after 998.

Aurelius prays to the gods for a miracle—a special tide

He n'istè what he spoke, but thus he said—   *didn't know*

With piteous heart his 'plaint hath he begun   *(com)plaint*

1030 Unto the gods, and first unto the sun.

He said, "Apollo, god and governor   *Apollo = the Sun*

Of every plant and herb and tree and flower,

That givest after thy declinatïon   *according to point in sky*

To each of them its time and its season

1035 As thine harbérow changeth, low or high:[1]   *place in zodiac*

Lord Phoebus, cast thy merciable eye   *Phoebus = Apollo*

On wretch Aurelius which that am but lorn!   *who am lost*

Lo, Lord, my lady hath my death y-sworn   *sworn*

Withouten guilt, but thy benignity   *unless thy goodness*

1040 Upon my deadly heart have some pity.   *my broken heart*

For well I wot, Lord Phoebus, if you lest,   *I know / if it please you*

You may me helpen—save my lady—best.

Now voucheth safe that I may you devise   *allow me to suggest*

How that I may be helped, and in what wise.

1045 Your blissful sister, Lucina the sheen,   *(the moon) bright*

That of the sea is chief goddess and queen

(Though Neptunus have deity in the sea,   *Neptune is god*

Yet empéress aboven him is she)

You know well, Lord, that—right as her desire

1050 Is to be quicked and lighted of your fire,   *given life by*

For which she followeth you full busily—

Right so the sea desireth naturally

To follow her, as she that is goddess

Both in the sea and rivers more and less.   *large and small*

1055 Wherefore, Lord Phoebus, this is my request: *Apollo=god of sun*

---

[1] 1031-54: Chaucer liked to show off his considerable astronomical knowledge. Here he shows that he knows all about the relationship among the sun, the moon and the tides. In the following section (1055 ff) Aurelius is asking that the laws of nature be suspended so that the sea can cover the rocks for two years. For a full discussion of the astrophysics involved see J.D. North, *Chaucer's Universe* pp. 423 ff.

Do this miracle—or do mine heartè burst—   *or cause my heart*
That now next at this oppositïon,
Which in the sign shall be of the Lion,   *sign of Leo*
As prayeth her so great a flood to bring
1060 That fivè fathoms at least it overspring
The highest rock in Armoric Britáin   *in Brittany*
And let this flood endurè yearès twain.   *two*
Then certès to my lady may I say,
'Holdeth your hest, the rockès be away!'   *Keep your promise*
1065 Lord Phoebus, do this miracle for me!
Pray her she go no faster course then ye.   *"her" = Moon*
I say this: pray your sister that she go
No faster course than you these yearès two.
Then shall she be e'en at the full alway,   *"e'en" = uniformly*
1070 And spring-flood lastè bothè night and day.
And but she vouchèsafe in such mannér   *agree*
To grantè me my sovereign lady dear,
Pray her to sinken every rock adown
Into her ownè darkè regïon
1075 Under the ground where Pluto dwelleth in,   *god of underworld*
Or never more shall I my lady win.
Thy temple in Delphos will I barefoot seek.
Lord Phoebus, see the tearès on my cheek,
And of my pain have some compassïon."
1080 And with that word in swoon he fell adown,
And longè time he lay forth in a trance.
His brother, which that knew of his penánce,   *distress*
Up caught him, and to bed he hath him brought.
Despairèd in this torment and this thought
1085 Let I this woeful creäturè lie—
Choose he for me whether he will live or die.   *for all I care*

The husband returns safely

Arveragus with health and great honoúr,
As he that was of chivalry the flower,
Is comen home, and other worthy men.

1090　Oh, blissful art thou now, thou Dorigen,
　　　　That hast thy lusty husband in thine arms,
　　　　The freshė knight, the worthy man of arms.
　　　　That loveth thee as his own heartė's life!
　　　　No thing list him to been imaginative
1095　If any wight had spoke while he was out　　*any person / was away*
　　　　To her of love; he had of it no doubt.　　*no suspicion*
　　　　He not entendeth to no such mattér,[1]　　*didn't think of*
　　　　But danceth, jousteth, maketh her good cheer.

The lover's pain

　　　　And thus in joy and bliss I let them dwell,
1100　And of the sick Aurelius will I tell.
　　　　In labour and in torment furious
　　　　Two years and more lay wretch Aurelius,　　*wretched*
　　　　Ere any foot he might on earthė go.
　　　　Nor comfort in this time ne had he none,
1105　Save of his brother, which that was a clerk.
　　　　He knew of all this woe and all this work,
　　　　For to no other creäture, certain,
　　　　Of this matter he durst no wordė sayn.　　*dared*
　　　　Under his breast he bore it more secree　　*secretly*
1110　Than ever did Pamphilus for Galathee.[2]
　　　　His breast was whole withoutė for to seen,　　*healthy on outside*
　　　　But in his heart aye was the arrow keen:　　*always was / sharp*
　　　　And well you know that of a sursanure　　*wound*
　　　　In surgery is perilous the cure,　　*hard to cure*
1115　But men might touch the arrow or come thereby.[3]　　*Unless one*

A possible remedy: magic

　　　　His brother wept and wailėd privily,

---

[1] 1094-97: "It did not even occur to him that anyone had been making advances to his wife while he was away." The passage says much the same thing twice.

[2] 1110: Characters in a medieval love poem.

[3] 1113-15: "You know that a wound only superficially healed (*a sursanure*) is very difficult to treat, unless you can get at the arrow" (buried in the flesh).

Till at the last him fell in rémembránce   *he remembered*
That while he was at Orleäns in France—   *university town*
As youngė clerkės that been likerous   *eager*
1120 To readen artės that been curious,   *arcane studies*
Seek in every halk and every herne   *hole and corner*
Particular sciénces for to learn—   *areas of knowledge*
He him remembered that, upon a day,
At Orleans in a study a book he saw
1125 Of magic natural,[1] which his fellow,   *fellow student*
That was that time a bachelor of law
(Al were he there to learn another craft)   *although*
Had privily upon his desk y-left.
Which book spoke much of th'operatïons
1130 Touching the eight and twenty mansïons   *daily positions*
That longen to the moon, and such folly   *belong to*
As in our dayės is not worth a fly
(For Holy Church's faith in our belief
Nor suffers no illusïon us to grieve).   *allows no*
1135 And when this book was in his rémembránce,
Anon for joy his heartė 'gan to dance   *At once*
And to himself he saidė privily:
"My brother shall be warished hastily!   *cured soon*
For I am siker that there be sciénces   *sure / skills*
1140 By which men maken diverse "ápparénces,"   *illusions*
Such as these subtle tregetourės play.   *magicians*
For oft at feastės have I well heard say
That tregetoures within a hallė large
Have made come in a water and a barge,

---

[1] 1125: *Magic natural* was felt to be distinct from "black magic" in which diabolical forces were invoked. "Natural magic," on the other hand, used observations of the planets and stars, and knowledge of their "influence" on human affairs to make predictions. The brother seems to feel that an astrologer practising "magic natural" who was also a *tregetour,* a magician who produced illusions, would be the perfect one for this job, "a piece of sheer ignorance on the brother's part" according to North, p. 427.

1145 And in the hallë rowen up and down;
　　　Some time hath seemed to come a grim lion;
　　　Some timë flowers spring as in a mead,　　　　　　　*meadow*
　　　Some time a vine, and grapës white and red,
　　　Some time a castle all of lime and stone,
1150 And when them likëd, voided it anon—
　　　Thus seemëd it to every mannë's sight.
　　　Now then conclude I thus, that if I might
　　　At Orleans some old fellow y-find　　　　　　　*fellow student*
　　　That had these moonë's mansïons in mind,
1155 Or other magic natural above,　　　　　　　*(See 1125, note)*
　　　He should well make my brother have his love.
　　　For with an "ápparence" a clerk may make　　　　*magic illusion*
　　　To mannë's sight that all the rockës black
　　　Of Britain were y-voided every one,　　　　　*taken away*
1160 And shippës by the brinkë come and gon,　　　*shore*
　　　And in such form endure a week or two.
　　　Then were my brother warished of his woe!　　*would be cured*
　　　Then must she needës holden her behest,　　　*keep her promise*
　　　Or elsë he shall shame her at the least."

The possibility of success rouses Aurelius enough to go to Orleans

1165 What should I make a longer tale of this?
　　　Unto his brother's bed he comen is,
　　　And such comfórt he gave him for to gon
　　　To Orleans, that up he starts anon
　　　And on his way forward then is he fare,　　　*he has set out*
1170 In hope for to be lissëd of his care.　　　　*relieved*
　　　When they were come almost to that city,
　　　But if it were a furlong two or three,　　*within a furlong = 1/8 mile*
　　　A young clerk roaming by himself they met,
　　　Which that in Latin thriftily them gret,　　*courteously greeted*
1175 And after that he said a wonder thing:
　　　"I know," quod he, "the cause of your coming."

And ere they further any footé went,
He told them all that was in their intent.
This Breton clerk him askéd of fellows   *asked about*
1180 The which that he had known in olden days,
And he him answered that they deadé were—
For which he wept full often many a tear.
Down off his horse Aurelius lights anon,   *dismounts*
And with this magician forth is he gone
1185 Home to his house, and made them well at ease.
Them lackéd no vitaille that might them please.   *victuals, food*
So well arrayéd house as there was one   *as this one was*
Aurelius in his life saw never none.

The magician displays some of his skills

He showed him ere he wenté to suppér
1190 Forests, parkés full of wildé deer.
There saw he hartés with their hornés high,   *stags*
The greatest that ever were seen with eye;
He saw of them an hundred slain with hounds,
And some with arrows bled of bitter wounds.
1195 He saw, when voided were these wildé deer,   *removed*
These falconers upon a fair rivér,
That with their hawkés have the heron slain.
Then saw he knightés jousting in a plain.
And after this he did him such pleasánce,
1200 That he him showed his lady on a dance,
On which himself he dancéd—as him thought,
And when this master that this magic wrought
Saw it was time, he clapped his handés two,
And farewell! All our revel was ago.   *gone*
1205 And yet removed they never out of the house
While they saw all this sighté marvelous,
But in his study, there as his bookés be,
They sitten still, and no wight but they three.   *nobody*
To him this master calléd his squire

1210 And said him thus: "Is ready our suppér?
　　　Almost an hour it is, I undertake,
　　　Since I you bade our supper for to make,
　　　When that these worthy men wenten with me
　　　Into my study there as my bookės be."
1215 "Sir," quod this squire, "when that it liketh you,　　*when you please*
　　　It is all ready, though you will right now."
　　　"Go we then sup," quod he, "as for the best;
　　　These amorous folk some time must have their rest."

They agree quickly on the magician's fee

　　　At after-supper fell they in treaty　　　*they negotiated*
1220 What summė should this master's guerdon be　　*fee, reward*
　　　To remove all the rockės of Britáin,　　　*Brittany*
　　　And eke from Gironde to the mouth of Seine.　*& also / [rivers]*
　　　He made it strange, and swore, so God him save,[1]　*tough*
　　　Less than a thousand pounds he would not have,
1225 Nor gladly for that sum he would not gon.[2]
　　　Aurelius with blissful heart anon
　　　Answered thus: "Fie on a thousand pound!
　　　This widė world, which that men say is round,
　　　I would it give, if I were lord of it.
1230 This bargain is full drive, for we been knit.　　*we are agreed*
　　　You shall be payėd truly, by my truth.
　　　But look now, for no negligence nor sloth,
　　　You tarry us here no longer than tomorrow."　　*do not delay*
　　　"Nay," quod this clerk, "have here my faith to borrow." *as pledge*
1235 To bed is gone Aurelius when him lest,　　　*when he pleased*
　　　And well nigh all that night he had his rest,
　　　What for his labour and his hope of bliss,
　　　His woeful heart of penance had a liss.　　　*a rest*

---

[1] 1223: "He drove a hard bargain, and swore that as sure as he hoped to be saved …"

[2] 1224-5: Scholars who think that the clerk's fee is steep "could do worse than themselves attempt the computational part" of his work. (North, 153)

They return to Brittany. December weather

       Upon the morrow, when that it was day

1240 To Brittany they took the righte way,   *direct route*

       Aurelius and this magicïan beside,

       And been descended where they would abide.[1]

       And this was, as these bookes me remember,   *remind me*

       The colde frosty season of December.

1245 Phoebus waxed old and hued like latten,   *colored / brass*

       That in his hote declination   *high point*

       Shone as the burned gold with streames bright.

       But now in Capricorn adown he light,   *sign of zodiac*

       Where as he shone full pale, I dare well sayn.[2]

1250 The bitter frostes with the sleet and rain

       Destroyed hath the green in every yard.

       Janus sits by the fire with double beard

       And drinketh of his bugle horn the wine,

       Before him stands brawn of the tusked swine,   *meat*

1255 And "Nowel!" crieth every lusty man.   *Noel, Christmas*

       Aurelius in all that ever he can   *in every way*

       Doth to this master cheer and reverence,   *shows proper respect*

       And prayeth him to do his diligence   *do his best*

       To bringen him out of his paines smart,   *sharp*

1260 Or with a sword that he would slit his heart.

The magician's preparations and the result

       This subtle clerk such ruth had of this man   *pity*

       That night and day he sped him that he can   *tried his best*

       To wait a time of his conclusïon—   *To find*

       This is to sayn, to make illusïon

1265 By such an "ápparence" or jugglery

---

[1] 1242: "And they dismounted where they intended to stay," i.e. when they reached their destination.

[2] 1245-9: The sun which had sent out streams of burning gold during the summer *(in his hot declination)* has grown feeble and brass-colored and now shines weakly in Capricorn (close to winter solstice).

(I can no termės of astrology) [1]
That she and every wight should ween and say   *everyone should think*
That of Britáin the rockės were away,
Or elsė they were sunken under ground.
1270 So at the last he hath his time y-found
To make his japės and his wretchedness   *tricks*
Of such a superstitious cursedness.
His tables Tolletanės forth he brought   *astronomical tables*
Full well corrected. Nor there lackėd nought,
1275 Neither his cóllect nor his éxpanse years,
Neither his rootės, nor his other gears,
As been his centres and his arguments,
And his proportionals convenient,
For his equatïons in every thing.
1280 And by his eighthė sphere in his working
He knew full well how far Alnath was shove   *a star or "mansion"*
From the head of thilkė fixed Aries above
That in the ninthė sphere considered is—
Full subtly he calculėd all this.   *calculated*
1285 When he had found his firstė mansïon,
He knew the remnant by proportïon,
And knew the rising of his moonė well,
And in whose face and term, and every deal,
And knew full well the moonė's mansïon
1290 Accordant to his operatïon,
And knew also his other óbservánces
For such illusïons and such mischances
As heathen folkė used in thilkė days.[2]

---

[1] 1266: That the narrator knows more "terms of astrology" than most of his audience is very clear from the passages that soon follow. According to North not one of the astronomical terms here used is misplaced or inappropriate. It is not necessary to understand these terms to get most of the point.

[2] 1292-3: This and lines 1125-34 above imply that some astrology was not considered legitimate, and the narrator—who knows so much about it—is now trying to distance himself.

For which no longer maked he delays,
1295 But, through his magic, for a week or tway
It seemed that all the rockes were away.

Aurelius's gratitude to the magician

Aurelius, which that yet despaired is
Whe'r he shall have his love or fare amiss,[1]
Awaiteth night and day on this miracle.
1300 And when he knew that there was no obstacle,
That voided were these rockes every one,
Down to his master's feet he fell anon
And said, "I, woeful wretch Aurelius,
Thank you, lord, and lady mine Venus,
1305 That me have holpen from my cares cold!"   *helped*

His demand to Dorigen

And to the temple his way forth hath he hold,
Where as he knew he should his lady see.
And when he saw his time, anon-right he   *right away*
With dreadful heart and with full humble cheer   *filled with dread*
1310 Saluted has his sovereign lady dear: *greeted*
"My righte lady," quod this woeful man,
"Whom I most dread and love as best I can,   *most respect*
And lothest were of all this world displease,   *most unwilling*
Ne're it that I for you have such dis-ease   *were it not / pain*
1315 That I must die here at your feet anon,
Nought would I tell how me is woe-begone.
But certes either must I die or 'plain.   *speak my grief*
You slay me guiltless for very pain.
But of my death though that you have no ruth,   *no pity*
1320 Aviseth you ere that you break your truth.
Repenteth you, 'fore thilke God above,   *before that God*
Ere you me slay because that I you love.

---

[1] 1297-8: "Aurelius, desperate (to know) whether (*Whe'r*) he will get his lover or miss out ..."

For, Madame, well you wot what you have hight	*know / agreed*
(Not that I challenge any thing of right	*demand / by rights*
1325 Of you, my sovereign lady, but your grace).	*your favor*
But in a garden yond at such a place,	*yonder*
You wot right well what you behighten me,	*you know / promised*
And in mine hand your truthe plighted ye	*you pledged*
To love me best. God wot you saide so,	*God knows*
1330 All be that I unworthy am thereto.	*although*
Madame, I speak it for the honour of you	
More than to save mine hearte's life right now:	
I have done so as you commanded me,	
And if you vouchesafe, you may go see.	*if you please*
1335 Do as you list, have your behest in mind,	*as you wish / promise*
For quick or dead right there you shall me find.	*alive or dead*
In you lies all to do me live or die,	*cause me to*
But well I wot the rockes been away."	*I know*

Dorigen's dismay

He takes his leave and she astonished stood.	
1340 In all her face there n'as a drop of blood.	*wasn't a drop*
She wende never have come in such a trap.	*never thought*
"Alas," quod she, "that ever this should hap.	*happen*
For wend I never by possibility	
That such a monster or marvel mighte be!	
1345 It is against the process of natúre."	
And home she goes a sorrowful crëatúre;	
For very fear unnethe may she go.	*scarcely walk*
She weepeth, waileth all a day or two,	
And swooneth that it ruthe was to see.	*pitiful to see*
1350 But why it was, to no wight told it she,	*to nobody*
For out of town was gone Arveragus.	
But to herself she spoke and saide thus,	
With face pale and with full sorrowful cheer	
In her complaint, as you shall after hear:	

She will die rather than be unfaithful

1355	"Alas," quod she, "on thee, Fortúne, I 'plain,	*complain*
	That unaware hast wrapped me in thy chain,	
	From which t'escapė wot I no succoúr	*I know no help*
	Save only death or elsė dishonoúr—	
	One of these two behooveth me to choose.	*I must*
1360	But natheless yet have I lever lose	*had rather*
	My life than of my body to have a shame,	
	Or know myselfen false, or lose my name;	*(good) name*
	And with my death I may be quit, ywis.	*indeed*
	Has there not many a noble wife ere this,	
1365	And many a maid y-slain herself, alas,	
	Rather than with her body do trespass?	*do wrong*
	Yes, certės, lo, these stories bear witness.[1]	

She cites many models of wifely chastity from classical history and legend

	When thirty tyrants full of cursedness	
	Had slain Phidón in Athens at the feast,	
1370	They commanded his daughters for t'arrest,	*be arrested*
	And bringen them before them in despite	*contempt*
	All naked, to fulfill their foul delight;	
	And in their father's blood they made them dance	
	Upon the pavement—God give them mischance!	
1375	For which these woeful maidens, full of dread,	
	Rather than they would lose their maidenhead,	*virginity*
	They privily been start into a well	*jumped*
	And drowned themselvės, as the bookės tell.	
	They of Messina let enquire and seek	*let = caused*
1380	Of Lacedaemon fifty maidens eke,	*also*

---

[1] 1366 ff: The following list of over 20 wives, maidens or widows who destroyed themselves rather than be sexually dishonored is an unusually extended list of *exempla,* one of the "colors" of rhetoric that the Franklin said he knew nothing about. The details of the cases adduced need not concern us. They are all taken from the same anti-matrimonial book by St Jerome that the Wife of Bath was at pains to refute in parts of her Prologue.

On which they woulden do their lechery.
But there was none of all that company [1]
That she n'as slain, and with a good intent   *and gladly*
Chose rather for to die than to assent
1385 To be oppressèd of her maidenhead.   *raped*
Why should I then to dien be in dread?
Lo, eke, the tyrant Aristoclides   *also*
That loved a maiden hight Stymphalides,   *called*
When that her father slain was on a night,
1390 Unto Diana's temple goes she right   *straight*
And hent the image in her handès two,   *grasped*
From which imáge would she never go.
No wight ne might her hands of it arace,   *tear*
Till she was slain right in the selfè place.   *same place*
1395 Now since that maidens hadden such despite   *disdain*
To been defoulèd with man's foul delight,
Well ought a wife rather herselfen slay
Than be defoulèd, as it thinketh me.
What shall I say of Hasdrubalè's wife
1400 That at Cartháge bereft herself her life?
For when she saw that Romans won the town,
She took her children all and skipped adown
Into the fire, and chose rather to die
Than any Roman did her villainy.   *should violate her*
1405 Hath not Lucrece y-slain herself, alas,   *killed*
At Rome when that she oppressèd was   *raped*
Of Tarquin, for her thought it was a shame   *By Tarquin*
To liven when that she had lost her name?
The seven maidens of Milesia also
1410 Have slain themselves for very dread and woe
Rather than folk of Gaul them should oppress.
More then a thousand stories, as I guess,
Could I now tell as touching this mattér.

---

[1] 1382-5: "But there was not one of that group of maidens who did not die gladly rather than agree to be robbed of her virginity."

When Habradate was slain, his wife so dear
1415 Herselfen slew, and let her blood to glide
In Habradate's woundès deep and wide,
And said, 'My body at the leastè way
There shall no wight defoulen, if I may!'   *nobody*
What should I more examples hereof sayn?
1420 Since that so many have themselven slain
Well rather than they would defoulèd be,
I will conclude that it is bet for me   *better*
To slay myself than be defoulèd thus.
I will be true unto Arveragus,
1425 Or rather slay myself in some mannér—
As did Democïonès's daughter dear,
Because that she would not defoulèd be.
O Cedasus, it is full great pity
To readen how thy daughters died, alas,
1430 That slew themselves for such a manner case!
As great a pity was it, or well more,   *or worse*
The Theban maiden that for Nichanor
Herselfen slew right for such manner woe.
Another Theban maiden did right so
1435 For one of Macedon had her oppressed,   *Because a Macedonian*
She with her death her maidenhead redressed.
What shall I say of Niceratès' wife
That for such case bereft herself her life?
How true eke was to Alcibiades   *also*
1440 His love, that rather for to dien chose
Than for to suffer his body unburied be?   *allow*
Lo, which a wife was Alcestis," quod she.   *what a wife*
"What says Homer of good Penelope?
All Greecè knoweth of her chastity.
1445 Pardee, of Laodomia is written thus,   *By God*
That when at Troy was slain Protheselaus,
No longer would she live after his day.
The same of noble Portia tell I may:

Withouten Brutus coulde she not liven,
1450 To whom she had all whole her hearte given.
The perfect wifehood of Arthemesie
Honoúred is through all the Barbary. *pagan lands*
O Teuta queen, thy wifely chastity
To allé wivés may a mirror be!
1455 The samé thing I say of Bilyea,
Of Rodogone, and eke Valeria."

Dorigen informs her husband of her plight

Thus 'plainéd Dorigen a day or two,
Purposing ever that she woulde die.
But natheless upon the thirde night
1460 Home came Arveragus, this worthy knight,
And askéd her why that she wept so sore.
And she gan weepen ever longer the more—
"Alas!" quod she, "that ever I was born!
Thus have I said," quod she, "thus have I sworn."
1465 And told him all as you have heard before;
It needeth not rehearse it you no more. *repeat*
This husband with glad cheer in friendly wise
Answered and said as I shall you devise: *tell*

His unusual response

"Is there ought elsé, Dorigen, but this?"
1470 "Nay, nay," quod she, "God help me so as wis, *indeed*
This is too much, and it were Gode's will." *if it were*
"Yea, wife," quod he, "let sleepen that is still.
It may be well paraunter yet today. *perhaps*
You shall your truthé holden, by my fay, *keep your word / faith*
1475 For God so wisly have mercy upon me,[1] *as sure as*
I had well lever y-stickéd for to be, *rather be stabbed*
For very love which that I to you have,

---

[1] 1475-8: "For as sure as I hope God will have mercy on me—because of the deep love I have for you I had rather be stabbed than that you should fail to keep your promise."

But if you should your truthe keep and save.   *Unless*
Truth is the highest thing that man may keep."
1480 But with that word he burst anon to weep,
And said: "I you forbid, up pain of death,   *on pain*
That never while thee lasteth life nor breath,
To no wight tell thou of this áventure.   *nobody / experience*
As I may best I will my woe endure.
1485 Nor make no countenance of heaviness,   *no show of*
That folk of you may deemen harm or guess."   *suspect*
And forth he cleped a squire and a maid: *he called*
"Go forth anon with Dorigen," he said,
"And bringeth her to such a place anon."
1490 They took their leave, and on their way they gon.
But they ne wisté why she thither went: *did not know*
He would to no wight tellen his intent.   *nobody*
Peráventure a heap of you, ywis,   *Perhaps / indeed*
Will holden him a lewéd man in this,   *stupid*
1495 That he will put his wife in jeopardy.
Hearken the tale ere you upon her cry.   *condemn*
She may have better fortune than you seemeth,
And when that you have heard the talé, deemeth.   *judge*

The lover meets Dorigen on her way to keep her rash promise

This squire which that hight Aurelius,   *was called*
1500 On Dorigen that was so amorous,   *in love with D.*
Of áventuré happened her to meet   *by chance*
Amid the town, right in the quickest street,   *busiest*
As she was bound to go the way forth right   *directly*
Toward the garden there as she had hight.   *where / promised*
1505 And he was to the garden-ward also,
For well he spiéd when she wouldé go
Out of her house to any manner place.
But thus they met of áventure or grace,   *chance or destiny*
And he saluteth her with glad intent,   *greeted*
1510 And askéd of her whitherward she went.
And she answeréd half as she were mad:

"Unto the garden as my husband bade,
My truthė for to hold—alas! alas!"   *My promise*

Impressed, Aurelius finally does the honorable thing

    Aurelius gan wonder on this case,
1515 And in his heart had great compassïon
    Of her and of her lamentatïon,
    And of Arveragus, the worthy knight,
    That bade her holden all that she had hight,   *she had promised*
    So loath him was his wife should break her truth.   *So unwilling*
1520 And in his heart he caught of this great ruth,   *pity*
    Considering the best on every side
    That from his lust yet were him lever abide[1]   *rather desist*
    Than do so high a churlish wretchedness   *high = low*
    Against franchise and allė gentilesse,   *decent & noble conduct*
1525 For which in fewė wordės said he thus:
    "Madáme, say to your lord Arveragus
    That since I see his greatė gentilesse
    To you, and eke I see well your distress
    That him were lever have shame—and that were ruth—[2]
1530 Than you to me should breakė thus your truth,
    I have well lever ever to suffer woe   *I'd much rather*
    Than I depart the love betwixt you two.   *than separate*
    I you release, Madame, into your hand,
    Quit every serement and every bond   *cancel every oath.*
1535 That you have made to me as herebeforn,   *before this*
    Since thilkė time in which that you were born.
    My truth I plight,[3] I shall you ne'er reprove   *I pledge / reproach*

---

[1] 1522-4: "That he would rather desist from satisfying his lust than commit such a low offence against decency and honor." The terms *churlish, franchise, gentilesse* are probably laden with class-conscious rather than moral connotation.

[2] 1529-30: "That he would rather (*lever*) be shamed—and that would be a pity (*ruth*)—than that you should break your word to me."

[3] 1537-8: "I pledge my word, I shall never reproach you for (not fulfilling) a promise (*behest*)."

Of no behest. And here I take my leave,   *About your promise*
As of the truest and the bestë wife
1540 That ever yet I knew in all my life.
But every wife beware of her behest.
On Dorigen remember at the least.
Thus can a squire do a gentle deed
As well as can a knight, withouten dread."   *without doubt*
1545 She thanketh him upon her knees all bare
And home unto her husband is she fare,
And told him all as you have heard me said.
And be you siker, he was so well apaid   *be assured / pleased*
That it were impossíble me to write.
1550 What should I longer of this case endite?   *write*
Arveragus and Dorigen his wife
In sovereign blissë leaden forth their life—
Never eft ne was there anger them between.   *Never again*
He cherished her as though she were a queen,
1555 And she to him was true for evermore.
Of these two folk you get of me no more.

The magician's generous response to Aurelius

Aurelius, that his cost has all forlorn,   *I'm lost*
Curses the time that ever he was born.
"Alas!" quod he, "alas that I behight   *promised*
1560 Of purëd gold a thousand pound of weight
Unto this philosopher. How shall I do?   *scholar-magician*
I see no more but that I am foredo.   *lost, ruined*
My heritagë must I needës sell   *inheritance*
And be a beggar. Here I may not dwell
1565 And shamen all my kindred in this place   *my family*
But I of him may get a better grace.   *Unless / better terms*
But natheless I will of him assay   *try*
At certain dayës year by year to pay
And thank him of his greatë courtesy.
1570 My truthë will I keep, I will not lie."   *My promise*

With heartè sore he goes unto his coffer,
And broughtè gold unto this philosópher
The value of five hundred pounds, I guess,
And him beseecheth of his gentilesse
1575 To grant him dayès of the remenant,[1]
And said: "Master, I dare well make avaunt   *I can boast*
I failèd never of my truth as yet,
For sikerly my debtè shall be quit   *certainly / paid*
Towardès you, however that I fare   *even if I have to*
1580 To go abeggèd in my kirtle bare;   *begging in my shirt*
But would you vouchèsafe upon surety   *grant / pledge*
Two years or three for to respiten me,   *grant delay*
Then were I well. For elsè must I sell   *I'd be alright. Otherwise*
My heritage. There is no more to tell."
1585 This philosopher soberly answered
And saidè thus when he these wordès heard:
"Have I not holden covenant unto thee?"   *kept my agreement*
"Yea, certès well and truly," quod he.
"Hast thou not had thy lady as thee liketh?"
1590 "No! No!" quod he. And sorrowfully he sigheth.
"What was the causè? Tell me if thou can."
Aurelius his tale anon began,
And told him all as you have heard before;
It needeth not to you rehearse it more.   *repeat*
1595 He said: "Arveragus—of gentilesse—   *out of "gentilesse"*
Had lever die in sorrow and distress   *Had rather*
Than that his wife were of her truthè false."
The sorrow of Dorigen he told him als'—   *also*
How loath her was to be a wicked wife,   *How reluctant she was*
1600 And that she lever had lost that day her life,   *had rather*
And that her truth she swore through innocence;
She ne'er erst had heard speak of 'ápparence'.   *never before*
"That made me have of her so great pity.

---

[1] 1575: "To give him time to pay the rest."

And right as freely as he sent her me,
1605 As freely sent I her to him again.
This all and some. There is no more to sayn."
This philosópher answered, "Levé brother,   *dear brother*
Ever each of you did gently to the other.
Thou art a squire, and he is a knight;
1610 But God forbiddé, for His blissful might,
But if a clerk could do a gentle deed
As well as any of you, it is no dread.   *no doubt*
Sir, I release thee of thy thousand pound,
As thou right now were cropped out of the ground   *As if*
1615 Ne ne'er ere now ne haddest knowen me.   *never before now*
For sir, I will not take a penny of thee
For all my craft, nor naught for my travail.   *skill / work*
Thou hast y-payéd well for my vitaille;   *food, victuals*
It is enough. And farewell, have good day"—
1620 And took his horse and forth he goes his way.

Demande d'amour [1]

Lordings, this question will I aské now: *Ladies & gentlemen*
Which was the mosté free, as thinketh you?   *generous*
Now telleth me, ere that you further wend.   *go*
I can no more, my tale is at an end.

---

[1] 1622-3: The *demande* is a question about love put to the readers of some poems or sections of poems.

ENDPAPERS: SELECT GLOSSARY

 Authority, Auctoritee, Authors: The literate in the Middle Ages were remarkably bookish in spite of or because of the scarcity of books. They had a great, perhaps inordinate, regard for "authority," that is, established "authors": philosophers of the ancient world, classical poets, the Bible, the Church Fathers, historians, theologians, etc. Citing an "authority" was then, as now, often a substitute for producing a good argument, and then, as now, always useful to bolster an argument. The opening line of the Wife of Bath's Prologue uses "authority" to mean something like "theory"—what you find in books—as opposed to "experience"—what you find in life.

Clerk: Strictly speaking a member of the clergy, either a priest or in the preliminary stages leading up to the priesthood, called "minor orders." Learning and even literacy were largely confined to such people, but anyone who who could read and write as well as someone who was genuinely learned could be called a clerk. A student, something in between, was also a clerk. The Wife of Bath marries for her fifth husband, a man who had been a clerk at Oxford, a student who had perhaps had ideas at one time of becoming a cleric.

Churl, churlish: At the opposite end of the social scale and the scale of manners from "gentil" (See below). A "churl" (OE "ceorl") was a common man of low rank. Hence the manners to be expected from a person of such "low birth" were equally low and vulgar, "churlish." "Villain" and "villainy" are rough equivalents also used by Chaucer.

Complexion: See Humor below.

Courtesy, Courteous, Courtoisie, etc.: Courtesy was literally conduct appropriate to the court of the king or other worthy. This, no doubt, included our sense of "courtesy" but was wider in its application, referring to the manners of all well bred people. The Prioress's concern to "counterfeit cheer of court" presumably involves imitating all the mannerisms thought appropriate to courtiers. Sometimes it is used to mean something like right, i.e. moral, conduct.

Daun, Don: Sir. A term of respect for nobles or for clerics like the monk. The Wife of Bath refers to the wise "king Daun Solomon," a phrase where it would be wise to leave the word untranslated. But Chaucer uses it also of Gervase, the blacksmith in the Miller's Tale. And Spenser used it of Chaucer himself.

Daunger, Daungerous: These do not mean modern "danger" and "dangerous." "Daunger" (from OF "daungier") meant power—in romantic tales the power that a woman had over a man who was sexually attracted by her. She was his "Mistress" in the sense that she had power over him, often to refuse him the least sexual favor. Hence "daungerous" often indicated a woman who was "hard-to-get" or over-demanding or disdainful, haughty, aloof.

Dreams: There was a good deal of interest in dream theory in the Middle Ages, and considerable difference of opinion: some held that dreams were generally inconsequential, others that dreams often were of considerable significance. Those of the "significant" school had biblical support from both testaments e.g. Pharaoh's dream of the fat cows and lean cows and Joseph's interpretation (Gen. 41) and many others in the OT, and in the NT, e.g. the other Joseph's dreams that assured him that Mary his wife was pregnant with Christ through divine intervention (Matt. 1:20, 2:13-20). They also had Macrobius's famous *Commentary on the Dream of Scipio* which distinguished between 5 different kinds of dream, 3 of them significant ("visio, somnium, and oraculum") and 2 insignificant ("insomnium" and " visum" or "phantasma"). The first 3 were felt to be prophetic in one way or another by Macrobius; the other 2 either simply carried on the worries or desires of the day, or were formed of disconnected and fragmentary images (phantasma) supposedly the result of indigestion. These last two, of least interest to the philosopher, might be of more interest to the psychologist and poet. Chaucer has several dream vision poems, in most of which he has some discussion of dream theory: *The Book of the Duchess, The House of Fame, The Legend of Good Women, The Parliament of Fowls,* especially the opening of *House of Fame* on the causes and significance of dreams. The argument of Chanticleer with Pertelote about the value of his dream in *The Nun's Priest's Tale* illustrates the common medieval disagreements, and brings up references to a number of the authorities that have been mentioned above.

The most influential sources of the tradition of writing dream poems were Boethius's *Consolation of Philosophy* and the *Romance of the Rose,* a French poem of the early 13th century. Chaucer had translated both of these in whole or in part.

Gentle, Gentil, Gentilesse, Gentleness: "Gentilesse" (Gentleness) is the quality of being "gentil" or "gentle" i.e. born into the upper class, and having "noble" qualities that were supposed to go with noble birth. It survives in the word "gentleman" especially in a phrase like "an officer & a gentleman" since officers traditionally were members of the ruling class. Chaucer seems to have had a healthy sceptical bourgeois view of the notion that "gentilesse" went always with "gentle" birth. See the lecture on the subject given by the "hag" in the Wife of Bath's Tale (1109-1176). But since "gentle" is used also to describe the Tabard Inn and the two greatest scoundrels on the pilgrimage, the Summoner and the Pardoner, one must suppose that it had a wide range of meanings, some of them perhaps ironic.

Gossip: (from Old English "God sib") literally a "God relation," i.e. a spiritual relation from baptism, a godchild or godparent. By Chaucer's time, it meant "confidant" with a flavor of our modern meaning to it.

Humor (Lat. humor—fluid, moisture)./ COMPLEXION: Classical, medieval and Renaissance physiologists saw the human body as composed of four fluids or humors: yellow bile, black bile, blood and phlegm. Perfect physical health and intellectual excellence were seen as resulting from the presence of these four humors in proper balance and combination.

Medieval philosophers and physiologists, seeing man as a microcosm, corresponded each bodily humor to one of the four elements—fire, water, earth, air. As Antony says of Brutus in *Julius Caesar*

> *His life was gentle, and the elements*
> *So mixed in him that Nature might stand up*
> *And say to all the world "This was a man"*

(V,v,73-75).

Pain or illness was attributed to an imbalance in these bodily fluids, and an overabundance of any single humor was thought to give a person a particular personality referred to as "humor" or "complexion." The correspondences went something like this:

Fire—Yellow or Red Bile (Choler)—Choleric, i.e. prone to anger
Earth—Black Bile—melancholic i.e. prone to sadness

Water   Blood—sanguine—inclined to cheerfulness, optimism
Air—Phlegm—phlegmatic—prone to apathy, slow

Too much red bile or choler could make you have nightmares in which red things figured; with too much black bile you would dream about black monsters. (See *Nun's Priest's Tale,* ll. 4120-26). "Of his complexion he was sanguine" is said of the Franklin in the General Prologue. Similarly, "The Reeve was a slender choleric man" (G.P. 589). The Franklin's "complexion" (i.e. humor) makes him cheerful, and the Reeve's makes him cranky. A person's temperament was often visible in his face, hence our modern usage of "complexion." Even when the physiological theory of humors had long been abandoned, the word "humor" retained the meaning of "mood" or "personality." And we still speak of being in a good or bad humor.

Lemman: A lover, a sweetheart. Not a courtly term, but used by the likes of Nicholas and Absalom about Alison in the Miller's Tale, for example. The Manciple has a long gloss on this "knavish" word used of poorer women, but not to be used of ladies (unless they are trollops too). It is, he says, the equivalent of "wench." See Manciple's T. 205 ff.

Likerous: Lecherous, though this sometimes seems a harsh rendering. In the Miller's Tale Alison has a "likerous" eye. "Lecherous" might fit there, though "flirtatious" is probably better. In the Wife of Bath's Prologue (732) it is used of Lucia who was so "likerous" of her husband that she killed him. "Jealous" seems a more accurate rendering here.

Lordings: Something like "Ladies and Gentlemen." The first citation in OED contrasts "lordings" with "underlings." "Lordings" is used by both the Host and the Pardoner to address the rest of the pilgrims, not one of whom is a lord, though the Host also calls them "lords."

Nones: For the Nones; For the Nonce: literally "for the once," "for the occasion," but this meaning often does not fit the context in Chaucer, where the expression is frequently untranslateable, and is used simply as a largely meaningless tag, sometimes just for the sake of the rime.

Shrew: "Shrew, shrewed, beshrew" occur constantly in the Tales and are particularly difficult to gloss. Readers are best off providing their own equivalent in phrases like "old dotard shrew" (291) or "I beshrew thy face."

Silly, Sely: Originally in Old English *saelig* = "blessed." By ME it still sometimes seems to retain part of this sense. It also means something like "simple," including perhaps "simpleminded" as in the case of John Carpenter in the Miller's Tale. The Host's reference to the "silly maid" after the Physician's Tale means something like "poor girl," and the "sely widow" of Nun's Priest's Tale is a "poor widow" in the same sense. The Wife of Bath refers to the genital organ of the male as "his silly instrument."

Solace: Comfort, pleasure, often of a quite physical, indeed sexual, nature, though not exclusively so.

Wit: Rarely if ever means a clever verbal and intellectual sally, as with us. It comes from the OE verb "witan," to know, and hence as a noun it means "knowledge" or "wisdom" "understanding" "comprehension," "mind," "intelligence" etc.